# OUT OF THE POCKET

**Published by:**
Library Tales Publishing, Inc.
1055 E. Flamingo Road #708
Las Vegas, NV 89119
www.LibraryTalesPublishing.com

For general information on our other products and services, please contact our Customer Care Department at 1-800-754-5016, or fax 917-463-0892. For technical support, please visit www.LibraryTalesPublishing.com

Library Tales Publishing also publishes its books in a variety of electronic formats. Every content that appears in print is available in electronic books.

ISBN-13: 978-0615912417
ISBN-10: 0615912419

1ST QUARTER

# MERCER 0
# WAR 7

**August 21, 2003** - I wish life had TiVo. Then I could rewind to all the memories I have of my dad and me playing catch in the street or water-skiing or going to a Cubs' game or getting Tropical Snow or watching *The Godfather*. Or at the very least, I could pause my life until he was finished fighting an oil war in Iraq. Then he would be here to coach me in football and help me wash cars at the Booster fundraiser and tutor me in Algebra II. My dad is risking his life 7,000 miles away from his first-born, and I can't do anything about it except pray and wait and wallow. How's that for an introductory journal entry?

**August 22, 2003** - I love running naked. I'm not perverted or anything; I just love streaking. I think I've been hooked ever since my dad asked me if I'd been skinny-dipping one day when I was eight. He then thought it'd be educational to throw me in the middle of Saylorville Lake. I was scared that the fishies would bite my prize jewels off, so I screamed and screamed until he yanked me out of the water, even as he was laughing. Anywho, that's probably why my friends and I go skinny dipping all the time in the summer and why I love to go streaking at midnight when it's raining. Call me Adam, but it feels so natural. Did you know that in warm weather, the 6th president of the United States, John Quincy Adams, used to go skinny-dipping in the Potomac River before dawn?

Why does school have to bite so bad? And I don't have ANY, count them, ANY, hot girls in my classes (well, okay, there is one girl). I'd go to school for the rest of my life if it meant I could have my dad back right now.

**August 23rd** - I guess I should address you, Ms. Boge, since you are the only one who's reading this. I've never been a big writer so journaling five times a week for your Creative Writing class might prove to be disastrous for my grade point average, but I will attempt to please you since you are pretty cool.

So, me. My name, as you know, is Mercer Michael Murray. As a 6'2, 170lb., brown-haired, green-eyed stallion, captain of the football team, and overall academic genius (at least in gym and art), I am lovin' being a senior. I have a freshman sister, Gina, and a little nine-year-old brother, Larry, both of whom I have to lug around EVERYWHERE because my mom works too much and my dad is fighting in Iraq. One of my best friends is David, the most genuine guy around. He's my wolf-brother for life. My other best friend is Mary, the sweetest person in the world. She's brilliant, and she's a stud athlete (swimming). I also hang out with my football buddies – they're the ones I go streaking with. I'm lucky to have good friends. Oh, and I forgot to mention that I love café mochas and my favorite food is Honey Crisp apples.

**August 23rd** - Today I'm going to tell you about my dad, Arthur Jerome (Artie for short). He is simply the most disciplined individual I know, AND he's got the biggest heart next to Mother Theresa. As you know, Ms. Boge, he has been the head varsity football coach at St. Thomas Aquinas High School since I was two. I grew up watching him coach, lead, instruct, and mentor over 1,000 young men. Now the Eagles here at St. Thom's haven't always had the best record, but he's won two 4A state championships over the past fifteen years. Anyway, Artie was called to active duty last March. It's too bad though; we were going to actually be good this year.

Do I have the right to be upset that my dad was deployed under some lame policy that allows military leaders to recall troops who have left the service but still have time left on their contract? I guess this is known as "inactive ready reserve" status, or IRR — they don't train, draw a paycheck or associate in any other way with the military. But the sheer number of IRR soldiers being mobilized is a sign that the military doesn't have enough people to fight the war. Here's another reason we shouldn't be in Iraq.

Nine months ago, we were decorating the Christmas tree, and the next day my parents were worrying about making sure the mortgage was covered, finding time to put up a security fence, and selling Dad's 2003 Chevrolet Suburban to avoid carrying insurance on it.

Since my dad is a math teacher, he has always been around more than my mom. She is a big shot lawyer who works more hours than any parent I know. So basically my dad was Mr. Mom. He can make a mean Chicken Parmesan, let me tell you. Now he's gone.

**August 24<sup>th</sup>** - It's a new day, Ms. Boge, and I'm ready to tell you about football. I'm the captain and the starting wide receiver on a team whose quarterback can't throw two feet in front of him. You might ask why I'm even playing receiver then, but that is where the offensive coordinator placed me freshman year, so I'm stuck with the position. I'm tall and thin and fast as a jackrabbit (plus I have spider-web hands), so they looked at the stats and pegged me for four years. Two years ago as a sophomore on varsity, when we had a quarterback with a decent arm, I was getting press every game. Iowa and Iowa State scouts were calling me and Notre Dame wanted me to visit for a tour of the campus. But then we got George as the quarterback, a quick and smart runner, who throws like a girl (sorry, Ms. Boge). My scouting went from a 10 to 0 real quick. No one called last year, at least not any D-I schools (that's Division I scholarship teams – the best you can get – in case you didn't know that, Ms. B), and I don't want to play at a D-II or D-III school. Call me a snob, but I just think I'm too good for them. Maybe I'll just go to Iowa and major in partying – seems to work for a good 95% of the college population. The problem is I don't drink either. One of my football buddies, Brian ("Bear"), has schools from all over the country knocking down his door, even USC and Miami. He's probably the most talented linebacker St. Thomas Aquinas has ever had. It's too bad my dad isn't here to coach him – Bear could have learned a lot more from him. Anyway, Bear is a cool guy. He's crazy and wild, and I have an absolute blast when I'm around him. He's the guy who taught me that streaking is an art form. He also gave me my nickname, 'Merck,' after the Roman god of speed (and commerce – he says I'll be a rich business man someday). Bear is the type to never do homework, but instead read about Greek and Roman mythology in his spare time. And he is the genius who introduced me to café mochas from Starbucks. (I use a lot of parentheses – what does that say about me?)

**To:** <u>artmurr@yaboo.com</u>
**From:** <u>Mercermur1@yaboo.com</u>
**Subject: school**
**August 25**

*Dear Dad,*

*Football is okay, but I still haven't had "the call" from Ferentz at Iowa. I know, I know, I have to wait until he can see me actually play this year. School is school. High school is all facts and memorization – when do we actually have time or the opportunity to THINK.*

*Since it was raining, we went streaking on the night before school started. Four of us jumped out of the bushes at the corner of 35th and University – cars honked and people cheered for us, especially me since I have the chiseled frame of a Renaissance sculpture. Of course we waited until the light was green – we certainly don't want to explain to a cop that some old lady rammed into a pole because naked teenagers ran in front of her. I'm obeying the law, Dad, except for the fact that we were in the buff.*

*I'm still single. It doesn't help that David doesn't date either – since he's an Evangelical Christian, he has vowed not to even kiss a girl until his wedding day – WOW, WOW, WOW! At least I'm too busy to date or have time for a serious relationship. Although there is this one girl…*

*Dad, when are you coming home? You've been fighting over there for seven months now (well, technically, six, since you trained for four weeks in the U.S.). You know, the Catholic Church is against the war, so if you came home, you could use your religion as an excuse.*

*I'm still lugging Larry and Gina around like you asked. I'm trying to be patient with them, but Larry talks too much, and Gina is embarrassing at school – she's only a freshman and she's hanging around with some guys in MY CLASS!*

*Mom is still coming home at 7:30 or LATER every night. I feel like I'm a single father. We are getting sick of eating Mac and Cheese and McDonalds and Subway, and the Honey Crisps aren't even out yet. I'm thinking about watching the Food Channel to learn how to cook.*

    *Mercer*

**August 26th** - Mom had to work late again, so I picked up Larry at piano after getting the shingles knocked out of me at football practice. The "Nanny" (she's actually this really hot college chick [oh, sorry - "girl," since "chick" is infantilizing women or something like that] whom Mom hired to take Larry and Gina places) gets off at 7:00 when I get home. I can't help it; I get so annoyed by my little brother. All he does is practice his piano, play chess, and read. Why couldn't I have had a little brother who played sports? We could have played catch in the backyard, I could have coached his YMCA basketball team, and we could have been best buds. But instead I get the shyest, quietest (except when he's around me – then I can't keep him quiet), brainiest little guy on the planet. He's actually smarter than I am. The only reason I even agree to pick him up is because of my dad. My mom is far away in la-la lawyer-land, but my dad scares the sweat out of me, even if he is 6,621 miles away. Plus, he asked me to help out with the kids since Gina can't drive yet. I guess I'm racking up points in heaven, as my dad always tells me. I miss him.

**August 27th** - Today's "journal topic" was to talk about a childhood memory. One of my earliest memories is going to the car wash. Yes, two bucks back then was enough to entertain me. Dad would bundle me up in the dead of winter, and we'd make an adventure at Amoco. He'd sing and make up stories about the brushes being the Orks and the soap being magic potion. I was only four, but I remember how I looked forward to those car rides. Still to this day, I get my car washed once a week. Since he's been gone, I go three times a week (sometimes just the inside). My friends tease me about my obsessively clean 1990 Expedition, but it makes me happy.

I also remember getting weird fried food at the Iowa State Fair. We'd order fried Twinkies, fried Oreos, fried Snickers bars, fried turkey legs – leave it up to Iowans to fry everything and anything. Next year I think I'll open up my own caramel apple stand with, yep, you guessed it, Honey Crisp apples.

**To:** Mercermur1@yaboo.com
**From:** artmurr@yaboo.com
**Subject: School is vital**
**August 27**

*Dear Son,*

*It's so dry here – what I wouldn't give for a quick jump in Saylorville Lake. In fact, why don't you go take one for me so I can live vicariously through you. Just keep your clothes on and make sure that if you bring any women, they keep them on too.*

*I know school can be boring at times, but it is the key to your future. It's not important that you play football – it's important that you get a good education. Then you can come back and coach and teach with me at St. Tom's.*

*I can't tell you much about what we are doing here, but know it's a good thing. Kids are learning for the first time in school, hospitals are being rebuilt, and people are praising Allah for giving them a taste of freedom. Of course, there are those Iraqis who think we shouldn't be here. Some just spit at us while others use more violent measures, but just know that we are fighting for democracy in a land that has never known it.*

*I've made a foreign friend here. His name is Ahmed. He is seventeen, just like you, but his dad was killed in a suicide bombing last April. He's fluent in English and is serving as a translator/semi-spy for us. Ahmed recognizes potential danger on the Iraqi streets that are not apparent to us. He'd like to e-mail you once in a while if you are willing. He's brilliant in math and wants to study chemistry in the U.S. Here is his e-mail: ahmed86@yaboo.com Drop him a line. I think it would mean a lot to him.*

*Remember the Ten Commandments. And I know I've asked you this before I left, but I'm reminding you again: I need you to take care of our family while I'm gone.*

*Dad*

**August 28**[th] - Ah, yes, the Ten Commandments. Let's start with Commandment I: "Thou shalt have no other gods before me." So basically this means don't put anything in front of God, which in my case would be football, girls, school, friends, money, lifting, food, and streaking - I'm just being honest. My dad told me this also means that you need to trust God. My

Dad's verse to live by is Proverbs 3:5-6, "Trust in the Lord with all your heart and lean not on your own understanding; in all your ways acknowledge him, and he will make your paths straight." For my dad, anything that couldn't be rationally explained (like why a two-year-old has to endure painful chemotherapy for months and then die anyway), he would just say, "God's ways are not our ways; He sees the big picture. We have to trust that." Easier said than done. I don't understand why my father has to fight for some other country and risk his life. How can I trust God with that? To tell you the truth, I'm pissed off. I'm mad that the best person I know has to fight a war 7000 miles away. He doesn't deserve it, heck, I don't deserve it. I know plenty of screw-off-delinquents in my high school who have the easy life with no worries. Why can't their fathers go? But I guess that's not fair either. And so I pray (yes, even though I have questions about religion and God, I pray at night, every night), that God will help me understand why Artie is in Iraq, and that He'll help me trust in His ways. It isn't easy.

---

**To:** artmurr@yaboo.com
**From:** Mercermur1@yaboo.com
**Subject: Why?**
**August 28**

*Dear Dad,*

*We read about a two-year-old girl who was recently beaten to death by her mother's live-in boyfriend, and the guy got off scott-free. Where is the justice?*

*Football season is going downhill fast, and we haven't even had our first game yet. Coach Fox knows that George, the quarterback, can't throw the ball, so we have ONE, count it, ONE pass play that we practice. And Coach won't move me to a different position! Dad, I seriously think he's stunting my potential because of you. You know he's always been jealous of you, and so now he's taking it out on me. I went in to talk to him about calling Ferentz at Iowa, but he just said that I need to be more of a team player and to stop thinking about myself. Dad, I know I'm good enough to play at Iowa. Can you e-mail him for me?*

*Mercer*

**To:** Mercermur1@yaboo.com
**From:** artmurr@yaboo.com
**Subject: Football isn't everything**
**August 29**

*Dear Son,*

*I'm sorry about football, Mercer, but don't blame the quarterback or Coach Fox. The likelihood of you receiving a scholarship to the University of Iowa is slim – you are talented, but Iowa is a top 25 team.*

*Your education comes first. Remember to strive for excellence in the small things (including homework) you do so you are prepared for greater responsibilities.*

*Today I witnessed a real life martyr. A U.S. soldier from a neighboring platoon saw a little girl playing with a piece of unexploded ordnance on a street near where he was guarding a station. He pushed her aside and threw himself on it just as it exploded. He's a hero and there aren't many left in this world.*

> *Dad*

---

**To:** artmurr@yaboo.com
**From:** Mercermur1@yaboo.com
**Subject: Thanks**
**August 29**

*Dear Dad,*

*I'm not going to stop hoping for Iowa – I know I'm good enough.*

*Why is math so hard for me when I have a father who's a math teacher? Mary has to tutor me practically every night. She never complains though. Maybe it's because she comes from a family of seven kids, so she's used to helping others.*

*David is doing well. He still doesn't know what he's going to do next year. We always argue about the war – he thinks we should be there and I don't. I support you, Dad, 100%, but that doesn't mean I have to like it.*

> *Mercer*

**August 29**ᵗʰ - I'm addicted to Starbucks' café mochas. My daily routine before school every day is to stop at Hy-Vee and pick up a venti café-mocha with skim milk (but I have to have the whipped cream). I slaved away all summer helping a landscape architect, and now all my money is going to coffee, and not just a cup of coffee, a $4 cup of coffee. I know it's insane, I know it's a waste, but I'm addicted. My name is Mercer Murray, and I am a mochaholic.

**August 30**ᵗʰ - I had to drive Larry to a chess tournament this weekend. He begged me to stay and watch him, but I wanted to see the Iowa game, so I told him to just call me when he was finished. Iowa beat Miami of Ohio 21-3. I feel bad because Larry actually got second in the whole tournament, but I am a die-hard loyal Iowa fan, and it would take a major tragedy to get me away from a game. When Iowa wins, it means my week is going to go well. I'm looking forward to scoring numerous touchdowns next Friday night (our first game), acing every test in school, and the girl of my dreams asking me to Homecoming. Nothing less than the best, I say.

My dad asked me to e-mail an Iraqi teenager named Ahmed (I'm not allowed to IM anyone – that's "instant message" in case you were wondering, Ms. Boge). His dad was killed by a bomb last April - I can't imagine. Still, it's weird writing to someone you don't know.

**To:** ahmed86@yaboo.com
**From:** Mercermur1@yaboo.com
**Subject: Hello**
**August 31**

*Dear Ahmed,*

*Greetings from Iowa, the most underrated state in America. My name is Mercer, and I am the seventeen-year-old son of Arthur, the Major you met. He said you might be interested in learning more about my country, so I thought I'd offer my opinion. America is the best place there is. You can protest the war and sign up to serve in it the next week. You can write about how bad the government is in the paper and run for office the next day (although anyone can run for office, it seems that only the rich ones actually make it because they can afford to campaign extensively – a glitch in the beauty of democracy). I'm grateful for the freedoms we have here, and I only hope that this war will grant you the same freedoms. Are you glad that the U.S. is there?*

*I guess I should tell you a little about myself. I'm seventeen, I'm a good football player, and I will probably attend the University of Iowa next fall, hopefully on a football scholarship. My mom is a lawyer, and I have a little brother (9) and a sister (14). I love pizza, café mochas, Honey Crisp apples, watching college football on TV, and hanging out with my friends. That's about it.*

*If you have any other questions, just ask. See ya.*

*Mercer*

*Dear Mr. Murray:*

*Salutations. My name is Ahmed Shojaat. Thank you most kindly for writing. I am seventeen also. I want to go to college to study chemistry. I have no brothers or sisters.*

*My father was killed in a bombing on April 1, 2003. My mother and I are trying to survive here. I do odd jobs, and my mother sells homemade bread. Sometimes we have to sell pieces of jewelry from her dowry. When my parents married, she buried it in the backyard in case we ever needed it. Now we do need it, although we only sell it in times of emergency.*

*I am lucky to have learned English in school. My father was a professor of chemistry at Baghdad University, so education has been a priority.*

*Thank you for telling me about your country. I look forward to learning more. Maybe I will visit someday.*

> *Sincerely,*
> *Ahmed Shojaat*

**August 31** - I feel so bad for Ahmed – I don't think I could take it if I lost my dad. He's my hero, you know. Did you know that he ran five miles five times a week without fail for something like twenty years? The only time he skipped it was the week after each of his kids was born. I hope to be the man he is someday.

The Aquatic Center closed for the summer today, so I decided to be a nice guy and take my brother, sister, and my neighbor, Andrew, age 2, to the pool for one last hurrah. Gina was off flirting with a couple of boys with fake tattoos, Larry was off under the shade-tent playing cards with his buddy, and I was sitting in a foot of water watching Andrew have the time of his life acting like a sea lion (I swear, it would be so great to be a kid again – no stress, no frustrations, no REALITY). All of a sudden, I saw these little pea-sized orange chunks float by. I figured it's probably some rocks or something, but then I remembered that rocks don't float. I looked around, only there was no one within a ten-foot radius of me so I knew it was either me or Andrew. The horror, the horror. I turned crimson and thought of all the things that could come from my body that might possibly be orange. Then I looked over at Andrew and saw a couple of orange chunks stuck to his leg. It took all of two minutes to grab Andrew (without calling too much attention to myself), yell to Larry and Gina, pack everyone up and head home. The last thing I need is the entire pool to realize that everyone had to evacuate because my two-year-old neighbor had carrots earlier in the day and digested them right through his swim diaper.

**September 1st** - Our first football game is this Friday. I'm ready to show the world what I've got, or at least show the University of Iowa. I really want a scholarship, not because we can't afford it, but because I've always dreamed of playing there and walking-on is demeaning to me (Mary tells me I need to get over myself). We'll see. We'll see how the coach uses my talent. I wish my dad was still the coach – he would have brought out the best in me.

---

**To:** artmurr@yaboo.com
**From:** Mercermur1@yaboo.com
**Subject: The One**
**September 2**

*Dad,*

*I'm in love. Her name is Beth and she is simply the most beautiful girl I have ever seen in my life. She's the ONE, dad. I just feel it. I'm hoping that she'll realize she loves me too and we'll get married right after college. Did you know that George W. Bush, 43rd president of the United States, and his wife Laura got married just three months after meeting each other? When you know, you know, right? Mary doesn't like Beth; she thinks she is stuck up, but I think Beth is just shy. Plus I think Mary is jealous of her. Beth is a knockout, and Mary is the cute, girl-next-door kind of good-looking. Mary's also a tomboy –she has worn her hair in a ponytail every day since I've known her, but she has a killer body, objectively (I can say that since she's one of my best friends, right?). Women are just weird. Mary is going to Marquette on a full-ride academic scholarship since she's salutatorian and since she received a 34 on her ACT. Talk about smart. She's as disciplined as you, Dad. She swims every morning and after school, plus she helps out with her six younger brothers and sisters. It's hard with Larry and Gina. I know that family is a priority, but sometimes they are so annoying.*

*Our first game is Friday night. I don't know how Coach Fox will use me, but I'm looking forward to it. Iowa scouts will be there looking at Bear, the most sought after linebacker in the COUNTRY, but I'm hoping they'll catch a glimpse at my prowess in the meantime. Say an extra prayer that it'll happen.*

*Mercer*

**To:** Mercermur1@yaboo.com
**From:** artmurr@yaboo.com
**Subject: Wait until marriage**
**September 3**

*Dear Son,*

*I'm going to remind you about our "chastity" talk one more time since I know how hard it is for you (remember that I was once a teenage boy). The moral purity of a woman doesn't belong to you unless she's your wife, so you shouldn't take it, no matter what.*

*Tell me why you are in love with Beth. Is she nice, funny, compassionate? Does she go to church? Ask David what he thinks about her – he's a good kid.*

*Ahmed is a big help here since he knows how to speak English. Because he knows the ins and outs of the city and he understands his fellow Iraqis, he keeps his ears open for anything shady. He's shared a lot with me about his dad and how wonderful he was. His dad was killed by Saddam loyalists – unfortunately, many academics are targeted here - so he wants to help us in any way he can.*

*It's so hot here that a Coke can burst open in the middle of the night – it scared me because it sounded like some sort of firearm. It's hard not to be on edge all the time.*

> *Dad*

---

**To:** artmurr@yaboo.com
**From:** Mercermur1@yaboo.com
**Subject: Re: Wait until marriage**
**September 3**

*Dad,*

*Sorry it's so hot over there. It's about 85 here, which isn't so bad unless you're in ten pounds of padding and clothing. I'm not complaining though – I love football.*

*I've never thought about why I actually like Beth. I guess I'm just mysteriously drawn to her. She's gorgeous and popular, and I guess she's pretty nice, although I've only talked to her once when I complimented her bowl in art class (she scoffed at me and walked away – apparently it was a tea pot – oops). She isn't really smart, and she gossips a lot, but I can't help it. She's a Betty.*

*I wrote to Ahmed. He seems pretty cool. He called me, "Mr. Murray." R-E-S-P-E-C-T – good guy, good guy.*

> *Mercer*

**September 4** - My dad just wrote me an e-mail stressing the importance of school, but right now, I just don't see it (sorry, Ms. Boge). I really struggle with math. But honestly, when am I ever going to use calculus unless I become an engineer? Let the "Ahmeds" of the world do the math; I'll entertain them with football.

---

**To:** Mercermur1@yaboo.com
**From:** ahmed86@yaboo.com
**Subject: Hello again**
**September 4**

*Dear Mr. Murray:*

*Hello, my friend. I hope all is well with you and your football games. We do not play football here, but some of the soldiers have been teaching me to throw a "spiral." I like your football very much. Our "football" is your "soccer." I am a goalie. We have not been able to play soccer in a long time. I miss playing it with my friends.*

*I am helping your father and his men, but I am also helping as an interpreter at one of the hospitals here. For a while people stole beds and supplies from the hospitals, but fortunately, the American soldiers have been guarding it so no one can steal anymore. A friend of my mother's went to the hospital last week to have a baby, but the baby was born dead. Her husband left her immediately because he believed it was the devil's work that the baby died. It may have been the devil's work, but I do not think that Allah would want her husband to abandon her. I would never leave my wife, no matter what. Do you want to get married someday? Normally, I would have been betrothed through an arranged marriage by now, but since our futures are so unknown, we cannot think of such things yet. Someday I want to get married and have six kids. I love children.*

*Please tell me more about your life in America. I am thinking about possibly studying there someday. Thank you for writing to me. I am able to use the computer at the University, so I will try to write as often as possible. It is good to have an American friend.*

   *Sincerely,*

   *Ahmed Shojaat*

**To:** ahmed86@yaboo.com
**From:** Mercermur1@yaboo.com
**Subject: Re: Hello again**
**September 4**


*Dear Ahmed,*

*I can't believe you don't play football there! I guess I'm just surprised be-cause Americans are practically obsessed with football. Someday when you come here to study, I'll teach you all about the best game invented.*

*Let's see, life in America. Well, I can tell you about my life in America. I am a senior at St. Thomas Aquinas High School, a Catholic (Christian) School in Iowa. I'm in love with the most beautiful girl I've ever seen, but I'm too scared to ask her out. I have two best friends, David and Mary, and I just hang out with them on the weekends. Most of my other friends drink on both Friday (after our football games) and Saturday nights, so I either go to the parties and drink Coke or I just stay at home and watch movies with my friends who don't drink. David doesn't drink because of his religion, Mary doesn't drink because her father is an alcoholic, and I don't drink because I accidentally got drunk once when I was twelve (I was at a wedding and the strawberry daiquiris, which I THOUGHT were non-alcoholic, were too good to pass up) and threw up in the bathroom all night (boy was my dad TO'ed!). I never want to be in the position where I can't control my thoughts or my actions again. Plus, I puked for pretty much the whole next day, so alcohol has no taste appeal for me. I must have eaten some Doritos that night as well because I can't eat Doritos anymore either. What do you do for fun on weekends? Are you still in school too?*

*Yes, I want to get married someday and I've already found the girl – she's so beautiful. I want to have four kids. That way no one will be left out on a roller coaster.*

*We have a big game tomorrow night. Wish me luck. By the way, please call me Mercer.*

*Mercer*

**To:** Mercermur1@yaboo.com
**From:** ahmed86@yaboo.com
**Subject: Re: Hello again**
**September 4**

*Dear Mercer,*

*Thank you again for writing. I look forward to checking the computer each day to read your e-mails. I wish you luck in your game tomorrow night. Someday you will have to explain the football rules to me.*

*Who is your future bride? What is she like? Will she make a good wife?*

*I am still in school, but we do not meet every day as you do. Since the war started last March, we have not been able to meet safely. Four of our teachers have been killed by bombings (both American and suicide bombers), so we never know when it is safe to go to school. I try to read my father's books to keep my mind active, but it is hard to concentrate. I want to come to America to study in peace.*

*It is difficult to tell you what life is like for me here since it changes every day. In the past, I would go to school in the morning, return for lunch between 2 and 4 o'clock, have my main meal with my family, maybe nap for an hour or two, especially in the summer months, do my homework and study and then enjoy time with friends and family. In the evenings, when everyday life was still relatively ordinary and calm, my friends and I would go out and walk the streets, have ice-creams or shawarma sandwiches, play games and visit numerous cousins, watch TV and listen to the latest hits (my favorite bands are U2 and an Iraqi band called **The Time**). We would also get pirated copies of your latest Hollywood movies. This provided a short education for me on life in America! Now I see my friends once in a while, but we cannot play many games. We are all too busy trying to provide for our families. It is dangerous, but being an interpreter for the Americans is good money. I need to take care of my mother.*

*I am glad you do not drink alcohol. I have never tried alcohol, and I do not ever want too. My parents have never drunk alcohol either. We honor Allah by not ever clouding our minds.*

*I hope that the Americans will bring peace to our country. I want to be able to go back to school soon. I miss learning.*

> *Sincerely,*
> *Ahmed Shojaat*

**September 5** - Okay, remind me never to complain of school again. My new Iraqi email friend, Ahmed, can't go to school every day because he doesn't know if his teacher is alive or if his classroom will be bombed. It's amazing how easy it is to take freedoms for granted.

Big game tonight. I better see some action on the field.

Today's journal topic was to describe myself physically. So let's start from the bottom. I don't mean to brag, but I have great looking toes. The nails are nicely shaped and I don't have any hair below the knuckle. In fact, I've had three people tell me that I should be a foot model.

Moving up the body, I have HUGE calves. It's a genetic thing. I'm pretty lean otherwise, but I have these softball calf muscles. Plus you can see thick veins running everywhere on my legs. I have light brown hair on my legs, but nothing too grotesque. Let's see, my knees. I have a dime-sized scar on my knee from where I had warts needled off when I was twelve. Nasty. Then I have these long thighs. My calves are actually a wee bit short for my 6'2 frame, but my thighs are LOOONG. I don't look like a Hobbit or anything, but it's a noticeable feature that I'll probably pass on to my kids. Moving on up, I'm proud of my six-pack. All summer I've been lifting and doing sit-ups/push-ups, etc., and the hard work shows. I also try to eat lean meat (but not around Mary because of her PKU – I'll explain later) and low-fat/high protein food. It pays off in the workouts. I have hairless, muscular arms with moles all over them (my father is 50% Italian so I have slightly dark skin) and a skinny neck (I refuse to do the neck machine too often where you look like your skin is a big turtleneck). I have a scar on my upper left chin from having a dime-sized mole removed when I was eleven. You'd think that a mole like that would have ruined my social life, but I was still a stud with the ladies (although I've never had a girlfriend). I have perfect teeth (with only a retainer for slight correction) and light green eyes with long black eyelashes. I have dark brown hair and I have dry skin that I have to "moisturize" or I will flake. I weigh 170 lbs., but I know I will have to gain weight when I get my scholarship to Iowa. That's okay. I've been pretty disciplined so far; all I'll have to do is drink a protein shake and eat more. So anyway, from my warts to my moles to my flakey skin, I'd say I'm pretty content with my appearance. I'm no Brad Pitt, but I'm not the Ugly Duckling either. I just wish I'd have enough confidence to go ask a girl out once in a while. Well, actually just one girl. Lions, and tigers, and bears, Oh my. You don't read this, right Ms. Boge?

---

**To:** Mercermur1@yaboo.com
**From:** ahmed86@yaboo.com
**Subject: Life in Bagdad**
**September 5**

*Dear Mercer,*

*How are you doing today, Mercer? It is 105 degrees F here, but it could be worse. Today my friends and I volleyed the soccer ball back and forth and watched my great uncle and his friend shuffle some dominoes. Then it was back to work.*

*I put my lips to a glass of tap water today and watched worms swim in the bottom. Sometimes I have to boil buckets of sewage-contaminated water from the Tigris River to wash my family's clothes. But parts of Baghdad - such as the impoverished Shiite neighborhood of Sadr City, once flooded with green rivers of sewage – now have functioning sewer systems. The insurgents are targeting our sewer system, leaving us frustrated that there are days we cannot flush our toilets. Over the past three weeks, three main water lines were attacked, leaving much of the city without water for days. We are trying to be patient, but the smell of sewage fills every other block, drinking water is often contaminated, and we sometimes have to sleep on our roofs to take a break from the sauna-like heat inside our homes. We wake up covered in dust. But my beautiful country will rise again.*

*Please tell me how things are in America. I hope you are studying and enjoying yourself.*

   *Sincerely,*

   *Ahmed Shojaat*

---

**To:** ahmed86@yaboo.com
**From:** Mercermur1@yaboo.com
**Subject: Marriage**
**September 6**

*Dear Ahmed,*

*I admit I've never had to go without clean drinking water. I complain that West Des Moines drinking water tastes "metallic," and that Des Moines water is much better, but it's not that bad. I wonder why terrorists haven't contaminated our water supply or milk supply or sent a bomb to the Super Bowl like in* The Sum of All Fears *(great movie by the way). I know my dad and the American soldiers will help your people so that clean water is never an issue again.*

*I think you misunderstood my comment about wanting to get married. I like this girl named Beth. I think she's the one I'm going to marry because, well, she's gorgeous. I haven't really talked to her that much, but I guess she'd make a good wife (generally we don't think about "dating" as if you had to marry that person). What do you look for in a girl? We don't have arranged marriages over here. Do you actually get to meet your future wife before you marry her? What if you didn't like her?*

*We lost last night. I only had 30 yards, which means that the coaches from Iowa won't be impressed. I don't mean to complain – I know you deal with a lot more stress than worrying about a football game, but I was bummed. I just want to play, you know? The good news is that Iowa won last Saturday. They beat Buffalo 56-7. If my Hawks win, I'm happy, at least for a little while.*

> *Mercer*

**To:** artmurr@yaboo.com
**From:** Mercermur1@yaboo.com
**Subject: Come Home**
**September 6**

*Dear Dad,*

*You've got to convince me that being in Iraq is a good thing because I'm struggling with it. You know they will never find weapons of mass destruction because there probably aren't any. And it's pretty convenient that Iraq just so happens to be the second largest supplier of oil in the world. I'm a true patriot as you've taught me to be, but I just hope this isn't another Vietnam (one of my teachers thinks so). Maybe I'm just bitter because I want you back home.*

*We lost last night, 21-7, and I only had 30 yards (five yard pass, 25 yard run). He threw the ball to me once! Why can't you come back and be the coach? Why can't the coach see my potential? Why can't I have a decent quarterback? UGH! I think we lost because I couldn't have my ritual Honey Crisp apple before the game – what is with these slow grocery stores?*

> *Mercer*

**September 6** - True story: once upon a time, England was old and small and the local folks started running out of places to bury people. So they would dig up coffins and would take the bones to a "bone-house" and reuse the grave. When reopening these coffins, one out of twenty-five coffins were found to have scratch marks on the inside and they realized they had been burying people alive. So they would tie a string on the wrist of the corpse, lead it through the coffin and up through the ground, and tie it to a bell. Someone would have to sit out in the graveyard all night (the "graveyard shift") to listen for the bell; thus, someone could be "saved by the bell" or was considered a "dead ringer." Oh, clichés, don't you love them? I thought you'd appreciate that Ms. Boge, since you are an English teacher and all. By the way, I'm curious to see if you actually read these journals. If you are reading this right now, circle your name in this paragraph.

**To:** artmurr@yaboo.com
**From:** Mercermur1@yaboo.com
**Subject: Why are we in Iraq?**
**September 7**

*Dear Dad,*

*Okay, Dad. So Bush says that we needed to go to Iraq because "the war is part of a greater conflict necessitated by the 9/11 terrorist attacks." But I think that the war in Iraq is just instigating more Muslims to commit more terrorist attacks and is confirming their belief that America is the bad guy. Aren't we just spurring them on to blow up Los Angeles? And what about all the suicide bombings now? Didn't we just give them a closer target? At least now they don't have to travel on American soil to kill Americans. Everyone hates America, Dad. And I don't just mean the terrorists. Tom, a friend of mine who is an exchange student, says that people in Denmark think Bush is an imperialist and that we have no business in Iraq. He also says that we are just "pissing them off more so they'll never stop." I don't know what to think. The al-Qaida/Saddam link has proven false, so the 9/11 argument washes out. And the weapons-of-mass-destruction argument also seems wobbly since they can't actually find any WMD's. I know Saddam is considered a WMD, but isn't it convenient that we go after him when he has the second largest oil supply in the world?*

*Mercer*

*Son,*

*The war on terrorism is a very long, painful, and tedious process. It is not decided in one battle in Afghanistan or one war in Iraq. Even if we kill bin Laden, jihad will continue. In the Arab/Islamic culture, fanaticism, intolerance, and corruption combine to perpetuate the idea that America is the enemy and killing the enemy is an honor. Terrorists don't need Iraq as an excuse to kill. Kids dream of being able to martyr themselves by destroying the American infidel. Unless that line of thinking is thwarted, especially in the young, terrorism will never stop.*

*Bringing democracy to Iraq is a strong start. We need to teach the people that a democratically elected government will not only end the oppression in Iraq, but will spread hope to the entire Middle Eastern world. When Iraqis are engaged in the fight against terrorism as we are, we have more power against the fanatics. Think of it as a recruiting mission: we are recruiting Iraqis to help us in the fight against terrorism just as terrorists recruit young Muslims.*

*It is good that you are thinking about this, Son. I know it is difficult to understand, especially since you can't see the progress we are making here, but trust me, we are doing the right thing.*

>    *Dad*

**September 8** - Mary came over today to help me with Algebra II. She's so smart – I wish math came as easily to me as it does to her. She's pretty disciplined though – homework is always first. I guess she has learned to be disciplined because of her special diet. Mary has a metabolic disorder called PKU, short for phenylketonuria. Basically she can't have a lot of protein since her body can't metabolize an amino acid (amino acids make up the protein found in food) called phenylalanine. Before they started testing for it, kids would end up being mentally retarded because the phenylalanine acts like a poison to their brain. She's been on a low protein diet since birth and has to drink special milk that doesn't have phenylalanine in it so she gets the protein she needs for growth. Mary has never had meat, chicken, regular cheese or even regular bread in her life. She counts all the phenylalanine in milligrams every day (she still needs some for growth), which comes out to be about five grams of protein a day (or 270 mg of phenylalanine). She's the most disciplined person I've ever met besides my dad, maybe even more than my dad. Not only is she disciplined with her diet, she's also disciplined with school, swimming, and even helping her brothers and sisters. I'm such a lazy oaf compared to her. Actually, I'm just a lazy oaf anyway. I need a mocha.

**Sept. 9** - I am obsessed with girls' hair. The girl I am going to marry (she smiled at me today in art) has the most beautiful hair I've ever seen. It's long and dark and thick and seems to swish in the sun like all those shampoo commercials. Hair is the "glory of man," as the Bible says, and I'm obsessed.

The nanny only works until 7:00 each day, which means that after 7:00 on weekdays and 24 hours a day on weekends, I'm the parent if my mom is unavailable. By parent, I mean chauffer and cook and nurse and psychologist. So I'm getting more upset with my mom for having all this added responsibility, but at the same time, I'm also more appreciative of her job as a parent. This wouldn't be a problem if my dad were here.

As long as I'm complaining, I might as well tell you, Ms. Boge (although I don't actually think you are reading this so I'll just tell myself) that my nanny likes David. She's 23 and gorgeous and she always stares at David. I'm used to it since he could be a model (at least that's what Mary and the rest of the girls at our school say), but when my hot nanny likes him, it bugs me. And the ironic thing is that he's oblivious to it all. He's so focused on "the plans God has made for him" that he doesn't notice he's a movie star living in Iowa. I guess that's why he's my best friend. I've never met anyone who is so humble and unassuming and yet so perfect at the same time – even his humor is never cruel. If only he'd give up that notion of going to the Marines after high school. He's such an amazing guy – why waste that on an oil war.

**To:** Mercermur1@yaboo.com
**From:** ahmed86@yaboo.com
**Subject: Re: Marriage**
**September 10**

*Dear Mercer,*

*I apologize for not writing sooner, but I have been helping my uncle with his children. It is difficult to entertain the young ones here because we have to keep them inside for their safety. We only have electricity two hours a day so cartoons are limited. It is sad because children need fresh air, especially in this heat. But we try to encourage them by playing games and telling stories. I am teaching my youngest nephew English. He is an eager learner.*

*When you say, "Iowa won," do you mean the University of Iowa? I would very much like to study chemistry in the United States someday. Maybe I could attend the University of Iowa. Yesterday, I spoke with my old neighbor, Thula, who is 10. She attended school for the first time last week because girls were never allowed to go to school here. I wish you could have seen her smile and speak about all she had learned in only three days. I do not really know if the Americans should be here or not, but at least some good is coming of it.*

*I caution you, my friend, to desire a girl simply for her looks. In my culture, when you date, it is in pursuit of a companion with whom you can spend the rest of your life. Then the love that will exist in marriage can be respected more by both partners. From what I have seen in movies about American culture, your dating couples act as married couples. It is my belief that you will be most happy with your marriage partner, and you cheat that partner by dating others. That is why I respect our arranged marriages. The parents know their children and most of the time make good decisions. Unfortunately, my mother is the only one who will be able to choose for me, but I trust her judgment. I am glad that I will be able to meet my future bride ahead of time, though.*

*Peace be with you, Mercer.*

*Ahmed Shojaat*

*Dear Ahmed,*

*I can't imagine being a kid and being stuck inside all day – it's nice that you try to entertain the kids. When I was a kid, I was always outside, even if it was freezing. There's something about fresh air that feeds the body. My dad says it's so hot in Iraq that some of his soldiers wear long sleeve shirts in order to sweat more because the sweat cools their skin. I won't complain about the Des Moines humidity again.*

*That would be awesome if you came to the University of Iowa for school. I hate school most of the time, but I need to remember that it is a privilege, especially after hearing the story of your neighbor going to school for the first time and you worrying about bombs while you're doing calculus. My September resolution is to whine less – we'll see how long that lasts.*

*Mercer*

**Sept 10** ˙ You know it's funny, but some of my favorite memories of my dad are when we work out together. My dad is the picture of a 45-year-old man in shape. And he knows how to push his body, given that he's been in the military most of his life. Ever since I can remember, we have run together, lifted together, pushed each other. Even though he's halfway across the globe, he still inspires me to challenge myself. Football is SO frustrating, but I stick with it because of him. I miss my Honey Crisps – I'm going through withdrawal.

**Sept. 11** - Today is the Anniversary of the 9/11 attacks. We had a special Mass remembering those who died for our country. I'm embarrassed to say this, but I had to leave (I hope people thought I was going to the bathroom, although Mary's eyes met mine, and I knew she knew why I was leaving). I cried in the bathroom – I didn't bawl or anything, but I broke down for a minute. 9/11 for me is all about my dad. I feel bad for the victims and their families, but my world was turned upside down when 9/11 occurred, even if it happened a year and a half later. My dad is in Iraq because of 9/11, and it torks me off. My eyes didn't hit the "redness" stage too badly, so I went back into the mass. I couldn't look at Mary – I knew I'd start crying again. Some stallion I am, huh.

**Sept. 12** - Big game tonight. We play Jordan Creek, our rivals. They have 3,200 kids in their school (we only have 1,300) so they have a bigger pool to pick from each year, but we've always stayed with them in most sports. I think this is our year. With my inspirational captain speech before the game, I think we can take them.

**Sept. 13** - Okay, so the inspirational captain speech didn't work. We lost, 42-7. Can you believe it? I didn't have any yardage – George threw the ball to me twice and both were horrible passes. Remind me in my next life to come back as a tailback. How are the coaches supposed to see my athletic skill if I can't even get the ball thrown five feet near me? I'm so frustrated right now. I'm going to either sprint five miles or punch a hole in my wall.

     9:00 PM - I didn't want to explain to my dad that I punched a hole in the wall so I sprinted the five miles instead (well, okay, I jogged and sprinted in between). My legs feel like fettuccine noodles, but I don't feel as stressed now. Plus, my Hawkeyes won – they beat Iowa State, 40-21, so the weekend wasn't a total wash. They are 3-0 now. I just don't know what I'm going to do if I can't play football at Iowa next year. Maybe I won't even go to college.

**September 15** - I got my journals back from last week. You obviously don't read them (since you didn't circle your name in the paragraph), so I could just blab on about anything, but I sort of like having this outlet to express how the world isn't cutting me any slack. I may be whiney, but I am the center of the universe, right? Maybe I'm like Truman in *The Truman Show*. Anyway, I'm going to write as if this is a foreign language to you – it makes it easier to be candid, just in case. Ms. Boge, I'm going to start dropping you hints about Honey Crisp apples to see if you read this. I need to know if you read this. I hope you aren't a good actress.

**To:** ahmed86@yaboo.com
**From:** Mercermur1@yaboo.com
**Subject: The weekend**
**September 15**

*Dear Ahmed,*

*I had a somewhat useless weekend. I didn't get any yardage in our game (and we lost), but I'm hopeful that I'll get some playing time soon.*

*My friends and I played Disc Golf on Sunday. It's sort of a new game where you throw a Frisbee (like a big disc) into a basket with as few throws as possible. We can't go to Bear's (my friend, Brian's) lake house in Okoboji (it's a lake resort area about three-and-a-half hours from here where we go boating, swimming, etc.) anymore because weekends are eaten up by football, but we still manage to dink around, doing stupid stuff. It's supposed to rain tonight, so we're going streaking again (that's where we run naked in the streets).*

> *Mercer*

**To:** Mercermur1@yaboo.com
**From:** ahmed86@yaboo.com
**Subject: Jihad**
**September 16**

*Dear Mercer,*

*Good Day to you, my friend. It is interesting to hear what you do in your culture. Do all Americans run around naked? We would never do anything like that. Modesty is very sacred in Islam. Women were not even allowed to go out without hijabs until recently, and many in rural areas still wear them every day.*

*I am happy that you are having fun in Iowa. I am still able to enjoy time with my friends on occasion. We play soccer or cards or listen to music in our homes. It is difficult to see many of my friends though since we all are trying to support our families. I am fortunate that only one of my friends has been killed.*

*I want to explain something, Mercer. Please do not think that all Iraqis or all Muslims approve of terrorism. It is so dangerous because of all the suicide bombings that are performed as jihad. The word jihad comes from the Arabic root word J-H-D, which means "strive." Essentially jihad is an effort to practice religion in the face of oppression and persecution. The effort may come in fighting the evil in your own heart, or in standing up to a dictator. Military effort is included as an option, but as a last resort and not "to spread Islam by the sword" as the stereotype would have you believe. Muslims are commanded in the Qur'an to "enjoin good and forbid evil" (9:112).*

*Muslims are also commanded not to begin hostilities, embark on any act of aggression, violate the rights of others, or harm the innocent. Even hurting or destroying animals or trees is forbidden. War is waged only to defend the religious community against oppression and persecution, because "persecution is worse than slaughter" and "let there be no hostility except to those who practice oppression" (2:190-193). Therefore, if non-Muslims are peaceful or indifferent to Islam, there is no justified reason to declare war on them.*

*I do not want you to think that all Muslims are bad. In fact, Islam is a peaceful religion. Those who distort its message do so for their own purpose.*

*Ahmed Shojaat*

**Sept. 16** - My name was announced as being chosen for Homecoming Court today. And while this is a great honor, I'm dreading the dance. I want to ask Beth SO bad, but what if she says "no." I just don't think I can handle that kind of rejection ("Back to the Future" line – great 80's flick). I've never really had to try with girls. In fact, the few times I've actually been out with girls to dances and stuff have been when the girl asked me. And even then we'd go in groups. In other words, I've never had a girlfriend. But now, I'm in love, and I'm scared that she'll blow me off.

**Sept. 17** - I can't believe it!!! This morning as I perused the job offerings in the counseling center, Heather called my name. I snorted – (another bad habit, but at least not within earshot) and went over to her. Heather is the long-legged, curvy, fake tan, fake-nails, whitened-teeth type who knows every guy wants her, that is, except me. The problem is that she was nominated for court too. One moment I was talking to her about cafeteria food and the next thing I knew, we were going to Homecoming together. Here's a prime example of why you should pay attention in conversations. Anyway, not only do I have to go to Homecoming with Iowa's version of Paris Hilton when I'd rather be watching college football, but I have to shell out cash for a girl I don't want to go with. The "Simple Life" it ain't.

**To:** artmurr@yaboo.com
**From:** Mercermur1@yaboo.com
**Subject: Dad?**
**September 17**

*Dear Dad,*

*I haven't heard from you in a week. Are you all right? Please write back soon.*

*Mercer*

# MERCER 3
# WAR 7

**September 18** - Okay, so now I'm going to Homecoming with Heather, the wonderbra Barbie, when I really wanted to go with Beth (although I can honestly say I might not have had the guts to ask her anyway), and Mary is all pissy with me because I'm going with Heather. I said, "But I don't even want to go with her." Then she huffed and she puffed and stormed off. The thing is, most guys would kill to have a good-looking chica like Heather for a date, and although I know she'll look good on my arm, I'm mad because I didn't get up the guts to ask the girl I really wanted to go with.

On the bright side, I went to Hy-Vee and they had HONEY CRISPS in!!! Yahoo! My life will now take a turn for the better.

**Sept 19** - Why do girls go shopping so much? Do they seriously think that guys get impressed by a new purse? I just don't get it, unless they are in competition with themselves. And that's another thing. Why do girls wear such tight clothing and then get all offended when guys oogle? I must admit that I like it, of course, (especially on the girl I'm going to marry,) but it bugs the crap out of me to see my sister wear tight shirts and short skirts. I HATE it when guys stare her up and down. It hits me somewhere in my gut, and I want to punch any male within eye contact. So why do girls do it then? By the way, the batch of Honey Crisps that I bought wasn't very good. Bad omen.

**Sept 20** - We lost AGAIN! The way things look now, we won't make the playoffs. We've NEVER started 0-3. It's definitely the coach. I knew he wasn't as good as my dad. See? Now I know

I'm not just crazy thinking that I should get more playing time. If I could transfer and play at Jordan Creek I would. I can't believe we lost to Sioux City, 3-7. I guess I should be happy we have a decent kicker. I must admit it was a good game – tough defense, but I was in on three pass plays and once again, our quarterback couldn't throw. The Hawkeyes beat Arizona State 21-2 today. They are now 4-0. At least one of my teams is winning.

**Sept 21** - David (my other best friend) just told me he's seriously thinking about joining the Marines after high school now. That means he might have to go to war too. I told him I thought he should go to college first, but he said school is just not his thing. I know he's never been studious or anything, but the Marines??? Why? Why would anyone actually CHOOSE to be in this war? I want my dad back.

Brian, "Bear," has decided to go to USC. He wants to get as far away from Iowa as possible and start "partying like the celebrities do," or something like that. Here's a guy who is probably the best athlete I will ever come in contact with, and he risks it all four nights a week by partying. I just don't get it? I want to punch him a few times and say, "Wake up, Bear, you're pissing your life away." But he'll probably end up a NFL hall-of-famer, so who am I to judge.

**Sept. 23** - Does something interesting happen to you every day? Nothing interesting happened to me today. I have no idea what I'm going to write about, so I'm going to say a lot of nothing. How do you feel about that as an English teacher, Ms. Boge? Oh wait, I forgot, you don't read these anyway so actually I'm writing to myself. Maybe I'll become famous someday and they will sell this journal for a cool "mil" and that will pay for my grandkids to go to college. I WILL be successful at something. I just don't know what that is yet.

**Sept. 25** - There was a pep rally at night today for all the Homecoming candidates. It was a BLAST! Each couple chose a costume and a song to come out and dance on the gym floor in front of everyone (or at least those cool enough to know that the Thursday night pep rally before our Homecoming game is THE place to be). Anyway, Heather, (who is actually kind of fun and crazy), chose Tarzan and Jane outfits and we lip synched "Jungle Boogie." It was so awesome. I'm a ham anyway (although I think Heather just wanted people to see her in her sleeveless, short tiger dress). I caught Beth's eye – you know where you catch someone looking at you and you stare back without smiling or anything. I kept it cool and stared right back. I tell you, girls have some serious power.

**Sept. 27** - We actually won a game last night. Granted it was against a team who has won a total of ten games the last five years, but a win is a win. I finally had one nice pass play (I juked an all-American safety and grabbed the ball out of the air with my fingertips!) for a 50-yard touchdown, but that was it, and there were no scouts in sight. I'm so pissed right now. I don't want to go to Homecoming tonight and see anyone. It's so unfair! All I want to do is play football as a Hawkeye. Is that so much? And NO ONE understands. David says, "Trust the Lord" for my plans, Mary says, "Football isn't as important as school," and my mom says, "I'm sorry, Mercer, but you'll have to find something else to put your energies into," (which, by the way, is about the only thing I've actually heard come out of her mouth all week). Put my energies into what? I don't like anything else. When you have a dream, you need to go with it, right? I need mocha.

By the way, all the nominees were announced again (in nice suits this time) at an all-school pep rally yesterday in the gym. Heather was announced Homecoming queen and George, the quarterback who can't throw, was announced king. They made the perfect couple.

**To:** Mercermur1@yaboo.com
**From:** ahmed86@yaboo.com
**Subject: Sad Day**
**September 27**

*Dear Mercer,*

*I am sad today, my friend. One of my childhood friends, Ali, died yesterday. He was trapped in his house and burned to death from the wreckage of more bombs. He could not get out. Both his legs were amputated when he was three as punishment because his father was anti-Saddam. Ali might have been targeted since he had been acting as an interpreter. This war is sometimes too much to bear. Plumes from mortar attacks and burning wreckage from roadside bombs threaten many here. Some will never leave Iraq out of loyalty, but my dream is to leave as soon as possible. All I see is bloodshed.*

*I looked on the website for the University of Iowa. Someday I will come to study in your country. Somehow I will make it happen.*

> *Ahmed*

---

**To:** ahmed86@yaboo.com
**From:** Mercermur1@yaboo.com
**Subject: Re: Sad Day**
**September 27**

*Dear Ahmed,*

*I am sorry about your friend. I can't imagine losing David or Mary or anyone close to me for that matter. By the way, have you seen my dad? I haven't heard from him in a couple of weeks.*

> *Mercer*

**September 29** - Sometimes I feel so stupid writing to Ahmed because my everyday problems are like two grains of sand compared to his Sahara. The guy's good friend just burned to death. I can't imagine living everyday in a place like that. Ahmed lost his father last April and now his friend. What else can happen? He wrote me this nice e-mail and I wrote back but it was like two sentences. I didn't know what else to say. How can I complain about anything or tell him about the Homecoming dance or game or anything so insignificant? I feel like such an ungrateful schmuck.

And one of those grains of sand happens to be my beloved Hawkeyes, who lost to Michigan State, 10-20, last Saturday. UGH! Do you ever have days where you think everyone else on earth is selfish? I'm irritated right now because every person I know, including my brother, sister, mom, best friend, and the grocery clerk, thinks the world revolves around them (sorry, "him or her"). Maybe I'm just mad because the Hawks lost, and they played like each player was out for himself. I never play like that – I'm all about the team. That is, if I get the ball. So now they are 4-1. At least they have a better record than we do.

I forgot to mention the dance. Homecoming wasn't a complete wash. Heather was drunk and spent the first hour of the dance puking in the bathroom and the rest of the night at home with an underage drinking ticket (her parents had to come get her – at least they apologized to me). David went with a group, so I just hung out with them (Mary didn't go). Beth wasn't there, but the D.J. played some decent jams. Then we went to a buddy's house and played pool and watched "Remember the Titans" and "Hoosiers." It wasn't the best of times, but it wasn't the worst of times either.

**To:** Mercermur1@yaboo.com
**From:** ahmed86@yaboo.com
**Subject: Another day of life.**
**September 30**

*Dear Mercer,*

*Today is another day that I am blessed with life. I was sad when I wrote to you last, but now I am hopeful at the thought of my future. Thank you for support-ing me.*

*I am most hopeful about my education. I was planning on attending Baghdad University where my dad was a professor, but since its future is unknown, I am trying to find a way to study in America. Yet, I would miss my university – I have such fond memories of listening to my father lecture.*

*Baghdad University doesn't have the history that many American universities have (it was officially established in 1952), but it is the oldest one in modern Iraq and in the area. My dad graduated from the University in early 1972 and received a scholarship to do his Ph.D. in England. Then he returned as a member of the faculty where up until 1990, he was active in research and teach-ing. Baghdad was once one of the most prestigious educational institutions in the region, perhaps only second to Cairo University in Egypt. Unfortunately, from 1990-2003, the University suffered a great deal because of Saddam's rule. Laboratory equipment was outdated and there was a great shortage of com-puters. Academic programs with other universities, including the U.S., were paralyzed, but my dad still taught and did the best he could with his research.*

*Now, Baghdad University is a shadow, although the war has brought some light to the people there. The salaries have been increased and they have better computer facilities including satellite and internet access. But the people are still afraid. It is unsafe to go to school. I do not want to worry every time I enter the classroom that I might be the target of a bomb or that military police might storm in or that the students who belong to certain religious factions might decide to be a martyr in my classroom. It is also difficult because we still have only about two hours of electricity every day, and we never know when it will come. With outdated materials, it is difficult to get a quality education, let alone concentrate, for fear of being injured or killed. Even the teachers are afraid. Most professors stay on campus no more than a few hours to do their teaching and then rush back home. There is no incentive to do research or mentor a promising student, so most faculty members just teach. In some ways, we were better off with Saddam's sanctions. I know it will get better, but I am not patient enough to wait. I want to study in the U.S. next fall. I am determined. Then I can come back and help my people.*

*Ahmed*

*Dear Ahmed,*

*I admire your never-give-up attitude. Thank you for telling me about the University of Baghdad. I can't imagine how hard it is to see an institution like that fall from its glory, but someday it will rise. I believe that the U.S. will see to that. I do know that America will bring good things eventually. In the meantime, I think you should come and be my roommate at the University of Iowa next year. I'll be playing football a lot, but I'll still let you help me with math once in a while. I'll make you a life-long Hawkeye fan and teach you about the pink locker room and everything. And I promise: I will be sober with you the whole time.*

*I have to go do my Algebra II homework. My other good friend, Mary, has been helping me, but I'm still struggling. So much for having a math teacher for a father. Speaking of my dad, tell him to e-mail me soon.*

> *Mercer*

**Oct. 4** - Maybe the season isn't in the toilet after all, at least not for our team. We are now 2-3 (we beat West last night 21-3) and the rest of the schedule looks promising. I know I'm supposed to be happy and all, but as the season wears on, I find myself more and more depressed. I can't BELIEVE that George can't throw a ball five feet. Larry, my no-athletic-ability whatsoever brother, can throw a ball five feet. Why is this happening to me? All I want is to play football, and I'm GOOD. It's not like I have unrealistic dreams or anything – I don't want to skip college and play in the NFL next year, but I want a chance to prove myself at the very least. It's so unfair. And to top it all off, the one person who could help me through this as a father AND a coach is fighting a war for no good reason.

**October 5** - Oh, what a game! The Hawks pulled off a big one against Michigan. They won 30-27. That makes me a little more optimistic for the week. Maybe I need to work out harder in practice to show the coach what I've got. I had to drag Gina and Larry and even my MOM out of bed for church this morning. My father never missed a Sunday Mass in his whole life, and neither will I.

**October 6** - It was 80 degrees today. Can you believe it? I almost got an iced mocha instead. October is "Respect Life" month. I'm sure you'd guess that I'm pro-life since I'm a cradle Catholic. I am definitely against abortion – but our priest made a good point that being pro-life shouldn't be limited to abortion, euthanasia, and the death penalty. We should respect ALL life, including respecting our family, our friends, and even our enemies. Respecting people doesn't mean you have to like them; it just means you should treat them with dignity since they are children of God. After I heard that homily, I prayed for forgiveness for being short with my mom. I need to respect her. I just wish I'd see her more.

---

**To:** artmurr@yaboo.com
**From:** Mercermur1@yaboo.com
**Subject: Dad!!!**
**October 6**

*Dear Dad,*

*Dad, I haven't heard from you in a while, although I guess I haven't written either. I've been writing Ahmed a lot. He's cool. It's hard for me to understand all that he has been through. I don't know what to say sometimes. I told him that he should be my roommate next year at U of I so he can tutor me in math.*

*Our team is doing better. We're 2-3 now, but I'm still not getting any yardage and thus, no press. I'm focused though, Dad. It's going to happen.*

*Larry and Gina are doing well. We're sort of passing ships, but they look healthy anyway. I'm learning to be a great cook. Chicken Curry is my specialty.*

> *Mercer*

**To:** artmurr@yaboo.com
**From:** Mercermur1@yaboo.com
**Subject: No WMD's**
**October 7**

*Dad,*

*They haven't found any Weapons of Mass Destruction. It's official. We are in Iraq for no good reason whatsoever and I'm PISSED. You are over there risking your life so a small population of white men can get rich off of oil. I'm moving to Canada.*

*Mercer*

---

**To:** artmurr@yaboo.com
**From:** Mercermur1@yaboo.com
**Subject: Math**
**October 7**

*And another thing, I'm getting a "D" in math. If you were here, I wouldn't be getting a "D" in math. Tell that to Mr. Bush.*

*Merck*

---

*To: artmurr@yaboo.com*
**From:** Mercermur1@yaboo.com
**Subject: Sorry**
**October 7**

*Sorry, Dad. I didn't mean to complain or be disrespectful to the president. I know, I know - you raised me better than that.*

*Mercer*

---

**October 11<sup>th</sup>** - We won last night. I had one catch for 17 yards. The Hawks won too, but I couldn't enjoy either victory. I'm moving to Texas where they appreciate good football athletes. I took my frustrations out on a new recipe – I'm actually getting good at this cooking thing. Everyone was gone though. No one appreciated my Chicken Cacciatore but me.

**October 12** - I feel a little better today. Mass put things in perspective. For some reason, I always feel cleansed after Mass. I confess that I'm a spoiled, arrogant little brat and remind myself that God loves me anyway. That's about all my theology involves at this point in my life.

After the game on Friday, Coach Fox asked if I wanted to practice with the defense this week since my "athletic ability is probably being underutilized." "Underutilized" doesn't even come CLOSE. I told him that I'd stick it out at wide receiver. Iowa is stacked for the next three years for defense. There's no way I'd get noticed if I switched now.

**October 16 -** I confess: I am a closet swearer. I don't swear out loud, but sometimes just saying an expletive in my mind makes me feel better. Like when I hit my head – if someone is around, I'll say, "Ouch," or "Oh, shoot." But if I'm by myself, I yell, "Oh, s8!t," in my head, and I feel better. The one thing you won't ever catch me doing is using the Lord's name in vain. I'm an "Oh, my gosh," kind of guy. Commandment II hits home with our family – God's name doesn't deserve to be used in any other way than in reference to Him.

**October 18 -** We won last night and I'm getting more depressed each week. We are now 4-3, which is good for the team, but I'm losing my steam here. I didn't have any yardage. In fact, I only went in on three plays. I was actually COLD on the sidelines. I can't even tell you the last time I remember being cold during a football game. Whine, whine, whine. Sometimes I can hear myself, and I want to slap myself upside the head. Oh, and to top it off, the Hawks lost to Ohio State 10-19. It is 85 degrees here today. I can't even enjoy the weather.

Beth smiled at me today. You know the "I think you're cute" smile. She's never done that before. I'm so glad you don't read these things, Ms. Boge, cause I'd be a wee bit embarrassed if you did.

**To:** Mercermur1@yaboo.com
**From:** ahmed86@yaboo.com
**Subject: Friends**
*October 19*

*Dear Mercer,*

*I apologize for not writing sooner, but we have been busy lately. We have been selling our furniture and books in order to buy food for our family members, and we are trying to store what food and money we can. I am grateful to the Americans for giving me work, but I wonder when they will leave. Then again, if the Americans leave, there would be civil war and chaos. My friend, Khaled, thinks that the Americans should leave because they are just drawing fire from insurgent groups. What do you think? I am grateful that Khaled is still here. He is thinking about joining the new army, but I have been encouraging him to go on to college. He is fiercely loyal to our country and will never leave, but I fear that his dreams of college are coming to an end. You would like Khaled. He is the jokester out of my group of friends, and he is also very loyal. He gets mad when anyone speaks badly about his friends. I never have to worry about Khaled betraying my trust either. It is nice to have a friend to confide in without doubt. What about your friends? What are they like?*

*I have not seen your father in a while. I think he might be out on a mission. I will let you know if I hear from him.*

    *Ahmed*

---

**To:** ahmed86@yaboo.com
**From:** Mercermur1@yaboo.com
**Subject: Re: Friends**
**October 19**

*Dear Ahmed, I know EXACTLY what you are going through. My best friend, David, is thinking about joining the Marines, and I keep encouraging him to go to college just like you are trying to encourage Khaled! David is a true patriot as well, and he's also very loyal. His mom is from Kerala in the southern part of India so he's my brown-skinned-brotha'. We've been best friends since seventh grade. He's never missed any of my athletic events or birthdays, and he's never said a mean thing to anyone. I just don't want to see him risk his life for this war. I know the Americans are trying to bring you democracy, but are you honestly glad they are there?*

*I will continue to pray for you, Ahmed. Someday we'll be eighty-year-old men rocking on a porch watching our grandchildren play touch football as we enjoy retirement.*

    *Mercer*

**October 20** - Sometimes I feel like such a social nerd. I think back to my reactions to people and the things I say and I'm so embarrassed. I cringe later at the tacky and misplaced things I blurt out. For example, today I asked Beth if she was a Hawk fan. She cringed and said she hated football. I laughed and said, "That's un-American." Then she looked at me like I just called her fat or something. Why can't I be like Conan with his witty comebacks? I talk a lot, but I'm not a smooth talker like David. He just knows what to say and when to say it and he is sincere too. No wonder my nanny is in love with him.

**October 22** - Thanks to the smartest and most giving person I know (besides David – how did I get so lucky to have not one but TWO giving people for best friends), I got a "C" in Algebra II on my 1st quarter report card. Mary is my guardian angel. Somehow I'll have to make it up to her.

Mom didn't bother going to conferences. This brings up Commandment IV, "Honor your parents." Shouldn't that go both ways? I listen to my dad, of course, but if I listen to my mom, shouldn't she give me some time in return? I guess she didn't go because I'm doing okay with grades. They are good enough to get into Iowa. Now I just have to figure out a way to get that football scholarship.

**To:** Mercermur1@yaboo.com
**From:** ahmed86@yaboo.com
**Subject: America**
**October 24**

*Dear Mercer,*

*Good day to you, Sir. I hope all is well with your football games. I will pray that Allah gives you the courage and strength to do your best at all times.*

*We visited the mosque today as we try to do every Friday for the weekly reading of the Koran and prayers. It is, how do you say, "ironic" that I am so religious. When my father and mother were first married (in 1979), many people grew up without observing the religious rituals, like prayers and fasting. Very few young women would wear the hijab (headscarf), although the traditional habay (black loose garment) was common among older women and women of the poorer classes. These days, Iraqis have become much more religious and teenagers are much more interested in religion than many of their parents ever were. One of the most obvious changes is that girls started to cover their hair when going to school. Unfortunately, it is now difficult to even go to school. I have been keeping up with my reading though. My mother has encouraged me to sell only the books that I have read. She is the biggest supporter of my education.*

*I do not know how I feel about the Americans being here, Mercer. At times I see progress, but other times I see more chaos. The one thing that I am holding out for is hope. I believe that democracy will be better for my people. It might take fifty years, but I believe it will happen.*

> *Ahmed*

---

**To:** ahmed86@yaboo.com
**From:** Mercermur1@yaboo.com
**Subject: Re: America**
**October 24**

*Ahmed,*

*You remind me of my blessings, and for that I thank you. I may not like school, but I don't have to be afraid to go there.*

> *Mercer*

**October 25** - We won again last night. We are now 5-3. If we win next week, we will go to the playoffs. I'm happy for the guys, but I'm still not getting any playing time. I'm sloughing off at practice too. Coach Fox pulled me aside and gave me the "teamwork" motivational speech, i.e., quit being lazy and act like a captain. I'm the captain. I'm the captain. I'm the captain, and I DON'T PLAY. I certainly can't inspire anyone if I can't inspire myself. I'm moving to Canada where they don't go to war and where they have socialized healthcare. Then I'll take Mary with me so they will pay for her $10,000 a year formula. We'll get an apartment, work at Starbucks, and read Poe. And then I'll wake up and pout some more about not being a Hawkeye, Mary will fall in love with some rich, handsome French guy who writes her poetry, and I'll get fired from Starbucks for forgetting to put whipped cream on some blue-haired lady's mocha. At least the Hawks won (they beat Penn State 26-14). They're looking good for a sweet bowl game.

**October 27** - As if it isn't bad enough that I haven't heard from my father in a month and a half, I read in the paper today that four coordinated suicide attacks killed forty-three and wounded more than two hundred in Baghdad on its bloodiest day since the fall of Saddam. Targets included the headquarters of the Red Cross and three police stations. Insurgents are increasingly victimizing civilians, Iraqi security forces, and aid agencies, not simply U.S. troops.

Basically, my life sucks. I haven't heard from my dad in forever; they are still killing at will, and my dad is one of the targets; my new friend, Ahmed, who is a much better person than I am, is also in danger; and I can't even get playing time to fulfill my ONE AND ONLY DREAM. Maybe if I join the Army, I'll have a purpose for my life. I feel like crying.

**To:** artmurr@yaboo.com
**From:** Mercermur1@yaboo.com
**Subject: I'm sleeping in a box**
**October 28**

*Dear Dad,*

*I forgot to tell you that this Saturday I am going to sleep in a box. Yep, Mercer Michael Murray is going to find out what it is like to be a homeless teen, if only for a night. The Iowa Youth Emergency Shelter is holding its annual "Reggie's Sleepout" at Drake Stadium. Over five-hundred people will sleep out in boxes and tents to raise money and awareness for the homeless in Iowa. I've already raised $500, including $50 from my friends (David and Mary gave $20 each - I hang out with good peeps). Mom gave me a check for $200 and a big hug with tears that made me water up.*

*The whole sleep out thing started because of a young man named Reggie. Reggie Kelsey aged out of the foster care system in 2001 when he turned 18, and within three and a half months, died in the Des Moines River. After being kicked out of his latest foster care placement, Reggie bounced from one shelter to another, and occasionally camped outside while working with Iowa Homeless Youth Centers' street outreach staff and others to try to qualify for federal disability payments. Reggie's Place Coffee Shop (David and Mary and I try to go there once a month to hang out with the kids) and now "Reggie's Sleep Out" were named in honor of Reggie and their commitment to prevent another tragedy like it. Cool, huh?*

*I'm going with the St. Pius youth group team, but David's youth group is also going, so we should have a blast! Did you know that there are over 20,000 homeless people in Iowa? Wow. It might be cold, but I'll bundle up tight. Pray for us.*

*Mercer*

**To:** Mercermur1@yaboo.com
**From:** ahmed86@yaboo.com
**Subject: Ramadan**
**October 28**

*Dear Mercer,*

*Today is a beautiful day, Mercer. Today we celebrate Ramadan, my favorite time of the year. Ramadan is a "month of blessing" marked by prayer, fasting, and charity. Muslims believe that during the month of Ramadan, Allah revealed the first verses of the Qur'an. Around 610 A.D., a caravan trader named Muhammad wandered the desert near Mecca (in today's Saudi Arabia) while thinking about his faith. One night a voice called to him from the night sky. It was the angel Gabriel, who told Muhammad he had been chosen to receive the word of Allah. Then, Muhammad found himself speaking the verses that would be transcribed as the Qur'an. Muslims practice sawm, or fasting, for the entire month of Ramadan. This means that we may eat or drink nothing, including water, while the sun shines. Fasting is one of the Five Pillars (duties) of Islam.*

*While we are hungry and thirsty, we are reminded of the suffering of the poor. Fasting is also an opportunity to practice self-control and to cleanse the body and mind. And in this most sacred month, fasting helps us feel the peace that comes from spiritual devotion as well as kinship with fellow believers. I must admit, I get very hungry during this time, but it is also my favorite time of the year. I feel cleansed and in control and hopeful for the future after the month of Ramadan. I pray more and feel closer to Allah and to my dreams.*

*Ahmed*

---

**To:** ahmed86@yaboo.com
**From:** Mercermur1@yaboo.com
**Subject: Re: Ramadan**
**October 28**

*Ahmed,*

*Wow! That is what I call discipline. You can't even have water? As Catholics, we fast as well during the season of Lent, although we don't sacrifice nearly as much as you do. We don't eat at all on Ash Wednesday and Good Friday (actually, I think we can eat small meals) and we don't eat meat on Fridays, but that's about it. I don't know if I could handle not eating all day – I admire you.*

*Mercer*

**October 30 -** It's "trick or treat" night here in Iowa. For some reason we trick or treat on the night before Halloween (at least in Des Moines anyway), something to do with deterring pranks. Anyway, a bunch of us football jocks dressed like cheerleaders and went door to door in Bear's neighborhood. I think some of the female "door answerers" liked our six-packs as displayed through the skimpy uniforms, but if a dad came to the door, we didn't get very far. Most told us we were too old and that we were ruining it for the little kids. But the little kids all laughed hysterically when they saw us. We stopped at Beth's house. She gave me the "eye" again, but then her dad chased us away. No wonder she doesn't go to the dances – talk about overprotective. Anyway, we got a good supply of junk food, and we had a blast. Of course, I didn't eat any candy – too much sugar won't help me catch any bullets. Big game tomorrow night, not that I will play anyway.

---

**To:** artmurr@yaboo.com
**From:** Mercermur1@yaboo.com
**Subject: Please**
**Oct. 30**


Dad – please write.

---

2ND QUARTER

## MERCER 10
## WAR 7

**November 1 -** Last night was the best night of my life. Not only did I have 120 yards (Yeah, baby!) and we won (now we are 6-3 and headed to the playoffs), but we went streaking after the game and got chased by cops. Now you may think this is a bad thing, but it was such an adrenaline rush. I ran to some family's backyard and hid in their doghouse (thank goodness it was 65 degrees – broke the "high" record for the day). I saw the flashlights of the cops and heard them asking each other where I went, but they couldn't find me. I stayed in there until 11:30ish until I was sure the coast was clear. Then I remembered I didn't have any clothes on, and I wasn't with my friends. What could I do? There weren't any leaves on the branches, so I grabbed some twigs. Better than nothing. Mom didn't even notice that I broke curfew. And the Hawks won again (they beat Illinois – 41-10)! What a great weekend.

---

**To:** artmurr@yaboo.com
**From:** Mercermur1@yaboo.com
**Subject: Car Bombs**
**November 1**

*Dad,*

*All we ever hear about over here is car bombs and IED's. Throw me a bone would you? Is anything actually getting accomplished?*

*BTW, I had a great game last night – 120 yards. We're headed to the playoffs.*

*Mercer*

**To:** Mercermur1@yaboo.com
**From:** artmurr@yaboo.com
**Subject: Not flashy**
**November 1**

*Dear Son,*

*I apologize for not writing for a while. Things are getting more complicated here. I will be praying for you tonight with your sleep out.*

*You may be scared by all the car bombings, but take faith. The media needs listeners, and car bombs are interesting. Searching vehicles at an entry control point with our Iraqi partners is not flashy, but those vehicle searches improve the security situation by keeping guns and bombs out of Iraqi cities. Looking for and finding weapons' cashes are not going to make the front page news, but again, cache finds keep the means to hurt innocent Iraqi citizens and Coalition Forces off the streets. Recently, one of our battalions found thousands of buried weapons and ordnance. We are getting the job done, son. Don't listen to everything you hear.*

> *Dad*

**To:** artmurr@yaboo.com
**From:** Mercermur1@yaboo.com
**Subject: Re: Not flashy**
**November 1**

*Dad,*

*If you don't write, all I have is the media. I am trying to see the positives in this war, for your sake and for Ahmed's, but when my dad is away from me, a new friend has to worry about how he's going to feed his mother, and my best friend is thinking of joining the two of you, I'm having a hard time remaining upbeat. In any case, I'm proud of you, Dad. I'm proud that you are my father and that you are saving lives.*

> *Mercer*

**November 2** - I read in the paper today that (aren't you impressed, Ms. Boge, that I'm reading the paper every day?) Iraqi guerrillas shot down an American helicopter, killing 16 U.S. soldiers and injuring 21 others. Additional attacks this month made it the bloodiest since the war began: at least 75 U.S. soldiers died. I'm so glad my dad wrote yesterday. I hate constantly worrying about him. I can't seem to concentrate anymore. My "C" in Math is now a "D-" at best. On the other hand, I've never had such power workouts during football practice. My coach thinks it's just because I'm the captain.

I made my family go to church again (after we came back from an AWESOME sleep out – thanks for pitching in, Ms. Boge, even if you don't read this). Commandment III: *Remember the Sabbath Day* is one that I intend to enforce.

---

**To:** artmurr@yaboo.com
**From:** Mercermur1@yaboo.com
**Subject: I slept outside in a box!**
**November 2**

*Dear Dad,*

*Reggie's Sleepout 2003! What a blast! It was dark, but at least there were enough lights to see FOUR HOURS OF LIVE MUSIC! We all slam danced and played air guitar, and then we broke for some chili and came back for more. Finally around 12:00 we went to our boxes (boys on one side of the 50-yard-line and girls on the other). Mine was made of two stove boxes from Lowes. I didn't design a cool one or anything, but the winners of the box contest were awesome. Someone made a two-story replica of 801 Grand (45 stories) - what an engineering feat! The sign on the outside said that 801 Grand in Des Moines holds 6,000 people; it would take more than three times that much to house all the homeless in Iowa. Good use of statistics. Anyway, they fed us and kept us entertained until the witching hour. Then it was time to bundle up and sleep with fresh air and stars. I did actually sleep, although I'm not sure how much. I brought three pillows - two for my lower half and one for my head. I fought with positioning all night and my boxes collapsed because, well, I don't know why, but they fell on me. No problem. They protected me from the wind and the ground - they served their purpose.*

*Next year I'm going to design the coolest box. Good thing I have a year to think about it. It was a good experience, even though I always knew in the back of my mind that I would get to take a nap in a nice warm bed the next day. I will continue to pray for those people. It's like John Bunyan said, "You have not lived today until you have done something for someone who can never repay you."*

**November 4** - President Bush won Senate approval for $87.5 billion in funds to continue the war. Not only do I have to sacrifice my dad, but it's costing me a lot of money to save some foreign country. Okay, I don't actually pay taxes yet, but I will someday.

I'm psyched about football now. I'm swatting behinds and yelling all the time in practice. I'm going to earn a scholarship, and we're going to win state.

**November 6** -You might have noticed, Ms. Boge, (that is, if you are reading this – I'm still holding back just a tad in case) that I don't talk about David much (he's my other best-friend, remember?). I haven't mentioned him a lot because I never see the kid. I'm too busy wallowing in pity over football, at least that's what Mary tells me when she asks why I don't talk to David that much anymore. It is football, but it's also the fact that I don't get home until 7:00 every night and I have to play parent four out of the seven nights in a week. Plus, David doesn't like streaking (the "body is a temple of the Holy Spirit" argument) and sometimes I need to just let off some steam, so I go out with my football buddies. Is that wrong? After football, David and I will hang around all the time again (winter is not a good time to be naked outside hiding in doghouses). Anyway, David is such a loyal guy. And it's not like he's sitting around waiting for me to call. He's got youth group and work to keep him busy. (If you ever wondered why an evangelical is going to a Catholic school, his mom and dad made an agreement when he was born – he would be raised in the evangelical church, but he would attend Catholic schools. It seems to have worked out well for him and people like me who need some good spiritual guidance.) I really should talk to him about this Marines thing though. I'm all for serving one's country, just not when it's my dad or my best friend.

David and I have the type of friendship where even if we didn't talk for months, we'd pick up right where we left off.

Mary says that doesn't mean I get to ignore him, though, and I agree. But it's just hard right now. David is a good guy – he'll understand.

---

**To:** ahmed86@yaboo.com
**From:** Mercermur1@yaboo.com
**Subject: Iraq – brief history**
**November 7**

*Ahmed,*

*I feel pretty dumb asking this, but could you give me a quick explanation of the whole Iraq "situation," at least twenty or so years back. They don't really teach it here, and the newspapers just talk about the current fighting. I am really trying to understand why my father is there. Thanks.*

*Mercer*

---

**To:** Mercermur1@yaboo.com
**From:** ahmed86@yaboo.com
**Subject: Re: Iraq – brief history**
**November 7**

*Dear Mercer,*

*It is ironic that you should ask me this. I was just thinking about how it is so different here now. I do not mean to complain, because good things are happening, but it is just different. I will try to explain our situation as I understand it, or at least how my dad explained it to me. Others may disagree, but I at least know the facts are right.*

*I grew up during "the war years," when the Iraqi government encouraged everyone to fulfill their duties as citizens. While men were drafted in large numbers to the military, women were strongly encouraged to produce multiple children. By 1988 (I was two) Hussein had declared victory in the Iran-Iraq war, but over 250,000 were dead and Iraq was left in severe debt. Saddam decided to gain money by invading a different foreign country. On the day I turned four, (my birthday is August 2, 1986), Saddam invaded Kuwait because he said that Kuwait was exceeding oil production quotas set by the OPEC. He also accused Kuwait of stealing oil from the Rumailah fields, and establishing military bases and civilian establishments inside Iraqi territory. Fortunately, Iraq only occupied Kuwait for seven months, but we were horrified at the injustice of the invasion (my father was one of the few who had access to the truth – most people were at the mercy of Saddam's propaganda promoting Kuwait as the betrayer). What followed were seven months of agony and nightmare as the Iraqi troops indulged in violence, torture, looting and destruction on a mass scale. For the Kuwaitis it meant complete loss of freedom, civic and human rights. When it became apparent that Baghdad had no intentions to withdraw, over eighteen countries and 690,000 troops joined the Operation Desert Storm (the Gulf War), a U.S.-led multinational military effort. The U.N. backed the operation, which took prompt and decisive action during the crisis by consistently issuing resolutions against and warnings to Baghdad. The Gulf War was a complete success, routing the Iraqis in forty-two days from Kuwait. Obviously the victory in the Gulf War was good for the people of Kuwait, but once again, the people of Iraq had to suffer because of our corrupt leader. It was particularly hard for children, as night after night of heavy bombing disrupted not only their sleep and family lives, but left many in shock and fear. I had ongoing nightmares for at least three months and a great sensitivity to certain noises that could be mistaken for bombs. I was lucky – the nightmares stopped, and I began to feel less anxious soon after the war was over, but some of my cousins were affected severely. Unlike other war-torn countries, 'post-traumatic stress syndrome' is not a recognized medical condition in Iraq. My cousins had to deal with nightmares for many years.*

*The U.S. decided to leave Saddam in office because many thought his own people would overthrow him. Then, when in six months, Saddam was still in power, the U.N. figured it would just cripple him with sanctions. On August 6 (1990) the U.N. Security Council adopted Resolution 61, which imposed strict economic sanctions on Iraq, providing for a full trade embargo, excluding medical supplies, food and other items of humanitarian necessity. This is when life began to change for our people. We were fortunate to have access to food, medical supplies, and other necessities because my father was an academic, but others suffered greatly, especially children, many of whom suffered and/or died from malnutrition. Saddam would not feed his own people, even the little ones.*

*Then in 1998, Saddam had enough. He expelled all UN inspectors and closed off the country. In December 1998, U.S. President Bill Clinton authorized air strikes on government targets and military facilities in response. Intermittent air strikes against military facilities and alleged WMD sites continued into 2002. Saddam suffered nothing, but his people suffered greatly. For too long, we have lived under tyranny and fear.*

*And so here we are. The Bush administration has justified its war against Iraq on three grounds: Saddam Hussein's alleged possession of weapons of mass destruction, his links to so-called terrorists, and liberating Iraqis from oppression and tyranny. I do not think the first two will ever be proven, but liberating us is enough for me. I want my people to live in freedom. Now many may call me a traitor for wanting to leave and study in the U.S., but I want to get a good education so I can go back and help my people. I will help my people. I have to help my people.*

    *Ahmed*

**November 8** - Today I raked the leaves. Now this may seem like no big deal, but when you have a front and back yard that cover an acre AND you have twenty years of tree growth, let me tell you, it sucks. Not only is my back killing me, but I have to live with the knowledge that I will have to rake again next weekend and probably the weekend after that and after that. At least it's only once a year though, but then again, if it isn't raking, it's shoveling and then mowing. The difference is raking is labor intensive. Thank goodness for the snow blower and the lawn mower. And what about toilets? I have to clean my bathroom every week, including the toilet. I guess I don't HAVE to clean my bathroom every week, but I am a clean freak. Anyway, I just realized that I will have to clean my toilet every week for the rest of my life. The same thing – spray, swish, flush, every week. Rake, shovel, mow, swish, flush, repeat. I guess it's kind of like life - you do the same thing over and over.

The bad news: my Hawks lost today at Purdue, 14-27. The good news: Mary got three first place individual finishes (50 free, 200 free, and 200 back) at state and a first place relay (200). St. Thom's got 2nd place overall.

**November 9** - Since David and I didn't go to the swimming meet yesterday, we took Mary out for a congratulatory breakfast after church. We had stacks of pancakes and hash browns (Mary can have the hash browns, but she has to bring in her own pancake mix because regular flour has a lot of protein – who knew?). I had the same thing she did. Mary knows I'm not a vegetarian or anything, but I never eat meat in front of her.

**November 10** -Today is Monday, the worst day of the week. I'm tired, but I'd call it more of an excited tired. In two days, I'll be celebrating a playoff victory with my friends while trying to do an interview with Keith Murphy on Channel 13 since I will have been the star player. Ferentz will take note and ask an assistant to call me the next day to "talk" about my future at the University of Iowa. See? It all works out.

I had to pick up Larry from Taekwondo practice at 7:30 since the hot nanny gets off at 7:00. I guess he's a brown belt now, which is actually really good. I forgot that he's been taking lessons since he was six. I actually admire him. He leads a pretty disciplined life and he's respectful, that is, if I can get him to shut-up once in a while. But then again, he's so quiet around others, I guess he needs to vent with his older, wiser, and smarter bro.

It's Veterans' Day today – we prayed for our veterans and soldiers in every class. I forgot about Veterans' Day, so when we were in first period, I was taken aback. I actually started shaking when we prayed – Mary stealthily grabbed the top of my hand and squeezed it. God Bless America.

---

**To:** Mercermur1@yaboo.com
**From:** ahmed86@yaboo.com
**Subject: Iraq**
**November 10**

*Dear Mercer,*

*I am trying to get a picture of what your daily life is like. For instance, what is your business district like? What is your high school like? Baghdad's streets are now filled with numerous street peddlers and beggars. Many people are trying to make a few dinars by selling things, shining shoes, or hustling foreigners. It is sad to see my former classmates work so hard for so little. It is also crushing to see the children begging on the street. They are so small, so much smaller and younger looking than their age because of malnutrition. I am fortunate to never have gone without food, although we have to sell more of our belongings now. My mother is strong. Sometimes I wish I could be more like her.*

*Ahmed*

**To:** ahmed86@yaboo.com
**From:** Mercermur1@yaboo.com
**Subject: Re: Iraq**
**November 10**

*Dear Ahmed,*

*Life here is pretty much the same day in and day out. To tell you the truth, I've been feeling angry lately. I'm mad that my dad isn't here. I'm also pissed that my dream of playing college football is slipping away.*

*Let's see, high school, huh? My high school is a little different than your average public high school, but it's filled with the same teenage problems. The biggest difference is that most of the people in my school are Catholic so we go to Mass as a school at least once a month. It's cool though – I like "God" time during school.*

> *Mercer*

**November 11** - HUGE playoff game tomorrow. This might be my last chance to show the Hawks what I've got. I'm going for the gold.

**To:** artmurr@yaboo.com
**From:** Mercermur1@yaboo.com
**Subject: We lost**
**November 12**

*Dad,*

*We lost. Jordan Creek beat us 21-20. I didn't have the ball thrown to me once. I hate my life.*

> *Mercer*

**November 13** - We lost last night to Jordan Creek in the opening round of the playoffs. It was 60 degrees – prime football weather, and we blew it. We lost 20-21. Now we could all blame the kicker for missing that extra point, but we all lost that game, well, except for me since I didn't get the ball thrown to me. Of course I didn't have any yardage – no news flash there. Maybe it was my fault as captain. Maybe my future was blown by a quarterback who couldn't throw. I'm speechless.

I trudged along the halls today waiting for the meaning of life to run into me, but it didn't. I see, hear, taste, smell, and feel nothing. I think my toes are even depressed. Mary tried to cheer me up with Skittles, Mountain Dew, and a homemade card, but I all I could muster was a smile. I couldn't even cry about it.

I did manage to read in the *Register* that the Bush administration reversed policy in a deal with the Iraqi Governing Council, agreeing to transfer power to an interim government much sooner, in 2004. Good. Let them take over their own government with their own people and get my father out of there so he can come home and be my dad.

**November 14** - Tonight is the first Friday night I've had off in over two months. You'd think I'd be happy. All I can think about is how I might have been cheated out of a dream. But I can't do anything about it. I know my dad would tell me to walk-on, but I don't know. I feel stupid. I'm too good for that. I have to get a job.

**November 16** - My Hawkeyes beat Minnesota yesterday 40-22. They are now 8-3 and it looks like they're going to the Capital One Bowl in Florida.

"Dancing Queen" by ABBA came on the radio today while I was spacing off trying to study for a math test. I smiled when I thought of the memory of my mom and me dancing to it. She once read this book about how penguin chicks stand on their parents' feet, so I decided to try it. Somehow we started dancing to the ABBA song with me standing on her feet. Of course I was only six at the time, but I think I danced on her feet until I was at least eleven. I miss my dad, but I miss my mom too.

**Nov. 17** - IT'S MY BIRTHDAY! I'm eighteen-years old. I woke up this morning feeling completely the same.

Mary surprised me today with brownies, Skittles (my favorite), a mocha, a bag of Honey Crisp apples, and a Picasso art book (Picasso – what a genius) today for my birthday. All I want to do is go home and sleep.

Beth is now going out with George, the no-passer quarterback. Unbelievable.

**MERCER   10**
**WAR      14**

November 18 - If you can believe it, my mom is actually gone MORE now. She has this big discrimination case against a bar owner. Her client lost his legs in an explosion last June while serving with the Iowa Army National Guard in Iraq. So he tried to go to this bar in West Des Moines called *Spirits,* but they wouldn't let him in because he had tennis shoes (they are special tennis shoes that amputees have to wear). His shoes weren't fancy enough (the bar prohibits tennis shoes and hooded sweatshirts) and the owner said that the guy didn't explain to the bouncers that he had prosthetic legs. Anyway, the guy hired my mom to sue the bar for violating Iowa law that says you can't discriminate on the basis of disability in public accommodations. She's on T.V. a lot. She looks pretty good for an old lady (she's got some killer green eyes, or so my dad says), although lately she's looking kind of skinny, in a not-so-healthy way. I just want her to be around more. I wish I could be Bilbo (without the hairy feet, of course) and live in a hole in the ground.

November 19 - I'm so bored with life. I go to school, come home from school, eat Cheetos and drink Coke on the couch while watching movies (they know me by name at the movie store now), order take-out for dinner, and go to bed. That is my daily routine. Gina calls me a slob every day, and Larry doesn't even bother to talk AT me anymore. I've lost all desire to do anything productive or beneficial to society.

**November 20** - I just read the best book EVER, in ONE DAY (that is a record). It's called *Friday Night Lights* and I heard they are making a movie out of it next year. It's all about a town that revolves around the high school football team. Now why couldn't I have been born in Texas? I was born to play football; I just know it. I got it at school today and read until 12:00, without even pausing for supper (I did go to the bathroom twice, but I brought the book with me - TMI).

**November 22** - The Hawks beat Wisconsin 27-21 to finish the season 9-3 (5-3 in the Big Ten). Not bad, not great, but not bad. Maybe I won't go to Iowa next year, although I haven't really applied anywhere else. Fortunately, there's still time to apply places. I have a 3.1 and a 24 on my A.C.T. (boy did I study for the math section – I got a 20! WOW!), so I shouldn't have too much trouble getting in somewhere. But what am I going to do if I don't play football? My whole life has revolved around football either through playing, watching, or observing my father coach. I guess I just assumed I'd play college football, become a P.E. teacher, and coach with my dad. Maybe I'll just start a chain of falafel stands and sit around and eat all day.

**November 24** - I applied for a job today as a front desk attendant at the *Boys' and Girls' Club*. The guy (a HUGE black man named Jerome) asked me something I've never been asked before in a job interview. He asked me what my relationship with my father was like. Of course, I went on about how we were best friends and how he was my hero and such. After this question, he shook my hand and offered me the job. Weird, huh?

**To:** Mercermur1@yaboo.com
**From:** ahmed86@yaboo.com
**Subject: Eid al-Fitr**
**November 26**

*Dear Mercer,*

*Ramadan ended today with the festival of Eid al-Fitr, literally the "Festival of Breaking the Fast." Eid al-Fitr is one of the two most important Islamic celebrations (the other occurs after the Hajj, or pilgrimage to Mecca). At Eid al-Fitr people dress in their finest clothes, adorn their homes with lights and decorations, give treats to children, and enjoy visits with friends and family.*

*These festivities are filled with a sense of generosity and gratitude. Although charity and good deeds are always important in Islam, they have special significance at the end of Ramadan. As the month draws to a close, Muslims are obligated to share their blessings by feeding the poor and making contributions to mosques. We celebrated Eid al-Fitr today, mostly with our hearts. We don't have any decorations or treats, but we thank Allah for our lives.*

*Ahmed*

---

**To:** ahmed86@yaboo.com
**From:** Mercermur1@yaboo.com
**Subject: Re: Eid al-Fitr**
**November 26**

*I admire you for fasting for a whole month! I would never be able to do that because of football, although now it looks as if my football dreams have come to an end. We lost in the playoffs and I didn't have any yards. No one has called me to play for them, except a couple of D-3 schools (the University of Iowa is Division 1 (D-1), the highest level. D-2 schools give out some scholarships and D-3 schools are colleges or universities that have teams but do not give out scholarships). It makes me happy that you can still celebrate Eid al-Fitr, especially since you are in the middle of a war. I wish I could celebrate. I feel like such a failure, and then I feel like such a loser because I'm so depressed over such a meaningless thing like football. I'm sorry, Ahmed. I have no reason to complain about anything.*
*Mercer*

**To:** Mercermur1@yaboo.com
**From:** ahmed86@yaboo.com
**Subject: Re: Eid al-Fitr**
**November 26**

*Dear Mercer,*

*Please do not apologize, my good friend. My father always told me that your feelings are never wrong; it is what you do with the feelings. It seems natural to be disappointed, but you will show your true character by how you react to your situation.*

> *Ahmed*

---

**To:** ahmed86@yaboo.com
**From:** Mercermur1@yaboo.com
**Subject: Re: Eid al-Fitr**
**November 26**

*Ahmed,*

*I don't think I have any character outside of football; that's the problem.*

> *Mercer*

---

**November 27** - Today is Thanksgiving. I slept in till 1:00. I am thankful for my faith, my dad, my mom, my sister, my brother, and my friends. Other than that, it's time to go back to bed.

Oh, by the way, I saw on the news that yesterday George Bush made a surprise visit to U.S. troops in Baghdad to serve them a Thanksgiving Day dinner. I wonder if my dad was there. He deserves to have some slop served by the man who sent him there.

---

**To:** Mercermur1@yaboo.com
**From:** ahmed86@yaboo.com
**Subject: Hope**
**November 27**

*Dear Mercer,*

*I do not know if you have heard yet, but your President Bush visited my city today! I cannot tell you how excited we all were, especially the soldiers. His visit created a surge of optimism and energy among the troops. I admire your President for making such a dangerous journey here to inspire the people who are fighting for our country. Saddam would never risk such a thing. I have not seen your father, but I am sure he is excited as well. I am pleased for my people. I believe that President Bush is a good man, and he is doing what is right to bring democracy to Iraq. I pray for him.*

*I do not know much about your tradition of Thanksgiving, but I know that I am thankful President Bush is here. I am also thankful that you are my friend, Mercer. I know you are feeling sad, but I know that you are a strong young man who will make his father proud just as I intend to do.*

*Ahmed*

**From:** Mercermur1@yaboo.com
**Subject: Re: Hope**
**November 27**

*Thanks, Ahmed. You always put things in perspective for me, if even for only a little while. I'm glad President Bush visited the troops too – I hope my dad got to meet him.*

*We celebrate Thanksgiving here in America by eating turkey, squash, pumpkin pie, cranberries, mashed potatoes, and other goodies. My dad usually cooks us up a great feast, but instead we went out for Chinese food this year. We celebrate Thanksgiving in remembrance of the Pilgrims when they first came to America from England. They had a hard winter and the Indians (Native Americans) helped them out and they all had a big feast to show their gratefulness (even though later on the settlers took their land from them, gave them diseases, and forced them on reservations to live). And so we celebrate Thanksgiving as a time of gratefulness for freedom of religion and for our blessings. I am very thankful for what I have, but I'm being a spoiled brat again. If I had my dad back here, everything would be perfect. Well, that and if I were to get a scholarship to Iowa.*

*Mercer*

**November 28** - It seems that all I want to do these days is sleep, eat junk food, see how much flab I'm packing on (what happened to the revved-up metabolism I had a year ago – I could eat ANYTHING I wanted), and write in this journal. It's funny, but I never liked writing before I had this thing. Maybe I'm writing to show you, Ms. Boge, that I'm a cool person who is just going through a hard time (but you don't read this anyway). Maybe I'm writing so I can go back and read it and laugh at the good ole' days. Or maybe I'm writing because I know no one will ever read this, and I'm the only one who really cares about my feelings so I'm my only support system. I know God hears me, but I sure can't hear Him right now – maybe I have to learn how to listen.

Thanksgiving was a disaster last night. My mom doesn't cook so we went to a Chinese restaurant for dinner. For seventeen years my father has cooked capon (I learned that everyone else in America has "turkey" when I was in first grade), sour cream mashed potatoes, balsamic/walnut salad, home-made ciabatta rolls, and banana cream pie (although the last four years I have made the banana cream pie –I think mine is actually better than my dad's. I didn't make it this year). This is the first year I haven't been with my father on Thanksgiving. So anyway, we went to *The Great Wall of China* for dinner. We all ordered our drinks and went through the buffet. Mom tried to small talk, but she acted nervous about it and I got annoyed. I was pretty much mute the whole time and only grunted yes/no answers when necessary. Gina blabbed on and on about dance and Algebra and going tanning to lose her "pasty look." Larry went on and on about chess and piano and how the teacher made him "homework helper." I just rolled my eyes and my mom gave me a dirty look. But I know she's just being polite to them. She's distracted – who knows if she even heard what they said. This made me even more mad – I have a right to be disinterested – I'm their brother, but she's their mother. She has no choice but to be interested and supportive and loving and actually CARE what they have to say. So by this time, I'm annoyed that Gina and Larry are so happy with their lives, I'm annoyed that she is trying to talk to me, and I'm annoyed that she isn't listening to them. I was about ready to blow. Then the waiter came by and Gina started flirting with him. So I told her to control her hormones or she'd end up with an STD. You see what I mean about saying the wrong thing at the wrong time? Of course Larry asked what an STD was and my mom snapped at me. I couldn't handle it. I threw my napkin on the table, stood up, gave my mom the death stare, and left. I stopped to look back at my mom, and I saw the bags under her eyes. Then I just started running, sprinting actually. I ran for my dad, I ran for my dreams, I ran for my guilt. I ran because I didn't know what else to do.

*Dear Dad,*

*In case mom hasn't already told you, I made a big scene at dinner last night. Our family just seems so fake. Mom looks like caca (no offense, Dad, but she's really skinny and she's got dark circles under her eyes and she doesn't even bother with make-up anymore unless she's going to be on T.V.), Gina is in la-la-girly land, and Larry is just Larry, the world's perfect child (he's so perfect that I get annoyed by the fact that I'm annoyed with him since he never does anything wrong). Anyway, I ran out on the family; actually I sprinted out the door and made a fool of myself and embarrassed everyone. What's wrong with me, Dad? I need you. I need you to go lift weights. I need you to listen. Please come home. We're falling apart.*

*Mercer*

**November 29** - Let me tell you why David is my best friend and a person whom I admire with the utmost respect. After sitting down at our normal table last Wednesday, the "cool" table in the lunchroom, David saw a froshie sitting by himself on one end of the table while about six freshman football players occupied the other end. We both observed the football players occasionally taunting the kid for his size (he was about five feet, 85 pounds soaking wet). Now I have an empathetic heart, but I'm slow to actually act on it. Not David. He saw what was going on, immediately went over to the kid and acted like they were best friends. He said, "Hey, man. What are you doing over here? Come on, why don't you eat with some REAL men," and proceeded to cast a disappointed yet cocky grin aimed at the other freshman football players who cowered and blushed. The kid followed David over to our table where we all proceeded to adopt him. His name was Freddie, and I'm confident that after a week of sitting with us, along with some prompting of our girls to flirt a little with him, little Freddie will not be the outcast of the freshman class for long. You see, David is always like that. He sees people's pain and does something about it, whereas I just see people's pain. But I guess I can work on it. I definitely respect people. David just does a much better job than I do.

**November 30** - I haven't written to Ahmed in a while (actually, it's only been three days, but I sort of miss the guy). I feel too guilty. I know I'm wallowing in pity here while he's fighting to stay alive, but I don't like feeling guilty for feeling sorry for myself. I do when I talk to him. I know I have no right to complain, but I'm just pissed and I want to stay pissed. Plus, the guy is PERFECT! He lost his dad, he takes care of his mother, he earns money for food for his family, and he never complains. Does he have ANY flaws?

On a lighter note, I learned another interesting tidbit. Back in the 1500's, baths consisted of a big tub filled with hot water. The man of the house had the privilege of the nice clean water, then all the other sons and men, then the women and finally the children, last of all the babies. By then the water was so dirty you could actually lose someone in it. Hence the saying, "Don't throw the baby out with the bath water." I really need to get a life.

**December 1** - I met with Jerome about the job with the Boys and Girls Club today. I'll be working behind the desk mostly, but I also get to coach a team of five-year-old boys. I start on January 5th. We have one practice a week and five games over the next two months. I guess Jerome is going to supervise me the first game and then let me handle the rest of them. Mary thinks this will pep me up a bit. I don't know. I feel like Sisyphus, up and down, up and down. Where's the meaning?

It's a new month. I CAN start over. I just have to figure out how to start starting over.

## MERCER    13
## WAR      14

**December 2** - Okay, it's time to get serious. I only need to start studying more, workout after school, write to my dad and Ahmed more, and treat my family better. How hard is that? It's time to be my own life coach.

I have serious guilt issues. I think about things over and over and over. I think about how much of a jerk I am to my family. I think about Ahmed's situation and how I have no right to complain. I feel bad for telling my dad I'm against the war. I need a piece of good news, you know?

My mom said she'll be home more now since the young National Guard soldier (the one who was suing the bar because of the dress code) settled out of court. We'll see.

**December 3** - We're reading this awesome book in Social Justice called <u>Amazing Grace</u> by Jonathan Kozol. It's all about the life of the poor in the South Bronx. Let me just tell you, I was clueless. I always thought that being poor in America wasn't really that bad. I mean, in Iowa you can go to a homeless shelter or the family violence shelter or apply for tons of government aid. But these people have nothing. The police don't even come if they are called. The welfare system is so screwed up, AIDS, drugs, and prostitution are rampant, and no one seems to care. People there feel as if the rich New Yorkers would feel better if the poor would all just disappear. Man, I really need to stop complaining. I'm so blessed, so blessed. So why can't I feel anything?

**To:** Mercermur1@yaboo.com
**From:** ahmed86@yaboo.com
**Subject: Thankfulness**
**December 3**

*Dear Mercer,*

*I feel like I will never get away from here. I am scared that something will happen to my mother like my father. I am scared that I will never be able to study in America. I am scared that my children will never know freedom. And yet, the beauty of the world around me reminds me to be thankful to Allah. North of Baghdad where the Tigris and Euphrates rivers come together, I see paradise. The gardens, the abundant fruit and vegetables – everything is lush and full and green. I see people working on tractors and grain bins and grain wagons. People are actually working again! Many people just want the chance to work again.*

*I am working, but I am working for the enemy in some people's eyes. I fear for my mother and aunts and uncles sometimes because I am working for the Americans. I heard of an interpreter whose family was murdered because he helped out the "infidels." But I need to help feed my family. They will die anyway without food.*

*Ahmed*

---

**To:** ahmed86@yaboo.com
**From:** Mercermur1@yaboo.com
**Subject: Re: Thankfulness**
**December 4**

*Ahmed,*

*I'm sure Iowa's beauty doesn't even compare to the cradle of civilization, but I do hope you can come and see it someday. Des Moines has a nice river and we have great bluffs on either side of the state. Plus, you have to come party with us up in Okoboji. I know you'll make it here, Ahmed. You are too smart to be selling jewelry for food. My dad will make it happen, somehow.*

*Mercer*

---

**December 5 -** It is cold, oh, so cold here. I'm freezing my butt off and my extra fat is not keeping me warm. I'm officially chubby, but I've actually lost three pounds. My six-pack is now a flab pack. I don't have the beer puffiness in the cheeks that Bear has, but I'm not chiseled anymore either. I'm tired all the time too. My grades are average, my interest is average, even my attention span in normal conversations is average. I need Oprah.

**To:** artmurr@yaboo.com
**From:** Mercermurl@yaboo.com
**Subject: Hello?**
**December 6**

*Dad,*

*You haven't written to your 1ˢᵗ born child since November 1ˢᵗ. Now I know you are alive because Mom says you write to her, and I know she's your wife and all, but will you just shoot me an e-mail with a subject line saying something? I'm in a funk, Dad. I'm starting to talk to Cheetos, even the little crumbs on my hand. Seriously, how are we ever going to get out of this war?*

*Mercer*

---

**To:** Mercermurl@yaboo.com
**From:** artmurr@yaboo.com
**Subject: Re: Hello?**
**December 6**

*Dear Mercer,*

*I apologize, Son. I have been working 18-hour days and computer time is scarce. It's a mess here, but I do know that the U.S. will bring democracy, someday. It might just be a little more difficult than we thought. Part of the problem is that we are fighting alongside some of the Iraqi people, but we are also fighting against them. It's sort of a civil war. The leaders of insurgent groups are paying out-of-work Iraqis to plant powerful roadside bombs to attack us. Most of the money comes out of Syria. We can't concentrate on going after individuals – we go after the guys who move the money.*

*The cash and insurgents, who come into the country across the Syrian border, move along the Euphrates River valley from the western edge of Iraq through Ramadi and on to Baghdad. The U.S. and coalition forces are attempting to cut off the route. These insurgent groups are affiliated with al-Qaida in Iraq and Abu Musab al-Zarqawi, a Jordanian militant who has ties to Osama bin Laden. They find people who are out of work and who need to feed their families. They'll say, "Go take this rice sack and put it in a hole. I'll give you $300." It's a no-brainer. In fact, improvised explosive devices (IED's) have caused more than 50% of the casualties here. These devices are becoming so powerful that they can overwhelm any military vehicle. Our battalion is assigned to find and disarm the devices – the key is to find the "initiation devices," the electronic equipment used by insurgents to detonate the explosives. Often they are base units for cordless telephones. Insurgents conceal themselves and watch as convoys pass. Then they use the phones to set off buried bombs. Sorry about the history lesson here, but I want you to get the truth first-hand.*

*I wish this were like the Gulf War when we easily crushed Saddam. But life doesn't always work like that. How are you doing in school? I'm sorry about football, but again, your education comes first. Iowa will be lucky to have you as a walk-on. Look at Dallas Clark.*

*Are you looking out for Larry and Gina? I still pray for you every night. Thanks for being the "man around the house."*

*Dad*

---

**To:** artmurr@yaboo.com
**From:** Mercermur1@yaboo.com
**Subject: Re: Hello?**
**December 6**

*Dad,*

*I can't tell you how good it is to hear your voice, even if it is only through e-mail. Sometimes I feel like I'm drowning here and you just threw me a line.*

*I'm still bummed over football, and I'm extremely out of shape, but at least I got a job. I don't start until January 5th, so that means I have nothing to do for a while but whine. My dream was to go to Iowa to play football. I'm fast, I'm athletic, I'm disciplined. I know playing football seems small in the background of fighting a war, but it's all I can think about.*

*Mary is doing well. She's still helping me with math again. I swear that girl is a saint. Someday she'll make some lucky stud a great wife (although when I told her that she looked at me funny). David is doing well, too. I hang out with his youth group some times on Wednesday nights. He's still talking about going to the Marines, but he's waiting to get the go ahead from God. Now there's a guy who's disciplined in prayer.*

*I'm talking to Ahmed a couple of times a week. I've learned a lot from him. He's so much more mature than I am, and he's patient too. In fact, he listens to me more than anyone here.*

*Bear is doing well. He still parties like a rock star and reeks of smoke all the time, but he's fun to hang out with. School is school. I like Government and Creative Writing though. Dad, I'm fat, actually, I'm flabby. I feel lethargic all the time and I'm addicted to reruns of "Friends."*

*Mercer*

---

**December 8** - Finals are coming up in a couple of weeks. How am I ever going to make it? I can barely do homework, let alone study for anything. I can't concentrate in class, and I don't care about anything school related except writing in this journal and getting in good discussions in Government. At least I'm reading the paper everyday (for class, we have to read the *Register* or the *New York Times* every day). I never cared much about politics until our oil daddies sent my father to go fight Crazy. I can slam the President in a journal, right? But then again, you don't read this, Ms. Boge, so I guess I can do whatever I like. I just better not ever lose this journal.

---

**To:** artmurr@yaboo.com
**From:** Mercermur1@yaboo.com
**Subject: Diplomacy**
**December 9**

*Dad,*

*I gotta tell you, Dad. We have a stellar Government teacher. She knows everything there is to know about the history of the world AND current events before they happen. I swear she must check the New York Times website every hour on the hour, even in the middle of the night. She told us that yesterday, Paul Wofowitz, deputy secretary of defense, issued a directive that barred France, Germany, and Russia from bidding on lucrative contracts for rebuilding Iraq, "creating a diplomatic furor." We had a great discussion on whether we need other countries' support to go to war. Mary is very pro-war so she argued that the United Nations was weak and had been negotiating way too long. David agreed and added that France, Germany, and Russia shouldn't be able to benefit financially from the war since they didn't support it in the first place. Then Bear spoke up, which shocked everyone since most people only know him as a meathead (even though he got a 35 on his ACT after drinking a bottle of vodka and getting two hours of sleep the night before). But like I told you before, Bear is brilliant; he just chooses when to express his intelligence. Anyway, he went off! He said that the Bush Administration deceived everyone because the reasons they gave for starting the war all turned out to be a lie (WMD's especially). Then he added that our very presence there only deepened the problems it was supposed to solve in the first place. He argued that the war on terror, barring the invasion of Afghanistan, is immoral and it is a political nightmare. The whole class stood in awe. Everyone thought Bear was just a dumb jock. Even David and Mary were shocked. Then the three of them started sparring arguments. I never knew Bear felt so passionately about the war. I don't think he has any connection to it – his mom and his dad are both at home and he's an only child. Anyway, it was a lively discussion – we all actually whined when the bell rang. This is what high school should be like.*

*Mercer*

**To:** Mercermur1@yaboo.com
**From:** artmurr@yaboo.com
**Subject: Re: Diplomacy**
**December 10**

*Mercer,*

*I can understand Brian's frustration. I myself am frustrated at the pace, but know that being here is the right thing.*

*Back in March, the U.S. determined that "diplomacy has failed" and that it would proceed with a "coalition of the willing" to rid Iraq of its alleged weapons of mass destruction. The U.S. maintained that Iraq was not cooperating with U.N. inspectors and had not met its obligations to 17 U.N. resolutions, including the total disarmament of Iraq. Months after the resolution was passed, Iraq was still not disarming. The Iraqi regime had used diplomacy as a ploy to gain time and advantage.*

*If you don't ever enforce consequences, you will never stop the behavior. Saddam would not listen to us or the U.N. or anyone. Were we supposed to let him do whatever he wanted? Not only to us but to his people? He needed to be brought down. HE was a weapon of mass destruction.*

*Dad*

---

**To:** artmurr@yaboo.com
**From:** Mercermur1@yaboo.com
**Subject: Re: Diplomacy**
**December 10**

*Just get him and get out of there, Dad.*

*Mercer*

---

**December 11** - My brother told me about how he was called a "fag" and was taunted today by some big-shot sixth grader. Now my first instinct was to go Zorro on this kid or at least threaten him until he peed his pants, but then I realized that Larry has to fight his own battles, or at least I need to let him "think" he's fighting his own battles, which means I will go have a word with this kid if I see him (without letting Larry see me). So anyway, I had to explain to Larry that kids are mean and that anyone who uses the word "gay" or "fag" out of context is immature (then he asked me what immature meant – parenting is hard!) and all the other older-brother advice, but he knew I was snowballing him. I know how hard it is to be called a "fag" or "gay."

When Larry told me, I think he liked my initial reaction, which was written all over my face. But then I calmed down and told him to ignore the kid (yeah, like that's easy). I don't know what to do besides threaten him.  Why don't they teach kids how to respond to bullies?

---

**To:** ahmed86@yaboo.com
**From:** Mercermur1@yaboo.com
**Subject: Bear**
**December 12**

*Ahmed,*

*I have to tell you this story about my friend, Bear (Brian). He's the crazy friend who is going to USC on a football scholarship. He's brilliant but doesn't study, he's the most talented athlete I've met, and he parties all week – go figure. Anyway, last weekend we were going to grab a bite to eat at Burger King when he decided to show off a little. So we walked up on the side of Burger King, and he saw a car in the drive thru. He said, "Wait here." He sneaked up behind the car, and as soon as he saw that the clerk was about to hand the food out, he ran up and grabbed it out of the clerk's hand before the guy in the car could get his food. He then sprinted ahead and ran onto the Farm Bureau (a huge insurance company with a twenty-acre campus) lot. He did all this knowing that a cop was behind the car in the drive-thru line. So the cop chased him (we all saw this but hid as soon as we figured out what Bear was doing) in his car, but Bear started running on the acre-long grass lawn in the Farm Bureau lot. The cop called for back up and started chasing Bear on foot. We lost sight of him so we went inside, ordered some food, and waited and waited. Finally, after about twenty minutes, Bear came waltzing in the Burger King in his polka dot boxers, a white undershirt (remember, it's December in Iowa – around 30 degrees), sat down at the table, and started eating a stolen cheeseburger while we all sat and stared at him. He looked up and said, "I was a little warm." We all started howling with laughter. I'm sure that was the best cheeseburger he's ever eaten. The next day in the Metro section of the paper, there was a small blurb about the "Burger Thief" and how someone should call if he/she knew any information. Bear cut it out and taped it in his locker.*

*So, I'm still bored, flabby, and frustrated. Any hope of you coming to America to force me to get my butt in gear?*

*Mercer*

---

**To:** Mercermur1@yaboo.com
**From:** ahmed86@yaboo.com
**Subject: Re: Bear**
December 12

*Dear Mercer,*

*I know what it's like to feel depressed. I am scared for my future. I know the Americans are fighting for our freedom, but at what cost? Many of my people are still looting without consequences. I don't understand why they would steal from their own people.*

*Sometimes I just feel like giving up, but my dad would never accept that. I must keep my eyes on the future and believe that I will accomplish my dreams.*

> *Ahmed*

---

**To:** ahmed86@yaboo.com
**From:** Mercermur1@yaboo.com
**Subject: Re: Bear**
December 12

*Ahmed,*

*You WILL get out of there, Ahmed, even if I have to come get you! Then I'll grab my dad and we'll go enjoy a nice American cheeseburger, fries, and a milkshake.*

> *Mercer*

---

**December 13** – It was warm and sunny today, 50 degrees for a high. We went on our traditional "cutting the Christmas tree and family picture" outing. This is the first year we wouldn't have Dad in the picture. I didn't want to go, but Mom said that Dad wanted us to carry on the tradition. I sawed the tree down today; Dad usually does this. Merry Christmas.

---

**To:** Mercermur1@yaboo.com
**From:** artmurr@yaboo.com
**Subject: Saddam in a hole**
December 13

*Mercer,*

*We caught Saddam.*

*Dad*

---

**To:** artmurr@yaboo.com
**From:** Mercermur1@yaboo.com
**Subject: Re: Saddam is in a hole.**
**December 13**

*Dad,*

*Hallelujah! Now you can cut the ham for Christmas, right?*

    *Mercer*

---

**December 13** - I am writing on this historic day to report that Saddam Hussein was captured by American troops today. The FORMER dictator was found hiding in a hole near his hometown of Tikrit and surrendered without a fight. The Iraqis will fight their own battles and Bush will bring my dad home. I am going to go lift now – I'm finally inspired.

---

**To:** Mercermur1@yaboo.com
**From:** ahmed86@yaboo.com
**Subject: Praise Allah!**
**December 13**

*Dear Mercer,*

*As your Paul Bremer said, "We got him." People cheered in the streets today. Bullets fired into the air like fireworks. Finally, the tyrant, the man who is responsible for the death of my father, is captured. We will celebrate tonight. I am happy to be sharing this with you, Mercer. Thank you again for your friendship. Praise Allah!*

    *Ahmed*

---

**December 14** - It's the day after the event that will bring my dad home and all anyone seems to talk about is that Bush has secured his victory in the 2004 presidential election with Saddam's capture. Who cares? It's 2003 and my dad is in a desert fighting people who consider it an honor to kill him. At least he is guaranteed only fifteen-month stints over there – wait – that means he isn't even guaranteed to see me graduate from high school! I think I'm developing a nervous twitch.

I didn't lift yesterday – I was too tired.

**December 15** - My dad will bring democracy to Iraq and he will bring Ahmed with him to come home and watch Hawk-eye games with me.

Mondays. What is it about Mondays? I think I'm going to start going to Mass on Saturdays so that Sunday is a complete day of rest including sleeping in, Honey Crisp apples, Cheetos, Coke (not Pepsi), Skittles, a long nap, and finally a café mocha while watching football.

**December 16** - I've got a beer gut and I don't drink beer.

**December 17** - In Social Justice class today, we talked about
the concept of a "Just War." We had a pretty lively discussion
about whether the war in Iraq fit the criteria. St. Augustine de-
fined war as a "state of conflict between two or more sovereign
nations carried on by force of arms." So the U.S. is at war with
Iraq (I guess it's the U.S., Great Britain, Israel, Italy, and Aus-
tralia, but we're the main force. It's ironic, though. We don't
even seem to be fighting Iraq - we're fighting nutty people who
get paid a lot to kill Americans). For St. Augustine the only
reason for waging a war would be to defend the nation's peace
against serious injury. The intention of the war is also very
important. He emphasizes the "idea of restoration of peace
as the main motive of war." St. Augustine thought war was
limited by its purpose, its authority and its conduct." What???
Uh, what??? So basically, you could argue that we went into
Iraq to restore peace, which would make the Iraq War justified.
However, he also said that the "lust of power" is condemned.
I guess it's all who you believe. Do you believe that we went
to Iraq to bring peace or to gain power? I know you don't read
this, Ms. Boge, but I'm curious about teachers' opinions.
    So then we learned about St. Thomas Aquinas's ideas, as
if they were ANY clearer! In his Summa Theologica, Aquinas outlined what is now considered to be "just war" theory.
The criteria for a just war are as follows: 1) The war must be
to "right a wrong." 2) The war must be winnable (of course,
which struggle is winnable and which is not is something best
judged with hindsight). 3) The suffering caused, or thought
likely to be caused, by the war is going to be less than the

suffering caused by leaving whatever evil you are trying to correct, like a despot on the throne, in place. You want to wage the war "efficiently" in terms of human suffering. Finally St. Thomas discusses the right intention for waging war. Only two possibilities are presented: either the furthering of some good or an avoidance of some evil. On the one hand, the U.S. is furthering good by bringing democracy to Iraq. But is bringing democracy to Iraq a good thing? Maybe it should be more socialist, like Sweden or France or Canada? At least their health care is paid for. On the other hand, how is endangering the lives of Americans furthering good, especially in a country that did not attack us in any way (I still don't buy the WMD theory). We haven't had any terrorist attacks since 9/11, so maybe we should be on the offensive. Yet, heightened security, not a war, might be the protection. Honestly, I don't care if this war is justified or not – I just want my dad home.

**December 18 -** Well, I'm almost finished with these entries for Creative Writing. I have to tell you, Ms. Boge, that I've enjoyed writing in this journal, ESPECIALLY since you don't read it (I hope). I'll miss writing stories (not the poems) and "free writing" every day in your class. Maybe someday I'll write a book about a soldier fighting in the Iraq War who ends up receiving a Congressional Medal of Honor. It's time to head to Starbucks to pretend to study for my first set of finals tomorrow: Government, Social Justice, Algebra II – no problem.

Did you ever worry about your friends, Ms. Boge? (I'll just pretend you are answering in my head.) I've been such a slug lately; I think I'm losing my friends. Not Mary or David of course, although I have to admit I'm not much fun to hang around these days, but my other friends like Bear and the football group. I haven't gone out with those guys in ages – even Heather snubs me in the hall now. Did I suddenly become unpopular, or am I just no fun anymore? Do I smell? Maybe I have an odor problem. Ah, who cares, right? I've got a couch to go lie on.

**December 19 -** Finals status report:
    Government: Multiple choice = D; Essay on the Iraq
        War: A+. Overall grade for test=C????
    Social Justice: Essay = B
    Algebra II: Estimated 30% on test – I should have been listening when Mary was tutoring me. I seriously hope I don't flunk.

I'm a slug. My motivational level is hovering at a "1" and I think I'm beginning to hallucinate. No wonder Beth doesn't like me.

**December 20 -** On a happier note, it turns out that the sixth grader moved on to some other poor slob this week, so Larry is off the hook. I don't know what the kid looks like, but I might have to find him someday and have a good heart to heart about bullying third graders. No violence, not even physical contact, just my foreboding muscles in his face.

**December 21** - Does anyone even care that Saddam has been captured? Nothing has changed. There are no announcements about reducing the troops or setting a deadline for getting out of Iraq. I haven't heard from my dad in six days and all my mom can say is, "Don't worry," even though she looks like she sleeps three hours a night and eats soy nuts for each meal. I can't concentrate on anything except *Survivor*, and I can't even look forward to that anymore because the bad chick, sorry, girl, won last Wednesday! Maybe I should go see a shrink.

**December 22** - Ms. Boge, I ACED your Creative Writing exam. I am destined to become the next Stephen King. Well, okay, not really, but I did like the story I wrote for your test. At least I'll have one "A" this semester.

Finals Status Report:

• Creative Writing – "A" – aced the story AND wrote  A  L  L  assigned journals

• Anatomy – did not study – lucky to get a "D"

• Spanish IV – did not study, but good at Spanish – C

This is my final journal entry for Creative Writing I. In approximately twenty-seconds I will turn this in to you. Surreal.

**To:** Mercermur1@yaboo.com
**From:** ahmed86@yaboo.com
**Subject: Finals**
**December 23**

*Dear Ahmed,*

*I made the perfect bowl for my Ceramics final. I'm giving it to my dad to put his keys and coins in. He won't be here for Christmas, but I'll save it for his birthday.*

    *Mercer*

---

**To:** artmurr@yaboo.com
**From:** Mercermur1@yaboo.com
**Subject: Re: Finals**
**December 23**

*Dear Dad,*

*Well, I've got good news and bad news. The good news is that I didn't flunk any courses. The bad news is that I got a 2.7 on my semester report card (technology spares no grace period with report cards anymore). I know, I know.*

    *Mercer*

---

**To:** ahmed86@yaboo.com
**From:** Mercermur1@yaboo.com
**Subject: Christmas**
**December 23**

*Ahmed,*

*Today was our annual "Christmas Basket" ceremony in the gym. It's a St. Thomas Aquinas tradition dating back to the Middle Ages (even before they discovered America, imagine that). All the seniors are split up into groups of five and assigned a homeroom in all the freshmen, sophomore, and junior classes. Then each homeroom adopts a needy family for Christmas. The family gives us sizes for clothes and shoes and a "Santa" list. Then the homeroom members (supervised by the wise and intelligent seniors) bring in "gifts" for Christmas, as well as money for food. The seniors get to go out and buy Christmas dinner and all the food is put in boxes for display on the gym floor. Then we have a candle lighting ceremony, where we read scripture passages and sing and give thanks and praise to God, and then members of each class light candles all around the balcony (the gym is slowly dark at first). You look around and see these candles, and then you see TONS of food on the floor (hams, cartons of oranges, stuffing, potatoes, pies, and much more) in huge boxes, and it is simply beautiful. After the ceremony, the seniors pick up the food and take it to the families. Our family had seven children, ages three months to sixteen years. They were so surprised when we kept bringing in presents and food and more presents and more food. Their whole family room was wall-to-wall red and green wrapping paper! We didn't get to see them open everything, but I know they were so thankful and happy. It feels good to give to others – I need to do that more often.*

   *Mercer*

---

**To:** Mercermur1@yaboo.com
**From:** ahmed86@yaboo.com
**Subject: Re: Christmas**
**December 23**

*Mercer,*

*I am proud that you are giving to others. Being able to give is a gift. We do not celebrate your Christmas holiday here, but it is fun to watch the American soldiers pass out gifts to the children. Toys, school supplies, food, candy, anything and everything for the kids. One of the soldiers gave me a nice sketch book and pencil set to doodle. It is much appreciated that he noticed I like to draw and write. I will journal my experiences so that others may know what war is about. The dangers, the death, the fear – will it all be worth it? Only Allah knows. Thank you, Mercer, for being a good friend to me. I look forward to checking my e-mail everyday to see if you have written. I will pray for you, my friend.*

   *Ahmed*

---

**To:** ahmed86@yaboo.com
**From:** Mercermur1@yaboo.com
**Subject: Finals**
**December 24**

*Ahmed,*

*Well, buddy, I barely passed my finals. I still pulled off a passing G.P.A. (grade point average), but I know my dad is going to be ticked. I just can't seem to find any motivation these days. I know I'm blessed. I know it, but I just don't care. All I see is my life going stale. My football career is over, my dad is in a desert fighting an unwinnable war, my mom looks anorexic, and I'm a jerk to my brother and sister for no reason. And I feel SO bad for whining because I really shouldn't be complaining about anything. What do you do when you get depressed?*

   *Mercer*

**To:** Mercermur1@yaboo.com
**From:** ahmed86@yaboo.com
**Subject: Re: Finals**
**December 24**

Mercer,

When I am depressed, which is quite often lately, I try to remember the
determination and hard work that my father had shown me. When I am tired,
his spirit seems to lift me up. When I am scared, my mother comforts me.
When I am sad, I try to hold it in until the next day. For some reason, morning
brings new hope for me.

Do not feel guilty, Mercer. You feel what you feel. You cannot apologize for
feeling something. But I caution you, do not become lazy. Allah did not give
you a brain to waste it or a body to just sit around. Go out and enjoy the fresh
air, smile and laugh with your friends, and hug your mother.

Enough lecturing. I am beginning to sound like my father. I hope I am not too
harsh with my words. I only want you to be happy.

Ahmed

---

**To:** Mercermur1@yaboo.com
**From:** ahmed86@yaboo.com
**Subject: Re: Finals**
**December 24**

Ahmed,

You are good for me. I know my dad would say the same thing.

Mercer

---

**To:** artmurr@yaboo.com
**From:** Mercermur1@yaboo.com
**Subject: Christmas**
**December 25**

Dad,

Merry Christmas! I know you don't have snow there, but at least you
don't have to shovel (although we don't either – what is with the lack
of snow these days – global warming?!!). Christmas was nice, I guess
– good food (I'm a gourmet cook now) and good cocoa. I got some cool
clothes and _The Lord of the Rings: Return of the King_ and Madden NFL
2004 for my PlayStation. Gina got clothes and a new CD player. Gina
and I complained to each other that mom was trying to "buy" us off

because she hasn't been around that much, but Larry wasn't feeling that vibe. He hit the jackpot – a BABY GRAND PIANO. Now at first I was a little T.O.'ed because a Grand Piano isn't cheap, but then I heard him play. Dad, Larry is good. Actually, he's AWESOME. He played every Christmas carol I've ever heard of without sheet music. So Gina started singing. And then we all started singing! The Murray family stood around my nine-year-old brother at his new Baby Grand and sang "Silent Night" and "Away in a Manger" for at least a half-an-hour. Mom left after twenty minutes – she didn't want us to know, but she was tearing up – so she went up to bed. Anyway, what else did we have to do on Christmas, so we just sang! Gina is actually a good singer – she added harmony and everything. Of course my manly baritone voice made the songs even more striking, but I'm not one to brag. We probably sang for an hour before the stomachs started rumbling (Dad, I made Chicken Kiev for dinner – do you know how putsy that thing is – it was AWESOME though), so we went in the kitchen and made sugar cookies from SCRATCH! All three of us. We found old cookie cutters and sprinkles (which were probably made in the 90's but our bodies can take it). Who knew that hanging out with the Murray fam could be so fun?

I called Mary to come over since her family has dinner around noon. I opened the door, and she practically tackled me with a hug – this was the first Christmas dinner that she could remember when her dad was sober! He's only been sober for three weeks, but Mary says that Christmas is a hard time for her dad (he gets depressed), so she was extra proud of him. Anyway, she was all smiles all night. She brought her low-protein cookie dough over and we decorated cookies (and ourselves – it's a good thing I discovered Oxi-Clean – man, I sound like Mr. Mom) with frosting. I actually enjoyed the simple pleasure of hearing laughter from my brother and sister. It's Christmas and I am thankful.

*Mercer*

---

**To:** ahmed86@yaboo.com
**From:** Mercermur1@yaboo.com
**Subject: Christmas**
**December 25**

*Merry Christmas, Ahmed! Today was a light at the end of a long, dark tunnel. I sang and baked and laughed. What more could you want in life? I wish you blessings on this day we celebrate the birth of our Savior. Feliz Navidad!*

*Mercer*

**To:** Mercermur1@yaboo.com
**From:** ahmed86@yaboo.com
**Subject: Re: Christmas**
**December 25**

Mercer,

I'D Miilad Said ous Sana Saida! That is "Merry Christmas" in Arabic. I have read a little bit about your Christmas holiday. It is interesting that your Jesus was born in Bethlehem and preached around Jerusalem. But I was wondering, who is Santa?

I am so happy that you had a good celebration. Was your family with you? My family is doing well here. My mom is still cooking and cleaning and trying to entertain my nieces and nephews. Sometimes I wish I had brothers or sisters, but I wouldn't want them to have to live through this fear.

       Take care, my friend.

       Ahmed

---

**To:** ahmed86@yaboo.com
**From:** Mercermur1@yaboo.com
**Subject: Re: Christmas**
**December 26**

Ahmed,

Someday you'll have to come to Iowa and pronounce "I'D Miilad Said our Sana Saida" but thanks for making me smarter. Ha!

We had a blast on Christmas. Larry played Christmas carols (songs) on the piano, and Gina and I joined him in song. Gina has a BEAUTIFUL voice – I never knew that. I mean, I knew she was in chorus and stuff, but she sang the first verse of "Go Tell it on the Mountain" and my jaw dropped. She could be on American Idol – she's that good (I actually told her that – it's Christmas so holding back the compliments just didn't fit into the plan). Anywho, then Mary came over and baked cookies with us and we all got in a frosting fight (I won, of course). Santa was good this year. Oh yeah, Santa. Santa is this big, joyous, fat guy with a huge white beard who dresses in a red suit and brings presents to all the children in the world (he climbs down the chimney to get in the house). It could be looked at as a great marketing scheme or simply good fun for the kiddos. I loved Santa when I was a kid. I didn't have a big brother to tell me he wasn't real so I think I believed in him until I was eleven. Then I overheard a friend make fun of his little brother because he didn't know Santa wasn't real – that day I went home holding back the tears. I was CRUSHED. But alas, I got over it, and went home to tell Gina (she was nine). She ran to her room bawling, calling me a liar the whole way up the stairs. Man, did I get a tongue lashing from my dad that night. Anyway, Santa is as American as football and Big Macs. Have you had a Big Mac? Don't start – they're *addictive (read <u>Fast Food Nation</u> by Schlosser - I didn't eat McDonalds for at least a week – but then I caved).*

*Peace.*

*Mercer*

**To:** Mercermur1@yaboo.com
**From:** artmurr@yaboo.com
**Subject: Re: Christmas**
**December 25**

*Mercer,*

*Merry Christmas, Son. Thank you for taking care of our family.*

*Dad*

# MERCER    21
# WAR       21

**To:** artmurr@yaboo.com
**From:** Mercermur1@yaboo.com
**Subject: Re: Christmas**
**December 26**

*Dad,*

*I think I'm experiencing the crash after a high. I had a great time yesterday, but today I've done nothing except sit around and play* **Madden** *NFL 2004. I feel like a tired, whiney, fat, old sloth, but I don't know what to do about it. What is wrong with me?*

> *Mercer*

**To:** ahmed86@yaboo.com
**From:** Mercermur1@yaboo.com
**Subject: Bored in Iowa**
**December 27**

*Ahmed,*

*I am SO SO SO bored. I woke up, brushed my teeth, watched mindless T.V. for two hours, played Nintendo for an hour, ate leftover Chicken Kiev (man, am I a good cook), took an hour nap, and now I'm e-mailing you. When I was a kid, I would play with my toys for hours on end until school started again. Now I don't have any toys.*

*I wish I were Peter Pan (with a roll of cash) - being a kid was so easy. I had an awesome childhood. My neighborhood friends and I would play kick-the-can, wiffle-ball, and have water balloon fights. We'd also build snow forts, go sledding, build snowmen, and eat snow (no yellow snow though). My parents were there, but they also made sure we were very independent as far as entertaining ourselves, so we were in our own little world. Anywho, life was good then. It's good now too – I just can't feel it. How does that work? So what was your childhood like?*

> *Peace,*
> *Mercer*

---

**To:** Mercermur1@yaboo.com
**From:** ahmed86@yaboo.com
**Subject: Childhood**
**December 27**

*Mercer,*

*I am so proud to have grown up in Iraq. How can I express the beauty of my country in words? I wish you were able to visit to see that she is more than desert and IED's. Iraq is the cradle of civilization and the home to many of the characters in your Bible. I am surprised they do not teach you more about it in school! We are taught a lot about America.*

*I enjoyed my childhood very much. I lived with my mother and father, my mother's mother, my uncle and his family, (including his wife and three daughters) and my father's mother. All the family members were good to me with gifts and many words of advice. We had dinner every night together with much stories and laughter. But then things turned for the worst. My uncle had to move north to find work, so his family and my mother's mother went with him. Because of more than a decade of economic sanctions, the Iraqi economy was exhausted.*

*Usually families would take care of each other, but it seemed there was always a competition between my father and my uncle to provide for his family. No words were exchanged, but once my father offered my uncle money to buy food, and my uncle slapped his hand away. They did not come over for dinner for a month. Then three months later, my uncle needed some money to pay the rent, but after paying for our own rent and food, my father had no spare money to give. Again, my uncle did not come over for dinner for a month. The struggle to survive here strains many relationships and not just in our family. My uncle and his family came over for dinner the Sunday before my father was killed. We laughed that day. Never hold on to anger – you do not know what will happen.*

*I found out later my cousins were too embarrassed to come over for a meal because they knew their own family could not return the favor. Hospitality, especially with food, is a very important element of our culture.*

*Marriage is harder now as well. As I said before, I would have been betrothed by now, but with my father's death and with the unknown future of our country, it is too risky. It also seems there are fewer men around because of the two wars and because of the economic sanctions (many men had to travel around to find work). Many women are raising their kids by themselves.*

*There is also a growing trend among young women to get married to older men. One of my cousins, Zahra, was only 16 when she had to get married to a man who was 39! Rumor has it that my uncle was pressured to give my cousin in marriage to settle a debt. Zahra seems sad now – she rarely comes to see us anymore. I remember my childhood as a happy one, but it has changed slowly over the years, especially because we were crippled by the sanctions. It is hard when one cannot work or provide or live without fear.*

*I am feeling more and more that I should study in America. I have requested an application to be sent to me and I have been e-mailing an admission's counselor. She said that she would send the paperwork required to take to a U.S. embassy in order to get the F-1 student visa. The only issue with Iraq is that certain countries considered in the "axis of evil" have more requirements. She said I have to register on a special immigration system and complete more paperwork. I want to bring democracy back with me.*

> *Ahmed*

---

**To:** ahmed86@yaboo.com
**From:** Mercermur1@yaboo.com
**Subject: Re: Iraq, my great country**
**December 28**

*Ahmed,*

*We'll get you here, buddy. Somehow.*

*That's interesting that you lived with so many of your family members. I don't have any living grandparents, and I only have one uncle who lives in D.C. (no kids). It would be awesome to have so many cousins to hang around. I suppose it wouldn't matter anyway - most people in American culture don't live with their extended family. I guess it's a privacy issue or maybe it's an independence issue?*

*Anywho, keep reading and writing and praying. I am REALLY going to need you as a math tutor next year.*

> *Mercer*

---

**To:** Mercermur1@yaboo.com
**From:** ahmed86@yaboo.com
**Subject: Hello**
**December 29**

*Mercer,*

*I will study in America.*

> *Ahmed*

**To:** ahmed86@yaboo.com
**From:** Mercermur1@yaboo.com
**Subject: Re: Hello**
**December 29**

*Ahmed,*

*My mom is a lawyer so maybe she can help if you run into any snafus.*

   *Mercer*

---

**To:** Mercermur1@yaboo.com
**From:** ahmed86@yaboo.com
**Subject: My friend**
**December 31**

*Mercer,*

*I apologize for the curt e-mail a couple of days ago. Two days ago a distant cousin came knocking on our door. Hamid, a chemistry major at Mustansiriya University, needed a place to live because he is wanted by the signature outfit of the Mahdi Army militia. Hamid told us that he tried to avoid a celebration to commemorate the birth of Hassan al Askari, a Shiite imam. When he tried to leave, he was asked for his* jensiya *(his national ID). In other words, they wanted to know his sect. He gave them his school ID instead and promised to bring his jensiya the next day. Hamid fled when one of the guards started to follow him because two of his classmates had recently been kidnapped and one was later found dead. They are still after him simply because he is Sunni. Hamid also told us that a student he knew scared an instructor into giving him a passing grade by claiming to be in the Mahdi Army and leaving threatening notes on the teacher's car. On the other hand, many Shi'ites see the Army as protection. It is a civil war, even if no one admits it.*

*I cry for Hamid. He cannot go back to learn at Mustansiriya anymore. He might be able to study at Baghdad University, but some of the same problems exist there as well. Many students and teachers have been kidnapped or killed since the war started and many have fled for safety. Even some current students choose instructors and classmates along sectarian lines. At Baghdad University, students see the College of Medicine and Pharmacy as Sunni schools, and the College of Education as Shiite (Hamid says it depends on if the dean or president is a Sunni or Shia). Students also have to worry about* allas *("chewers") – informants who may be watching them.*

*I need to study in America. I need to be in a place where I am not worried about someone listening to my conversation or worried that a suicide bomber might enter the café where I am having lunch with my friends. The nightmares must only last a little while longer.*

   *Ahmed*

**To:** ahmed86@yaboo.com
**From:** Mercermur1@yaboo.com
**Subject: Re: My friend**
**December 31**

*Ahmed,*

*I don't know what to say, Ahmed. I'm so sorry – for your cousin, for your family, for your country. We'll get you here somehow, even if my dad has to sneak you over.*

*I just finished The Kite Runner. Have you heard of it? Do you want me to send it to you? Good book. I think you'd find a lot of similarities since the kid grew up in Afghanistan.*

> *Mercer*

---

**To:** artmurr@yaboo.com
**From:** Mercermur1@yaboo.com
**Subject: It's a new year!**
**January 1**
*Dear Dad,*

*I have to tell you that my senior New Year's Eve was pretty lame. David, Mary, and I went to a party at Bear's (his parents let him have parties all the time as long as no one drives), but it was just a bunch of really smashed people falling all over each other (Beth wasn't there either), so we left with some other friends at 11:30 and hung out at David's house. I am such a downer, Dad. I'm surprised David and Mary still hang out with me. But today is a new day and what better day to start over than on January 1st. 2004 is going to be AWESOME!! My New Year's Resolutions are as follows:*

1) *get in shape*
2) *stop eating Cheetos*
3) *study more*
4) *stop eating Skittles*
5) *be a better friend to David and Mary*
6) *stop drinking mochas*
7) *volunteer at "Kids Against Hunger" at least once a month*
8) *stop feeling sorry for myself*
9) *ask the girl of my dreams (if she's still not going out with George) to prom(it's in May, but I have to gear myself up)*
10) *stop whining*

*I'm ready, I'm disciplined, I'm psyched. Peace out.*
> *Mercer*

**To:** artmurr@yaboo.com
**From:** Mercermur1@yaboo.com
**Subject: It's Day Two**
**January 2**

*Dad,*

*Oh, ya, ya, ya. The Hawks pulled a major upset in the Outback bowl and beat Florida **IN FLORIDA** 37-17. They finished the season 10-3. It was one of the best games I've ever had the privilege to watch. I'm still hoping I can play with those guys next year – we'll see.*

*Reality check. Here is how I did on my resolutions:*

1) *I started to do bench presses in the basement, but Bear called and I forgot to finish*
2) *I didn't eat any Cheetos, but Kettle Potato Chips just happened to call my name*
3) *I didn't have to study, but I did go to the library and checked out* How to Win Friends and Influence People *by Dale Carnegie.*
4) *I didn't have any Skittles to eat – YEAH!!! I accomplished one resolution!*
5) *I called David – he came over and we played Madden 2004 while eating Kettle Potato Chips*
6) *I did not have a mocha – until 3:00 when I drove by the Starbucks drive-thru as I was dropping off Larry at the library for his "book club." I would have stayed, but it was an hour and I just couldn't see myself sitting in a library for an hour.*
7) *I plan to go to "Kids Against Hunger" tomorrow with David, Mary and Mary's siblings. Here's resolution number two accomplished!*
8) *I did not feel sorry for myself today.*
9) *I have four months to drum up the courage to ask Beth to prom – I'll work on it.*
10) *I did not whine once today. Woo hoo! Resolution #3 accomplished!*

*Not bad, huh? Merck is making a comeback.*

*Mercer*

*P.S. Seriously, why did you pick the name "Mercer"? I'm not whining.*

**To:** ahmed86@yaboo.com
**From:** Mercermur1@yaboo.com
**Subject: Kids Against Hunger**
**January 3**

*Ahmed,*

*It's a new year and I'm pumped. I started out my Saturday by putting together food packets for hungry kids in the U.S., Africa, and Central America, and I feel good. David, Mary, her siblings, and I went to Holmes Honda to pack food to be shipped off. Do you know it only takes 25 cents to make six servings of food? 25 cents won't even buy you a pack of gum anymore! The problem is getting the food to the people – corrupt governments are everywhere, aren't they? School starts again on Monday. I'm ready to go back. One of my New Year's Resolutions is to stop whining, so if you hear my whining, call me on it, okay?*

*I've also read TWO whole novels over the break – this is a first for me. Since I'm sitting around anyway, I figure I might as well get my R.A.C. (Reading Across the Curriculum) out of the way (we have to read a book of our choice a quarter for credit). I just finished <u>The Da Vinci Code</u> – excellent book. I knew all the stuff about the Catholic Church and Jesus having a kid was bogus, but it was a thriller anyway. Do you want me to send it to you?*

*We're still praying for you, Ahmed. I'm looking forward to seeing you face to face.*

> *Mercer*

---

**To:** Mercermur1@yaboo.com
**From:** ahmed86@yaboo.com
**Subject: Re: Kids Against Hunger**
**January 3**

*Mercer,*

*You are such a good person, my friend. Thank you for offering to send the books. It will be expensive, so I will try to get them here first. Anytime I can learn about other cultures, I am excited.*

> *Ahmed*

**To:** artmurr@yaboo.com
**From:** Mercermur1@yaboo.com
**Subject: Gina**
**January 4**

*Dad,*

*This may sound stupid (but it's NOT WHINING), but Gina wore the SHORTEST SKIRT I'VE EVER SEEN today to church. Granted she had on tights or pantyhose or whatever you call those things, but I was SO embarrassed. I see the way guys look at her, EVEN IN CHURCH. Am I wrong here?*

*Mary, David, and I went to Barnes and Noble for a "last coffee without actually needing the caffeine" meeting. We were going up to order and Mary offered to treat since she just babysat her neighbors last night and made $100 (what???? Maybe I need to start babysitting). So she asked me what I want and I said, "Grande café mocha, please, miss," and she said, "Do you want fries with that?" I paused because I didn't get it at first, but David started chuckling right away. I blushed a little and smiled at my friends. David and Mary are awesome – maybe they should go out? Nah. We'll be friends always – that's good enough.*

       *Mercer*

---

**To:** Mercermur1@yaboo.com
**From:** artmurr@yaboo.com
**Subject: School**
**January 5**

*Dear Son,*

*Good luck back at school today. Remember, trust in God's timing. (Acts 1:7) "He said to them: It is not for you to know the times or dates the Father has set by his own authority." I love you.*

       *Dad*

*P.S. Will you ask your mom to send a case of Vaseline? We use it to coat our mouths when we shower to keep out contaminated water – there is a cholera scare going around.*

**To:** artmurr@yaboo.com
**From:** Mercermur1@yaboo.com
**Subject: My last semester**
**January 5**

*Dad,*

*This is the last semester of my high school career, and I can't really tell you how I feel about that. I definitely have senioritis, but who doesn't.* In Dale Carnegie's book, How to Win Friends and Influence People, *the first chapter says, "Don't complain, criticize, or condemn." Good advice, but tough to follow.*

*I want to go on to experience new adventures in college (with any luck while playing football) and go to classes where they actually make you think. I know I'm lucky to have had pretty good high school memories though, mostly revolving around good friends.*

*I will try to trust God's timing – but I don't have to like it, right? I'm off to school – 7:00 A.M. is too early to be up, let alone writing e-mails.*

> *Mercer*

**January 6 -** Well, Ms. Boge, I'm back in your class. I liked Creative Writing I so much, I decided to sign up for Creative Writing II. I figure you probably read these journals the first couple of weeks, so I'm going to be pretty low key with my commentary, but I also know you'll get overloaded with short stories and essays so you won't pay attention to the content of the journal entries, but that's a GOOD thing. It's better for me to feel free in writing, at least that's what you tell us. I'm telling you though, you missed some juicy stories last semester. Nothing that can get you fired or anything. Never mind. I'm sure all this teenage angst is boring to you. In any case, I'm glad to be in your class again.

I started my job yesterday too. It was basically just orientation to the layout of the *Boys' and Girls' Club* and to the procedures behind the desk, but I did have a chance to see the kids playing basketball, pool, and goofing off in the game room. I have practice on Wednesday nights. Tomorrow is the first time I meet the little rug rats. I'm ready.

I've got another full load: Creative Writing II, Ceramics II, Christian Lifestyles, Spanish IV, Economics, Anatomy II, and Lifetime Sports. I can tell you that I'm looking forward to everything except Anatomy II and Economics. Five good classes out of seven is pretty good, I'd have to say. My teachers are cool – not a lot of homework, except from you, Ms. Boge. But then again, I like to write.

**January 7 -** Today was my first practice with the five-year-olds at the *Boys' and Girls' Club*. Jerome came to help me – at first I didn't understand why he was there. I mean, how hard could it be to have basketball practice with eight little kids, right? Anywho, I waltzed in Gym C fifteen minutes early, to show them who was in charge. At first, I was confident and cool and collected. Then I saw all the parents giving me the once over. Did I have something in my nose? The kids were all running around the side-lines, falling down on the ground laughing. Then I saw the parents glare at me again. Was there whipped cream on my upper lip (I *had* to have a mocha before my debut.)? I swear I was sweating for ten minutes before the change of the guard. So as soon as the hand hit 6:00, I blew my whistle (man, that was a power rush) and called the little hooligans over. I was thinking that roll call would take two minutes, tops. Ten minutes later, I was still trying to sort out who was on my team. One boy was in the wrong gym, one had to go "poopy," one started crying for his mom (who just left, of course), another actually THREW UP, and one girl refused to tell me her name. I looked at Jerome, who was just smirking away. Once we figured out where everyone was supposed to be, we started with some simple dribbling in place. After thirty seconds of balls flying everywhere, including at people's heads (more crying), I decided we better start out with some simple passing. After thirty seconds of more balls flying everywhere (at least there wasn't any crying), I decided maybe we should spread out a little more and just pass the ball two-feet away from a partner. This worked. So now it's 6:35 and I don't know what to do for the next twenty-five minutes. I had all these drills in my head, but I hadn't expected such mediocre skills. Here's why you should plan ahead and study your audience. Jerome saved me again with some age-appropriate games. 7:00 came and I was exhausted (mentally – I'm not THAT out of shape). Who knew that five-year-olds could be so much work? I had a blast though – I can see why my dad likes coaching so much. My favorite kid (I know you are not supposed to have favorites, but I'm only human), Colin, came over and gave me a hug before he left. I smiled, something I haven't done in a while.

**January 8 -** I had such a good day yesterday, and now I feel like guano. I'm worried about my dad; I can't seem to concentrate on anything. I am SO SO glad we don't have a lot of homework; otherwise, I'd feel even more stressed. Why do I have to have a dad who is fighting a war? I don't understand what I did to deserve this? My dad could die. He could die.

**January 9 -** I'm losing brain cells. I look at the board in class and think about IED's. The only class I look forward to (I don't even enjoy Lifetime Sports – how cruel is that) is Creative Writing II (no, I'm not trying to kiss up – I know you never read these anyway), where I can journal or write a story. I now know that I will never write a story without a happy ending.

**January 10 -** Mary came over around 7:00ish and physically dragged me (man, is she ripped) to the St. Thom's boys' and girls' basketball games. I'd always been their biggest supporter, but this year I haven't even been to one game. What's the point? My dad is in a desert – how can basketball provide any source of comfort for that? Anywho, I watched and clapped once in a while. Mary tried to get me into it, but my heart just wasn't willing. When will this end?

By the way, I got my acceptance letter from the University of Iowa today. No football scholarship. Figures.

**January 11 -** I can thank my awesome Government teacher for making me read the paper everyday – now it's a habit. At least I haven't lost my motivation for that, although I have to admit I only focus on the Iraq stories. I read about how the Grand Ayatollah Ali al-Sistani, the most influential Shiite cleric in Iraq, said members of the country's interim government must be selected by direct vote. He opposes the U.S. plan to hold regional caucuses. Then I thought about the difference between electoral votes and a direct vote – I guess I did learn something in school. I hope the U.S. holds out on this one. The founding fathers, with limited historical knowledge, knew what they were talking about. Even though we've had four cases where the winner of the most popular votes lost the presidency (including the last election), the Electoral College process works. If we had a direct vote, all the candidates would hang out in California, Texas, and New York and would change positions according to the latest opinion poll.

On a brighter note, the U.S. plans to hand control of the government to Iraqis on June 30. My dad will probably have to stick around to make sure things are running smoothly, but at least he'll be out of there soon. Gotta keep going, for tomorrow is another day. Is that good or bad?

**January 14** - I am going to be a coach someday – I don't know at what level, but I know that I've found my calling. We had our second practice tonight and I LOVE MY KIDS! Even though I've been a slug lately with school (my dad's voice is always in the back of my head, saying, "Striving for excellence in small tasks prepares one for greater responsibilities." I'll do my homework tonight – I promise), I actually prepared for practice today. I called Jerome earlier in the week and I talked to the other five-year-olds' coach to get some ideas. Let's just say I am gifted. The kids were in awe of my stud-like abilities and my words of wisdom. Actually we just played around – in an organized fashion though – and laughed and laughed and laughed some more. My buddy, Colin, is a blast. He has the wit of Conan and the charm of Bond and he's only five! He makes me laugh, but I admire him because of his effort. Whether we are doing a dribbling drill, a passing drill, or shooting around, Colin is focused and always gives 100%. Maybe it's because he has to work harder, considering his physical handicap (he has cerebral palsy) or maybe he just has a driven nature. In any case, he's an inspiration to me and to his teammates.

I went to David's youth group tonight after practice at Jordan Creek Evangelical Free Church. I gotta tell you, they are cool people. Pastor John always remembers my name and asks how I'm doing, and they ALWAYS pray for our soldiers in Iraq. It's actually fun too – we play some sort of game (where I can show off my athletic prowess), and then we listen to a speaker or discuss a Bible passage. I've learned a lot from going – I just wish I could feel better. I know, I know, God wouldn't give me anything I couldn't handle. But what if I don't want to handle this?

3RD QUARTER

**To:** Mercermur1@yaboo.com
**From:** ahmed86@yaboo.com
**Subject: Hope**
**January 15**

*Mercer,*

*I hate living in fear. I wish I were courageous like the American and Iraqi soldiers. They do not seem to be afraid of anything. The insurgents are the ones who seem afraid, yet they give us no hope. They say they are fighting for our freedom from the infidels, but they only offer more violence and chaos. They have no plans to advance our society – only more terror and instability. If they keep us in fear, they have the power. I do not want to be afraid anymore. I want to fight before they kill again.*

*Ahmed*

---

**To:** ahmed86@yaboo.com
**From:** Mercermur1@yaboo.com
**Subject: Re: Hope**
**January 15**

*Ahmed,*

*I cannot imagine being so terrified all the time – I don't know if I could handle it as well as you do. My dad doesn't let on that he's scared that much, but I know he is. From what I see, you are just as brave as my dad or any other soldier.*

*Mercer*

**January 16** - Today we had the first snow of the 2004. It was only three inches, but we made a lanky snowman anyway (we, as in my neighbor, Andrew, age two– the kid who made carrot poops in the pool - and Larry and I). I hang-out with Andrew to give his mom a break sometimes. She's a single mother who works as an executive at Principal. I've never even seen the dad.

Anyway, I want him to have a rich and imaginative childhood like I did, so I try to be a fun neighbor. Today Larry joined us and it wasn't so bad. He was really patient with Andrew. The credit goes to my parents. So the snowman was decked out in yellow and black Hawkeye attire, of course. We have to teach little Andrew who's the boss in this state. Sometimes I wonder if I make football out to be more than it is. But what else is there?

Mary and David stopped by to drag me to another basketball game. I actually clapped this time. If Colin can give 100%, I can at least give 45%. Half-time sparked an idea that might make me come out of my funk. During my freshman year, three "cool" senior guys would dress in funky outfits and sweep the floor with the five-foot-long brooms during time-outs and half-time. It was sweet. Maybe if I did that with some buddies, I might actually enjoy going to the games. We'll see.

After the game a bunch of us came over to watch *Star Wars: Episode II, Attack of the Clones*. I am a *Star Wars* freak. I still have all the old figures from my childhood (they might be worth a lot of money someday), and I own all the tapes. Episode III doesn't come out until 2005. I can't wait to find out how they are going to turn Anakin to the Dark Side.

**To:** artmurr@yaboo.com
**From:** Mercermur1@yaboo.com
**Subject: 500 dead**
**January 17**

*Dad,*

*I know that people die in war, but 500!!!! I just read this morning that the number of U.S. soldiers killed in Iraq since the invasion in March climbed to 500 when a roadside bomb killed three U.S. soldiers and two Iraqi troops. What are we doing? I know the three big reasons that Bush gave, but war? Why did we have to go to war? Why couldn't we wait for the U.N.? Why did I have sixteen years of peace only to obsess about an oil-war during my senior-year in high school? Why won't Bush give a timeline to get out of there? He said that the new government will take over on June 30th – what does that mean for you?*

> *Mercer*

---

**To:** ahmed86@yaboo.com
**From:** Mercermur1@yaboo.com
**Subject: My dad**
**January 17**

*Ahmed,*

*I wrote a whiney e-mail to my dad and now I feel guilty. I just read that the American casualty count is up to 500 and maybe reality is finally setting in. I've tried to go on and be the poster-boy for high school life, but I can't anymore. How do I live with this constant worry? Maybe I should go see someone. I can't talk to my mom because she is a wreck herself – she DEFINITELY needs to see someone. And to top it all off, I'm supposed to take care of Gina and Larry. I HAVE to because my dad asked me to. I feel like I'm on the Tilt-a-Whirl all the time, just one loop away from blowing chunks.*

*I have to go take Larry to a Taekwondo tournament and drop Gina off at a friend's house. I'll write again later. Oh, I forgot to tell you, Beth broke up with George. My prospects for asking her to prom are looking up.*

> *Mercer*

---

**To:** Mercermur1@yaboo.com
**From:** ahmed86@yaboo.com
**Subject: Re: My dad**
**January 17**

*Mercer,*
> *You are a good person.*

> *Ahmed*

**January 17** - It's Saturday night, 11:59 P.M. and I'm writing a journal entry for Creative Writing II. How lame is that? Bear and I hung out tonight (Mary and David went sledding at Sleepy Hollow with David's youth group). We cruised the loop, he mooned some cute girls, and then we stopped over at our buddy John's house for a pick-up poker game. I won ten bucks – hooahh. I had to drive Bear home because he drank too much, as usual (at least he doesn't drive), and we stopped at the drive-thru at Burger King on the way. This is why I laugh when I'm with Bear: at the drive thru, he says, "Uh, yeah, I'll have a number three with a coke and a number four with a coke. Yeah, hey, can I get that to go?" The lady didn't get it – she just said, "Yes, sir, please pull around." Maybe it would have worked better if she thought he was serious and actually corrected him. Why must I analyze EVERYTHING? Why can't I just enjoy LIFE?

---

**To:** Mercermur1@yaboo.com
**From:** ahmed86@yaboo.com
**Subject: Life**
**January 18**

*Mercer,*

*I am sorry I had to be so brief yesterday. I wanted to quick check my e-mail before I had to pick up my niece at school - her mother feels more comfortable if I pick her up to keep her safe. I was looking for an e-mail from the Iowa admission's counselor, but I was also happy to receive your e-mail. I know it is hard to hear that American soldiers are dying, but they are dying for me and for my family and for my people. I am so thankful. I will continue to pray for your dad's safety.*

*Did you know, Mercer, that more than three-million children are enrolled in primary school now? Schools are being rebuilt, and lives are being changed. Most Iraqis are very grateful for the Americans. I thank your dad every time I see him. He is a great leader.*

*I have to go read for my class tomorrow. It is a good feeling to have homework.*

*Ahmed*

**January 18** - Ahmed just wrote an e-mail and ended it with, "It is a good feeling to have homework." Can you imagine? I am never going to complain about school again. Okay, I probably will, but I will try to be more conscious of the fact that school is a blessing.

Mary called me up and said, "Let's go grab our Sunday night mocha at Chit 'n Chat and wax poetic in accordance with the prophecy." That girl, I tell you, always keeps me on my toes. David joined us later, and we laughed about old times. It feels good to laugh again.

**January 19** - I read in the paper today that the U.S. asked the U.N. to intercede in the dispute over the elections process in Iraq. So the U.N. isn't good enough to trust for permission to actually GO to war, but now they are good enough to ask to help with elections? Oh, the webs we weave.

On a brighter note, today we had an awesome speaker to celebrate Martin Luther King Jr. Day. Alveda King, a niece of Martin Luther King, Jr. talked to us about civil rights and "dream blockers," which include teen pregnancy, abortion, sexually-transmitted diseases and the sexual revolution. She was supposed to speak at Wilson High School, but the principal decided to cancel it because some parents complained. I think it boiled down to the fact that King is pro-life and people didn't like that. But even if you are pro-choice, knowing the opposition makes you a stronger debater, right? If I went to Wilson, I'd be TO'ed. I love debating, especially about moral issues like abortion and capital punishment. I love being challenged to actually THINK and not simply memorize. Anyway, she received a standing ovation from good ole' Aquinas kids so maybe she didn't feel so bad.

We talked about Martin Luther King, Jr. in Christian Lifestyles too (and Economics and Creative Writing as well). We were talking about MLK, Jr.'s "peace" strategy and Mr. Schmidt put a quote on the board. I liked it so much, I copied it down. "A nation that continues year after year to spend more money on military defense than on programs of social uplift is approaching spiritual death." Exactly. Mercer's translation: stop spending money on wars that take fathers and mothers away from their families. I don't know the nuances of social programs and personal accountability, but I do agree that we should be lifting people up instead of tearing them down. Then again, maybe we are trying to create "social uplift" in Iraq. Mr. Schmidt also asked us MLK, Jr.'s famous question, "What is your life's blue-print?" He asked us to think about our goals for the next year, five years, ten years, and the next twenty years. Then he asked us to write them down for a homework assignment. I'm actually looking forward to writing them (after I finish my journal, of course).

We continued to talk about MLK, Jr.'s advice once you have the blueprint. He said, "And when you discover what you will be in your life, set out to do it as if God Almighty called you at this particular moment in history to do it. Don't just set out to do a good job. Set out to do such a good job that the living, the dead or the unborn couldn't do it any better." I LOVE this quote. It is totally something my dad would say. He's always telling me to give 100% in everything I do, whether it is cleaning a toilet or writing a paper. I hope I can teach my kids to do that someday. It sounds relatively easy, but it's actually hard to do in EVERY aspect of your life.

Finally we talked about MLK, Jr.'s views on education in Econ. He said, "The function of education, therefore, is to teach one to think intensively and to think critically. But education which stops with efficiency may prove the greatest menace to society. The most dangerous criminal may be the man gifted with reason, but with no morals...We must remember that intelligence is not enough. Intelligence plus character - that is the goal of true education."

So how do you teach this in a public school? Oooo, did we get in a good discussion about this one. Mr. Coughlin sends his kids to public school, so he offered some insight (the *Character Counts* program sounds good), but when it comes down to it, morality is taught by the parents. So what if the parents don't teach it? Is it the school's responsibility? How do they teach morality without mentioning God? Good stuff, good stuff.

**January 20** - The Iowa caucuses were held yesterday and Kerry pulled off the victory, to everyone's shock (people will remember the "Dean Scream" for a while). Maybe Kerry will win the presidency, and he'll pull the troops. That could be a good thing for me, but a bad thing for Ahmed. I'm glad I'm not president.

**Subject: Martin Luther King, Jr.**
**January 20**

*Ahmed,*

*I don't know if you have ever heard of Martin Luther King, Jr., but he was one awesome dude. In 1964, King became the youngest person to receive the Nobel Peace Prize for his efforts to end segregation and racial discrimination through civil disobedience and other non-violent means. Anyway, in one of his speeches, he asked, "What is your life's blueprint?" So our religion teacher asked us to write out our "blueprint" for the next year, the next five years, the next ten years, and the next twenty years. Here's what I came up with for my "blueprint."*

> *By the end of....*

*2004 – I will be practicing with the Hawkeye football team for our Rose Bowl game. I probably won't play, but I will travel.*

*2009 – I will be a twenty-four-year-old English teacher at St. Thomas Aquinas High School in West Des Moines, Iowa. I will be the offensive coordinator with my dad beside me as the head coach. I will have lunch with my father every day, and I will be engaged to my high school sweetheart.*

*2014 – I will be a twenty-nine-year-old head coach at St. Thomas Aquinas High School. I will be the best writing teacher in the school and will be completing my second novel. I will have a one-year-old boy named Joseph who sleeps through the night at six weeks (even at the age of eight I remembered my brother CRYING and CRYING and CRYING in the middle of the night – I need sleep too much). My mom and dad will be retired and I will take my family to go fishing at their lake house on the weekends. I will serve as president of the Iowa Homeless Youth Shelters, and I will be an usher at church every other Sunday. Oh, and Gina will live within two miles of me with her family and Larry will visit every month from Harvard, where he is on the genetics team finding a cure for PKU.*

*2024 – I will be a thirty-nine-year-old head coach at St. Thomas Aquinas High School. I will be writing my third best-selling novel and coaching all three of my sons' basketball teams. I will take my daughter to dance twice a week and I will support my wife's decision to go back to school for her law degree. My dad will pick me up every morning at 5:00 A.M. to jog five miles while my mom welcomes us back with a mocha (she'll have figured out the Starbucks' mocha recipe by then). Larry (the famous geneticist who found the cure for PKU) and Gina (a dance teacher and elementary school teacher) will live down the street with seven cousins for my kids to play with. I will be president of the Boys and Girls Club Foundation, and I will still be an usher in church every other Sunday.*

*How does that sound? I think you should write your goals for the future too, Ahmed. It's kind of fun.*

*Mercer*

**To:** Mercermur1@yaboo.com
**From:** ahmed86@yaboo.com
**Subject: Re: Martin Luther King, Jr.**
**January 20**

*Mercer,*

*I am glad to know you. I need to talk to people who are motivated and who push me to do my best. It is difficult at times to keep looking forward. Here is my "blueprint."*

  *By the end of...*

*2004 – I will be completing my first semester as a chemistry major at the University of Iowa in Iowa City, Iowa. I will work in Iowa City to save money for a trip home to see my mother and my family.*

*2009 – I will be a twenty-four-year-old graduate student at Berkeley University in California. I will complete my dissertation by 2010. I will be betrothed to a friend of the family who is in medical school at Berkeley.*

*2014 – I will be a twenty-nine-year-old chemistry professor at the University of Baghdad and a representative in our government. My wife will be a pediatrician and will also raise our three daughters. My mother will live with us, and we will worship together as a family every Friday with my cousins' families. Our country will be a democracy. Well-nourished kids will go to school without fear, communities will thrive in a free market, and Baghdad will become the newest hip tourist spot.*

*2024 – I will be a thirty-nine year old senator in the Iraqi government. My people will have had access to water, food, electricity, health care, education, and employment for the past five years during my service. I will continue my involvement in the U.S. Embassy in Baghdad (created in 2009), and Iraq will trade its wealth of oil to the world. My seven sons and daughters will all be in school studying medicine, law, and education. My wife and I will look forward to vacations on the Tigris.*

  *Is that a plan? It is attainable.*

  *Ahmed*

---

**To:** ahmed86@yaboo.com
**From:** Mercermur1@yaboo.com
**Subject: Re: Martin Luther King, Jr.**
**January 20**

*Ahmed,*

*I know you will be a great influence on your country's future. I'm looking forward to reading both our sets of goals in thirty years as we sip mochas on my beach house porch.*

  *Mercer*

**January 20** - I went to the game against Jordan Creek tonight. My Anatomy lab partner, Ryan, hit a last second three-pointer to beat Jordan Creek by one point. I couldn't help but jump up and down and hug everyone and storm the floor – we redeemed our football loss, at least that's how I looked at it, but then I went home after the game and ate a pint of Chunky Monkey. Keep your eye on the prize, Mercer.

**January 21** - Practice again with my Urban Bellies (our team sponsor, Urban Belly, a hip kids and pregnancy clothing store, paid for the t-shirts so we call our team the Urban Bellies). Colin actually inspires the other five-year-olds – who knew that kids so young could be inspired? He's slower than the other kids – noticeably slower – but they all wait for him. They want to pass to him, and they all yell at him to shoot all the time.

After practice I handed out Blow Pops – everyone gave me a hug for that. Then Jerome and I talked for a bit while watching the other five-year-old team practice (we were the better team, of course). I asked him why he asked me the question about my relationship with my father during our interview. He said that people who have a good relationship with their father, especially boys, are more responsible and respectful, in general. He said that he would have hired me anyway, but it gives good insight during an interview. I asked him what kids are supposed to do if they don't have fathers; he said the care-giver should seek out strong male role models. Oh. So I am a role model – heavy. That means I'm supposed to be a role model for Larry and Gina too. And the Urban Bellies. And Andrew, my neighbor. I guess I better stop being such a jerk then.

**January 22** - Mary mentioned, sort of in passing, that I should start running after school with her to get back in shape. Back in shape? I got all defensive and said, "Why, do I look fat or something?" She said, "No, Mercer, you look good, you always look good." Then she said she thought I would feel better if I started running again with her. I told her, "No thanks," and then I started talking about dissecting the pig in Anatomy II. The truth is that I would love to run with Mary, but I know she'd kick my butt. She is a slim G.I. Jane (seriously, she's got some guns) and I'm Homer Simpson with hair (at least right now). I know she would slow down with me, but I am just too embarrassed to be slower than a girl.

**To:** Mercermur1@yaboo.com
**From:** ahmed86@yaboo.com
**Subject: Life in Bagdad**
**January 22**

*Dear Mercer,*

*I am glad you asked me to write out my goals. It is always good to foresee what my future could be like if I stay on the path. I admit I become discouraged at times. I look around at my people, and I cry for them, but then I see a child run by with a soccer ball, and I see hope. I look at my mother and how hard she has worked for me and our family without ever complaining, and I see hope. I look at my communication with the University of Iowa, and I see hope.*

*It is still dangerous here though, especially for interpreters. It is hard to tell who is an insurgent, who is a suicide bomber, and who is my neighbor. Women in rural areas always had to wear headscarves, but in the city, many women had disregarded the religious convention. Now, however, it is dangerous for a woman to NOT wear a headscarf: many women who don't wear headscarves are being kidnapped by men who think their behavior is disrespectful to the Muslim religion. They also are expected to stay indoors and look after the children, and they have to behave like someone who is shy or embarrassed instead of walking with their head held high. They can't even lift their eyes to someone's face. It seems we are reverting back to our old ways sometimes.*

*Ahmed*

---

**To:** ahmed86@yaboo.com
**From:** Mercermur1@yaboo.com
**Subject: Re: Life in Baghdad**
**January 22**
*Ahmed,*

*You are a CHAMPION! I am a slug, but you are my hero! You always look at the positive side, even when bad things happen.*

*It is interesting that women have to wear headscarves and have to look down like someone who is shy. That would never happen in America, at least not now, although women only got the right to vote in 1920. I understand the religious obedience, but it does seem demeaning. I'm not putting down your culture or anything; I just think that in America, people wouldn't stand for it. But they would respect it if a Muslim woman wanted to honor Allah in that way. Now I'm just blabbering on – I don't want you to think that I don't respect Islam. I'm just saying that most Americans would see the headscarves as unequal treatment for women.*

*Ahmed, please be careful. I read in the paper today that CIA officers in Iraq are warning that the country may be on a path to civil war. So much for the upbeat State of the Union address by President Bush. Just don't get caught in the crossfire – watch your back. What is the deal with the Sunnis and the*

*Shi'ites anyway? Why do they hate each other so much? In two days I coach my first basketball game for five-year-olds. Say a little extra prayer for me.*

   *Mercer*

---

**To:** Mercermur1@yaboo.com
**From:** ahmed86@yaboo.com
**Subject: Re: Life in Baghdad**
**January 22**

*Mercer,*

*Do not worry, my friend, I do not take offense. It is good for me to understand the ways of American culture before I spend the next eight years there, no? I do want you to understand that women wearing headscarves is a way to honor Allah and to keep marriages strong. The Koran teaches us that men should serve their wives and that wives should honor their husbands. The only problem comes when men do not serve their wives and think they are entitled to more. It is like you said: unequal treatment. I see both sides. I do not think I will want my wife to wear a headscarf, but if she chooses to wear one, I will support her decision. It has to be her decision though.*

*I have much to learn about America! I am looking forward to the lessons.*

   *Ahmed*

---

**January 23** - I was actually geared up for the boys' and girls' basketball game tonight – I thought I might learn a few coaching strategies for my rug rats' game tomorrow, but alas, (does anyone even use the word "alas" anymore?), the game was in Sioux City. I guess I'll have to rely upon my own coaching acumen to pull a victory. Onward Christian Soldiers.

---

**To:** artmurr@yaboo.com
**From:** Mercermur1@yaboo.com
**Subject: Coaching**
**January 24**

*Dad,*

*I LOVE COACHING!!! We won, 12-10, but that isn't the important thing (although it is pretty important). I laughed so much I almost peed my pants. Did I tell you that I was coaching my first game today for the five-year-olds? These kids have taught me more about life in two weeks than I've learned in all of my math and science classes combined. Kids were running up and down the court, fixing their shoes in the middle of the game, scratching themselves EVERYWHERE, and one even ran off to go to the bathroom when we were on offense. I can't even tell you how much fun I had. When I subbed one little* boy, he started crying when he realized that I had to take another player out. My star player, Anna, who scored ten of the twelve points, gave the opposing team's shooters hugs after every made shot. But the best part was the winning basket. My man, Colin, who has such an awesome spirit, hadn't received the ball yet. With fifteen seconds left in a tie game, Max passed it to him. Colin passed it off to Anna and ran toward the hoop. Anna dribbled, got double-teamed, and somehow rolled the ball to Colin. He picked it up, dribbled a bit, and shot the ball as the buzzer went off. SWOOSH! I think that was the best moment of my entire life. Colin has cerebral palsy, so he'll never be a high school hoops' star, but he was a champion that day. I will never forget the expression on his face.

Dad, I miss you, but I've been sitting around pouting for months now and it's time to stop. You are doing your job, and I need to do mine. If Colin, who has many more obstacles to overcome than I do, can do his best, then I can too. It is time.

Mercer

**MERCER   24**
**WAR     21**

**January 25** - I ran today. I could only stomach three miles at a 9:00 minute pace, but it felt good to get moving again. Mercer's back.

**January 26** - Alarm – 5:30 A.M. Dark, cold, lonely. A three-mile run at 5:30 in the morning bites. It's time to recruit.

**January 27** - I woke up and almost hit the snooze button, but then I remembered that I am recruiting today. Gina didn't know what hit her. I went into her room at 5:30 and started jumping on her bed (I guess I should have warned her last night, huh?). She FREAKED out and started yelling at me. I told her she was flabby and needed to get in shape so we were going to go running this morning. She paused and actually started getting dressed. Man, I am a good coach. We ran three miles; I told her the route and waited for her outside back at the house. I patted her on the back and told her I'd treat her to a Starbucks, skinny latte for the chubby, of course. She slugged me in the gut and assessed my own jelly-belly. Tomorrow, we'll do the same.

**January 28** - Gina and I ran again this morning – it's so much easier when someone goes with you. Gina hates me right now, but she'll thank me later. Mom actually ate breakfast with us. We told her about our early morning run, and she went off about how proud she was of us and how she used to run with dad. At that thought, she started welling up and left to be excused. I feel so bad for my mom – I can see she's not doing too well. It was nice to talk to her though. I made a training schedule for Gina. I'm helping get her in shape for dance team tryouts in April. She's really not flabby – she's actually too skinny. I hope she doesn't take me seriously.

---

**To:** ahmed86@yaboo.com
**From:** Mercermur1@yaboo.com
**Subject: No WMD's**
**January 28**

*Ahmed,*

*I read in the* Register *that David Kay, the former head of the U.S. Weapons inspection teams in Iraq, informed a senate committee that no WMD's have been found in Iraq and that prewar intelligence was "almost all wrong" about Saddam Hussein's arsenal. So, did the U.S. receive bad intelligence or did the Bush administration manipulate the intelligence to build the case for war, or both? My dad is risking his life for oil – maybe I should walk to school today.*

*Mercer*

---

**To:** Mercermur1@yaboo.com
**From:** ahmed86@yaboo.com
**Subject: Re: No WMD's**
**January 28**

*Mercer,*

*I know you are frustrated that they have not found WMD's, but I believe that Saddam had them. It is good that the U.S. is here. I have to believe it is good.*

*I am sorry I did not answer your question about the Sunnis and Shi'ites in the previous e-mail, but I had to ask my mother to confirm my understanding of the sects' history. Here is the best explanation I can give you:*

*The hatred is not principally about religion – it is about power. Sunnis and Shi'ites may disagree on some matters of dogma and some details of Islam's early history, but they agree on the important tenets of the Muslim faith, like the Koran and the Prophet Muhammad. However, they use the small differences as justification for division: they both want the power to rule.*

*Islam's split began in A.D. 632, immediately after the Prophet Muhammad died without naming a successor as leader of the new Muslim flock. Some of his followers believed the role of Caliph, or viceroy of God, should be passed down Muhammad's bloodline, starting with his cousin and son-in-law, Ali ibn Abi Talib. But the majority backed the Prophet's friend Abu Bakr, who became Caliph. Those loyal to the custom of the caliphate eventually became known as Sunnis, meaning followers of the Sunnah, or Way, of the Prophet.*

*Since the Caliph was often the political head of the Islamic empire as well as its religious leader, Sunni Islam is the dominant sect. Today about 90% of Muslims worldwide are Sunnis. But Shi'ism would always attract some of those who felt oppressed by the empire.*

*Shi'ites soon formed the majority in the areas that would become the modern states of Iraq, Iran, Bahrain and Azerbaijan. Crucially, Shi'ites outnumber Sunnis in the Middle East's major oil-producing regions - not only Iran and Iraq, but also eastern Saudi Arabia. But outside Iran, Sunnis have historically had a lock on political power, even where Shi'ites have the numerical advantage. Sunni rulers maintained their monopoly on power by excluding Shi'ites from the military and bureaucracy; for much of Islamic history, a ruling Sunni elite treated Shi'ites as an underclass, limited to manual labor and denied a fair share of state resources.*

*The rulers used religious arguments to justify oppression. Shi'ites, they said, were not genuine Muslims but heretics. Of course this was just an excuse to encourage prejudice. Sunnis likened reverence for the Prophet's bloodline and the Shi'ites' fondness for portraits of some of the Imams to the sin of idolatry (even though the Sunnis hung pictures of Saddam in all the schools). When Saddam came into power in Baghdad in 1979, Iraq's Shi'ites had enjoyed a couple of decades of peace. Then came Khomeini's 1979 Islamic revolution in Iran. Saddam was afraid the same thing would happen in Iraq, so he ordered the murder of Iraq's most popular ayatullah, Mohammed Bakr al-Sadr. After the war with Iran ended, Shi'ites were once again shut out of most senior government and military positions. With the defeat of Saddam's army in the 1991 Gulf War, Shi'ites saw a chance to rise against the dictator. But they received no protection from the allied forces, and Saddam was able to smash the revolt. By some estimates, more than 300,000 Shi'ites were killed; many were buried in mass graves. For the rest of his reign, Saddam kept the Shi'ites firmly under his thumb.*

*And so here we are. I do not know if the U.S. understood the deep hatred that many years of oppression can hold. The CIA is right, Mercer, civil war is inevitable. The bridge over the Tigris between the Sunni neighborhood, Adhamiya, on the eastern bank and the Shi'ite district of Khadamiya, on the western bank is already being patrolled heavily. People do not trust each other. We all worship the same God, but we do not trust our fellow Muslims. It seems this hatred is not limited to the extremists anymore. I do not understand it. I do not want my children growing up with such hatred. I am a Shi'ite and I am proud of it, but I love my country and its entire people, not just those who believe what I believe.*

*I know that is a long explanation. I had to research a lot of it. It is good for me to know as well. I have to do my math course work now. I will write again tomorrow.*

*Ahmed*

**To:** ahmed86@yaboo.com
**From:** Mercermur1@yaboo.com
**Subject: Re: No WMD's**
**January 28**

*Ahmed,*

*Did anyone ever tell you that you should be a history professor? I learn more from you in an e-mail than I do reading a whole chapter in my history book. The Sunni/Shi'ite problem sounds a lot little the Protestant/Catholic conflict in Ireland. Since the 17^th^ century, Protestants and Catholics, both Christian religions, have been warring over government control much like the Sunnis and the Shi'ites. In 1920, the British passed the Government of Ireland Act, which divided Ireland into two separate political entities, each with some powers of self-government. Eighty years later, there is still tension, although it's not as violent. Maybe that's what the Sunnis and Shi'ites should do. Maybe Iraq should be split into different states like Ireland. I like the idea of having states' rights as well as federal rights. Maybe the Iraqi government can split up the power so no one feels oppressed. Just a thought.*

*I'm going to go do something mindless like watching T.V. I ran today, Ahmed. Mercer, the stallion, is making a comeback.*

      *Mercer*

---

**To:** Mercermur1@yaboo.com
**From:** ahmed86@yaboo.com
**Subject: Sunnis and Shi'ites**
**January 29**

*Mercer,*

*I forgot to tell you about some other differences between Sunnis and Shi'ites. They are minor but interesting. Typically, Sunnis pray with one arm folded over the other, just below the rib cage. Shi'ites prefer to keep their arms straight down at their sides. During prayer, members of both sects kneel, bend and touch their forehead to the ground. When calling the faithful to prayer, Sunni mosques invoke God and the Prophet Muhammad, Shi'ites additionally mention Ali, the Prophet's son-in-law.*

*In Iraq now, such overt signs of faith can be fatal. Sunni insurgents have been known to stop cars with stickers of Ali and murder the passengers. Vehicles are also given sectarian designations by their license plates – cars with plates from Anbar are assumed to be owned by Sunnis, while those with plates from Basra or other southern provinces are automatically believed to be driven by Shi'ites. The safest plate to have is one from Baghdad.*

*I have read a little about the trouble in Ireland. It does sound very similar. I am glad to hear they are at peace. It gives me hope for my people.*

*I am glad you ran today, Mercer. Someday in America I will join you on your runs. For now, I must remain close by or inside for safety. Take care.*

*Ahmed*

---

**To:** Mercermur1@yaboo.com
**From:** ahmed86@yaboo.com
**Subject: School**
**January 30**

*Dear Mercer,*

*I went to school today. Each day in the classroom is a gift. Ten years ago, my elementary school had very few textbooks, and broken windows were everywhere. Pictures of Saddam were on all of the walls. For some kids the after-school activity was begging on the street. I went back to see my elementary school yesterday, and while the walls are still crumbling and the toilets are filthy, the teachers have chalk and erasers, and the kids have pencils and notebooks. Now pictures of Mickey Mouse with messages encouraging cleanliness adorn the walls.*

*Ten years ago, Saddam was holding a presidential election in which he was the only candidate. We didn't have free speech here. Saddam opened the doors to foreign journalists to show off the vote, but under stringent supervision. My friend, Mustafa, is 15, but he's still in elementary school. He's making up for all the years he lost when he dropped out to work during Saddam's rule. He doesn't see the Iraqi war as an invasion – he thinks the Americans liberated Iraq from the tyranny of Saddam. Before the invasion, when 2,500 dinars were worth $1, teachers earned about 3,500 dinars a month (or $1.40 U.S. dollars), today, my aunt, an English teacher with 12 years of experience, earns about $166 a month. Good things are happening.*

*We used to have to say, "Long live our leader, Saddam Hussein!" several times a day at school, and all of us would have to clap at the mention of his name. Now it seems like a joke – our fearless leader was found in a hole in the ground with lice in his beard. How could such a man command so much power and be reduced to such a state?*

*Ahmed*

**To:** ahmed86@yaboo.com
**From:** Mercermur1@yaboo.com
**Subject: Re: School**
**January 30**

*Ahmed,*

*I can't imagine having pictures of George Bush everywhere as if we worshipped him. It's so different. Thanks for telling me more about the differences between the Sunnis and the Shi'ites as well. You are a much better teacher than our textbooks. I hope they can work out their differences before things get out of control.*

*Have you seen my dad lately? I haven't heard from him in a while. Keep an eye out for him, okay? Thanks, Ahmed. I'm glad you are there for him.*

*Mercer*

---

**To:** Mercermur1@yaboo.com
**From:** ahmed86@yaboo.com
**Subject: Food**
**January 31**

*Mercer,*

*I am hungry. There is no other way to put it. I have not had any meat for a week, which isn't so bad, but there is not enough rice or bread to feed our family. I must risk my safety and go back to the American camp to help them so I can earn some money.*

*Since September 1990, the main source for food has been the government food ration. The amount of food ration monthly per person after the oil-for-food agreement in June 1997 was 7kg flour, 1.25 kg rice, 0.05 kg sugar, 50g tea, 0.75g cooking oil. Of course, in addition to that, there were open markets, supermarkets and small corner shops (and the black market) where we could find almost all food products. We were fortunate – my father had a good job; most people could not afford to buy much extra food from the market or from shops, as they did not have much cash. Many Iraqis were unemployed, but even those who had jobs received extremely low salaries.*

*I actually dream about food every night now. I dream about saucy vegetable and meat dishes, grilled kebabs (skewered chunks of grilled meat), fish from the Tigris (masgouf), and kubbeh (minced meat, pine nuts, raisins and spices covered with rice or grains). Our main staple food in Iraq is timn (long grain rice). It is prepared in different ways and with different flavors. Another important staple food is bread. No meal passes without lots of bread on the table. Vegetables like green beans, fava beans, okra, aubergine, tomatoes and zucchini are the basis of many tasty vegetable dishes that are poured over the rice.*

*I miss meat, especially lamb. Lamb kebabs, big chunks of lamb with green beans or okra, and quzi (stuffed roasted lamb) were my favorite.*

*I am not weak from hunger yet, but I still miss my favorite meals. I try to be like my mother, who never complains. I try to be strong for my nieces and nephews, whose bellies are empty. I will go find work so that they will not have to go without food much longer.*

*Thank you for listening to me, Mercer. You remind me to be blessed for my health and my family and for the food that I do have. May Allah bless you.*

*Ahmed*

---

**To:** ahmed86@yaboo.com
**From:** Mercermur1@yaboo.com
**Subject: Re: Food**
**January 31**

*Ahmed,*

*Soon you will be pigging out on Big Macs, fries, Coke, Skittles, café mochas and my famous Chicken Kiev. We're going to fatten you up here in America.*

*Mercer*

---

**January 30** - David and I went to the ball game tonight fully loaded with our duffel bags. We put them in the bathroom and took our places in the front of the senior section. After about four minutes, we left inconspicuously and found the janitors. We changed and strategically placed ourselves in opposite corners of the gym. During the first time out, we fulfilled our school-spirit duty. Remember, no one has done this for three years, so people were a bit surprised, but we came out in coconut bikinis and grass skirts (we had shorts underneath) and started sweeping the floor (you know, so the players have better traction). The CROWD WENT WILD!! I don't know about David, but I was good about keeping a straight face. Even the principal laughed. We came out for two more time-outs and then changed back into normal clothes. After about four minutes into the second half, we went back into the bathroom and changed into adult Star Wars costumes (Darth Vader and a Storm trooper). The CROWD WENT WILD AGAIN!!!! What a blast – I wish Mary could have been here to see it. I did catch Beth's eye though – she smiled "the smile." Merck is the alpha male once again.

January 31 - Today was our 2<sup>nd</sup> b-ball game for the Urban Bellies. We won again, 10-8 – of course Anna made all the shots, but she's really good about passing the ball around. She just happens to be the only one who can make a shot. Colin had a good steal and then an assist to Anna. I didn't 'almost pee my pants this time,' but it was still a blast. One of the parents treated us all with Gatorade after the game – it was actually fun just to sit around and drink some electrolytes with a bunch of five-year-olds. It made me miss my dad though. He would have loved to see me coach.

Feb 1 - We went to a big Super Bowl party that David's youth group put on today. They had a huge inflatable climbing wall, an inflatable slide, and an inflatable Sumo Wrestling ring with huge pads for the participants to wear. It was sweet. The Patriots won, but I didn't watch the game much. Everyone was all in a tizzy over the halftime snafu involving Janet Jackson and Justin Timberlake and the wardrobe malfunction. I was oblivious – I was too busy taking Mary down on the Sumo mat.

---

**To:** Mercermur1@yaboo.com
**From:** artmurr@yaboo.com
**Subject: Nation building**
**February 2**

*Dear Son,*

*Mercer, I don't think I tell you enough how thankful I am for your leadership in our family. I know you are struggling, but I am so proud of how you are helping Mom and Larry and Gina. I am asking a lot of you, I know, but I also know that you can handle it.*

*Building a country is a slow process. Brigade and battalion commanders, captains and lieutenants are taking on responsibilities as diplomats, politicians, development consultants and educators. We are building communities to help build a nation.*

*Such a feat cannot be accomplished in a short time or without loss. I am so proud of our troops – they go above and beyond and they do not complain.*

*We all carry a card around with us with the Seven Army Values written on it – loyalty, duty, respect, selfless service, honor, integrity, and personal courage. I see all of those things in you, Mercer. You are serving your country by supporting your father and by taking care of our family.*

*Dad*

**To:** artmurr@yaboo.com
**From:** Mercermur1@yaboo.com
**Subject: Re: Nation Building**
**February 2**

*Dad,*

*It is so good to hear from you. I know that Mom fills me in on what you're doing and everything, but it's nice to get a personal e-mail too.*

*I don't know if I tell you this enough, Dad, but I'm proud to be your son. I'm proud when I hear your name said as "Major Arthur Murray." I'm proud when teachers ask about you and say too many compliments about you to remember. I may complain about the war, but I'm proud that I can say my father is fighting in Iraq. I brag about you all the time to my friends and in my journal, but sometimes I guess I forget to tell you how inspiring you are. The past couple of months I have been complaining about my own life without giving thought to how hard it must be for you. If I were my son, I would have scolded me as a spoiled brat a long time ago.*

*I saw on TV today that President Bush is getting pressured by both Republicans and Democrats to figure out the intelligence failures, so he called for an independent commission. What are you going to do, Dad, if they find out that the intelligence was all wrong? I know you will still fight, but won't you be a little upset that you are fighting a war without a reason?*

*All is good here in Iowa. We won our second game yesterday. Anna made all the points – she'll be a great ball player someday. She reminds me of Mary with her drive and patience and strength. Good peeps.*

*I'm running again. I've even convinced Gina to get in shape with me. She wants to get in shape for dance team tryouts anyway. She is really skinny, so I'm filling her up with protein shakes.*

*Mercer*

---

**To:** ahmed86@yaboo.com
**From:** Mercermur1@yaboo.com
**Subject: Cold!**
**February 2**

*Ahmed,*

*It is FREEZING here today. It's supposed to get to a high of 10 degrees here – AH!!!! My fingernails are blue, my belly button has icicles falling from it, and my ears are bleeding because they are so dry. What's the weather like there?*

*Mercer*

**To:** Mercermur1@yaboo.com
**From:** ahmed86@yaboo.com
**Subject: Re: Cold**
**February 2**

*Mercer,*

*I guess I should be grateful for the weather here. Today it was 62 degrees F and the sun was shining. I seem happier on sunny days, unless it's 115 degrees F in August. I remember hanging around the army camp last August, just hoping they would need some translating help or something so that I could go inside in the air conditioning. I was laughing at a soldier who fried an egg on the sidewalk and had another soldier take a picture of him and the egg. It was hot, very hot.*

*We were outside for an hour today. It was a nice break from trying to entertain all the time. I am receiving more and more homework every day. I am happy.*

    *Ahmed*

---

**To:** artmurr@yaboo.com
**From:** Mercermur1@yaboo.com
**Subject: Hawkeyes**
**February 4**

*Dad,*

*I e-mailed Ken O'Keefe, the offensive coordinator at Iowa yesterday. If I'm coming back, I'm going after my dream. He e-mailed me back today and said he remembered me! He praised my sophomore year and told me to send him my highlight tape. Then he said he'd welcome me to come out as a walk-on next fall. That was crushing. I thought I might have a chance, albeit small, but at least a shot. I don't know if I'll send him the tape or not. Don't worry though, I sent him a thank you e-mail. What do you think I should do?*

    *Mercer*

---

**To:** Mercermur1@yaboo.com
**From:** artmurr@yaboo.com
**Subject: Re: Hawkeyes**
**February 4**

*Mercer,*

*Send the tape. But don't forget to send a hand-written thank-you note.*

    *Dad*

# MERCER 24
# WAR 21

**February 5** - I can't believe it, but the semester is a quarter of the way finished. I'm checking Edline weekly – Mercer Murray is getting A's' and 'B's.' I know that the semester is just getting off to a start, but I'm determined to come back strong. My goal is to get straight 'A's' this semester. The only classes that might give me trouble are Anatomy and Econ. Larry found my grade sheet (the one they send home to the parents quarterly) and complimented me over and over. I blew it off, but I really do appreciate his encouragement, especially from someone who at the age of nine is smarter than I am.

I have to go get my highlights tape ready to send off to Coach O'Keefe.

---

**To:** Mercermur1@yaboo.com
**From:** ahmed86@yaboo.com
**Subject:** Fish
**February 5**

*Mercer,*

*I just caught a fish from the Euphrates. I sautéed the flesh in congealed goat's blood and put it on a plate, with innards and bones on display. It's a delicacy here. Most of our dishes have tomato paste as the basic ingredient, but it is difficult to buy it here now. We used to be able to buy it before the war, but supplies are limited. I have faith that will change soon. I hope I don't talk about food too much. Good food is one of the few pleasures we have.*

*Although violence is still a way of life here, I feel better knowing that it is justified, at least in the context of war. I remember the fear we lived under when Saddam was in power. A few years ago, Uday, Saddam's son, set up his own militia called the Fedaeen. The militia had all the financial backing of the*

---

*state and no one could interfere. One of the ways they discouraged any sort of defiance was to publicly behead young women in the streets. Saddam also appointed Uday head of the Iraqi Olympic committee where he tortured athletes who failed to win. This is not civilized. I am ready to not be afraid of my government.*

*Ahmed*

---

**To:** ahmed86@yaboo.com
**From:** Mercermur1@yaboo.com
**Subject: Re: Fish**
**February 6**

*Ahmed,*

*I can't say that innards sautéed in congealed goat's blood sounds appetizing to me, but I guess it's what you grow up with. I'm glad you get to eat fine food, at least once in a while. Do you want me to send my dad some tomato sauce? I think he could get it to you.*

*Mercer*

---

**To:** artmurr@yaboo.com
**From:** Mercermur1@yaboo.com
**Subject: Urban Bellies**
**February 7**

*Dad,*

*The Urban Bellies won our 3rd basketball game today! This time three people scored, although Anna was still the star (man, it is nice to have a good athlete). I can't believe the "season" is already half over. Five games just aren't enough to develop their skills.*

*Anywho, school is going well. I'm studying every night – my goal is to get straight A's this semester. Larry will probably have to tutor me, but at least it will keep him out of trouble. I sent off the tape to the Hawkeyes. I'll let you know.*

*Remember how you told me that you can tell a lot by a person by watching a person laugh – do they hold back or is it a real, enjoyable laugh? I thought about this when I was talking to Beth today (actually, exchanging phrases is more accurate). She sort of laughed in the conversation, but it was more of a "polite, you-are-a-dork kind of laugh." I felt like a complete tool – why do I get so tongue-tied when I'm around her? I'm so much more comfortable around Mary and David, who roar at my jokes. I'm so confident with everyone else. Why can't I be confident around her? I'm still asking her to prom though – Carpe Diem. It'll just take a while to build up the nerve.*

**February 8** - I gotta tell you, Ms. Boge, that I'm excited about this short story assignment: 500 words or less and starts with, *"It was Christmas Eve; Nancy dozed before the fireplace, wondering if he would come, as promised."* I know it's not due until March 1, but I'm going to go all out on this one. Now I just have to think of who the "he" is and what "he" promised. I love a challenge.

**To:** ahmed86@yaboo.com
**From:** Mercermur1@yaboo.com
**Subject: Track**
**February 9**

*Ahmed,*

*I overheard Beth say she was starting track practice today. Hmmm, track. I've always been encouraged to go out for track, but I thought it was just a waste of time when I could be training for football (and goofing off). But now, I might have a reason. I have been running lately, so maybe I should give it a shot? What do you think?*

*Mercer*

**To:** Mercermur1@yaboo.com
**From:** ahmed86@yaboo.com
**Subject: Re: Track**
**February 9**

*Mercer,*

*I think it is a good idea to go out for track and field. You will be able to see Miss Beth's character. Remember though, looks are not everything. I want my wife to be beautiful also, but her character is the most important thing. Good luck.*

*Ahmed*

**February 10** - Mercer Michael Murray is now officially on the track team. Coach Ferguson said he was happy to have me. I convinced my sister Gina to go out, too. She is actually a pretty good runner. The long distance teams had the same workout, so after I ran the "assigned" five miles, I trekked back a mile or so and ran with her to the finish. I kept pushing her to run faster and finish strong. I was impressed – she was the third girl to finish. Who knew?

**February 11** - Basketball practice today was pretty lackluster without Colin. His mom called and said he was sick. I never realized how much one person could be so vital to a team, even at the age of five.

**February 12** - I told Mary I was going out for track, and she paused and asked me why. I told her that it was to get in shape and she said, "But why now? I offered to run with you? Is it to get in shape or is it because of Beth?" I blushed. Then I got T.O.'ed and said, "Whatever, Mary." She stormed off. I NEVER fight with David – girls are weird.

---

**To:** artmurr@yaboo.com
**From:** Mercermur1@yaboo.com
**Subject: Track**
**February 12**

*Dad,*

*I went out for track on Tuesday. I'm ready to be a Renaissance sculpture again.*

    *Mercer*

---

**February 13** - I love milk. I think I drink a gallon a week. Milk is the perfect food. Why can't life be more like milk?

It's the day before Valentine's Day and Y.E.L.L. (Youth Embracing the Love of Literature), the school's literary club, sponsored a flower drive. Earlier in the week, members sold cards for a buck and then today we received them in homeroom. I got one from Mary thanking me for being such a great friend. David got at least ten from all these girls who are in love with him. Mary got a few from some random friends, and Beth got a few. Unfortunately, I didn't send any. I definitely should have sent Mary one – she has been the best friend anyone could ever ask for. I probably should have sent Beth one to at least give her a "hint" that I like her and might ask her to prom. Maybe I should have asked her to Prom in the card? Oh well, opportunities pass me by all the time. What's another one.

---

**To:** ahmed86@yaboo.com
**From:** Mercermur1@yaboo.com
**Subject: Valentine's Day**
**February 14**

*Ahmed,*

*It's Valentine's Day here today. It's a holiday to celebrate romance and couples and all that mushy stuff, which is fun if you actually have a significant other. I think it's just a marketing scheme to make people buy roses and candy and jewelry, but maybe I'm just bitter. Valentine's Day bit the big one for Mercer. Bear had another party, so David, Mary, and I decided to check it out. After mingling some, I went to find Bear, and find him I did. He was making out in a corner with Beth. Talk about head blow, gut blow and shin kick. I turned and was about to walk out when I almost toppled over Mary. She looked at my face, looked at the PDA in the corner, and looked back at me. She put her hand on my arm, but I was not in the mood for a pity pat. I went back to the kitchen, shoved some popcorn in my mouth and went over to David to try to change the subject in my head. Mary followed me - I was good about acting like nothing was wrong. When David asked if I wanted to go home (two AGONIZING hours later), I had the car running before he could get his coat. Maybe I should have sent Beth that flower yesterday. Some Valentine's Day.*

*Mercer*

---

**To:** Mercermur1@yaboo.com
**From:** ahmed86@yaboo.com
**Subject: Re: Valentine's Day**
**February 14**

*Mercer,*

*I know it is hard, but do you respect a girl who would kiss someone in public so openly? In some Islamic cultures, Miss Beth could be stoned. I do not mean to judge her. It seems that American culture allows for such behavior, but I hope that Miss Beth just made a mistake.*

*Ahmed*

**To:** ahmed86@yaboo.com
**From:** Mercermur1@yaboo.com
**Subject: Re: Valentine's Day**
**February 14**

*Ahmed,*

*I respect your opinion, Ahmed, but what about Bear? Shouldn't he be at fault as well? Don't you think it's unfair that the female takes all the blame? I've also heard about women in your culture being raped and then punished for being raped because they had sex with someone who wasn't their husband. Where is the justice in that? I'm not saying that what Beth did was right, but I think it's just more acceptable in our culture. I wasn't mad because she was making-out in public, although I wouldn't feel comfortable doing that (they were both drinking though). I was mad because she broke up with George, and I thought I had a shot of asking her to prom. I don't know what to think. Now I guess I'll just go to prom with my buddies like last year.*

*Everything was going so well, Ahmed. I am studying more, I'm running again, and my five-year-olds are kicking butt. Why does this have to happen now?*

　　　　*Mercer*

---

**To:** Mercermur1@yaboo.com
**From:** ahmed86@yaboo.com
**Subject: Re: Valentine's Day**
**February 14**

*Mercer,*

*You are right. Our laws are not equal for men, but I believe the new government will change that. Some people are set in their old ways though.*

*Mercer, I advise you to pray for your future wife. You do not know who she is; only Allah knows. Pray that both of you will make the right decisions to find each other.*

　　　　*Ahmed*

**February 15** - The romance side of Valentine's Day was crushing to my existence, but on the upside, my Urban Bellies are undefeated. I never thought I'd care so much about five-year-olds and an undefeated season. Maybe it's my ego, but I am psyched for our final game next week. Colin came up to me after the game and said, "If they had a "Coach of the Year" award, you would win it." I welled up and hugged him. I will enjoy being a father someday.

Mary called me yesterday to apologize for being rude. She said she was happy I was going out for track and that she would come to all my track meets. What a good friend.

---

**To:** ahmed86@yaboo.com
**From:** Mercermur1@yaboo.com
**Subject: Allah**
**February 16**

*Ahmed,*

*It's back to the grind. Tests, papers, worksheets, and ceramic bowls. At least we are playing ping-pong in Lifetime Sports - I am ranked #1, thank you very much. My candle burns at both ends, and I'm lovin' it.*

*I think it's a good idea to start praying for my future wife. I was so blinded before that I thought for sure Beth was "the one." But I guess I have a lot of time and a lot of girls to meet before I take that step. My dad always told me to pray for my future wife. He said he prayed about mom five years before he even met her. It's just hard, you know? Sometimes I just want someone to call my own right now.*

*You told me to pray to Allah, but I don't really know that much about Allah. Isn't Allah the same as God? I remember something about Allah being the god of Abraham so that would mean that we worship the same God, right? What is the difference then? Who do you think Jesus is?*

*Mercer*

---

**To:** Mercermur1@yaboo.com
**From:** ahmed86@yaboo.com
**Subject: Re: Allah**
**February 16**

Mercer,

My dad was wise to teach me about Christianity. He recognized that Christianity and the Bible are referenced everywhere in literature, philosophy, and culture. It is sad, but many of my fellow Muslims do not understand their religion anymore, let alone Christianity. In unfree societies, one is not taught to think, only to hear and obey.

Here is a short history of the Islam religion. Way back when, the angel Gabriel appeared to Muhammad, a descendant of Abraham and Hagar. Muhammad could not read or write, but the messages from Allah (God), brought by the angel, were written down by others during the next 23 years of his life and later put together in a book called the Koran, in Arabic "The Reading." The religion was called Islam, which, in Arabic means "submission to God, peace, safety, purity." Followers were called Muslims. Muhammad completes a succession of prophets, including Abraham, Moses and Jesus, each of whom refined and restated the message of God. The Koran therefore corroborates, updates and expands the Old and New Testaments.

Like Judaism and Christianity, our religion was founded by a descendant of Abraham. We believe in Moses and Jesus, the Torah, and the Ten Commandments. We believe in angels, in heaven and hell and the Day of Judgment, in the return of Jesus, in the books and messengers of God, and in predestination and free will. However, we don't believe Jesus is God. One of the main tenets central to Islam is that there can only be one God – Allah - and that he is the source of all creation. Hence, there is no God but God, and Muhammad is his messenger. We believe that Jesus as a deity is blasphemous because it is seen as a form of polytheism. We also believe that Jesus was not executed on the cross and that he escaped crucifixion and was taken up into Paradise. We believe Jesus was a great prophet, though. Muhammad was the last prophet that Allah sent and his message is considered the final, universal message for all of humanity.

The Five Pillars of Islam is the term given to the five duties that every Muslim must fulfill. These duties are Shahadah (profession of faith), Salah (ritual prayer), Zakat (a 2.5% alms tax – Shi'ites pay an additional tax called the "Khums"), Sawm (fasting during Ramadan), and Hajj (pilgrimage to Mecca). These five practices are essential to Sunni Muslims. Shi'ia Muslims subscribe to eight ritual practices which overlap with the Five Pillars. As a Shi'ite, we also have jihad, (not in the sense the media has portrayed it – jihad is "struggle in the way of God" or "to struggle to improve one's self and/or society"), which is also important to the Sunni, but not considered a pillar. The second is Amr-Bil-Ma'rūf, the "Enjoining to Do Good," which calls for every Muslim to live a virtuous life and to encourage others to do the same. The third is Nahi-Anil-Munkar, the "Exhortation to Desist from Evil," which tells Muslims to refrain from vice and from evil actions and to encourage others to do the same.

*I always feel as if I am lecturing. It will be easier to tell you more when we are in person. What are your duties as Christians?*

*Ahmed*

---

**To:** ahmed86@yaboo.com
**From:** Mercermur1@yaboo.com
**Subject: Re: Islam**
**February 16**

*Ahmed,*

*I'd like to tell you that I actually follow all of our "duties," but I'm not the best example of a Catholic Christian. If you listen to the teachers in Catholic school, you are supposed to go to church every Sunday and on Holy Days of Obligation, confession once a month, and receive the Sacraments. I think we are supposed to tithe as well. Oh wait, I Googled it. This is what we have to do: 1. To attend Mass on Sundays and Holy Days of Obligation and rest from servile labor. 2. To receive Holy Communion at least once a year, between the first Sunday of Lent and Trinity Sunday. 3. To receive the Sacrament of Reconciliation (confession) at least once a year. 4. To observe the fast days and abstinence days established by the Church. 5. To observe the marriage laws of the Church. 6. To contribute to the support of the Church. I guess I wasn't that off.*

*If you ask David though, who is an Evangelical (Protestant) Christian, he would say the only thing you have to do is accept Jesus as your Lord and Savior and become saved (which Catholics believe too, just not only one time in our lives – we praise Him as Lord and Savior every day), and then let the Holy Spirit do the talking. The Holy Spirit will guide you to WANT to go to church and read the Bible and do good works and want to grow closer to God. They don't have the duties like communion and confession and fasting. I think Catholics and Protestants have more in common than most people think. Anywho, I like going to David's youth group once in a while. They make the Bible relevant to my "teenage world."*

*It's interesting that Muslims think it is blasphemous to consider Jesus as God. I remember when a couple of Mormon missionaries came to my door once and I talked with them a bit. They implied it was "ignorant" to believe that God can be three persons. That was the end of that conversation. It's hard to explain how God can be God the Father, the Son, and the Holy Spirit, but it's something I've never had trouble believing. If God can make the earth and the stars and the oceans and know every little detail about every hair on my head, then He can certainly exist in three different states. My dad said it was sort of like how we all have different roles. I am a son, a brother, a nephew, a friend, etc..., but I am still one person. Anyway, I'm glad to know that Muslims don't think I'm going to hell, even if they think I'm wrong about Jesus.*

*How's that for YOUR history lesson? Ha! I've got to go pray for my future wife now.*

*Peace out,*
*Mercer*

## MERCER 24
## WAR 21

**February 17** - Can I just tell you how glad I am that I don't have any math courses this semester? Mary is in her second year of calculus so she's taking enough of the burden of math on for the rest of us. I swear that girl is SO disciplined. Can you imagine eating salad and fruit and veggies and low-protein bread at every meal? I've never heard her complain either. I'd throw fits if I couldn't have my Big Macs and Chick-fil-A sandwiches (not around Mary though). Plus she studies and takes care of her brothers and sisters and tries to keep her dad sober (which he has been since Christmas – Mary is happy). What pressure for a seventeen-year-old. It's a good thing she has me as such a good friend.

**Feb. 18** - Tonight was our last practice – I am going to miss my little plebes. At the end I stressed the importance of giving your best, even on the bench. Then I mentioned that it would be GREAT if we had an undefeated season, but that I was proud of all of them no matter what.

**February 20 -** We were the sweepers again tonight. This time David and I came out as Batman and Superman. But the big hit was when Mary (this is the first time St. Aquinas has ever had a girl sweeper – we're breaking down the walls) came out in a Supergirl suit and swept the floor after us. Oh man, did the crowd light up. We hung around and swept again for two more time-outs and then decided to let the crowd bask in our aura. Both St. Thom's teams won, of course.

**February 21** - It's 11:59 P.M., but I had to write tonight. If ever there were a momentous day in the history of Mercer Michael Murray's life, it was today. My Urban Bellies scored on Colin's last second shot to win. All great moments seem to happen in slow motion for me. After the swish of the basketball, I leaped up and grabbed Colin and swung him around. Then I put him on my shoulders and all his teammates cheered. Now, fifteen seconds is a long time for five-year-olds to do anything, but for fifteen seconds, these kids were feeling pure joy. Sports may get a bad rap sometimes for being commercialized or whatever, but the thrill of that swished-shot will live on.

We all went out for pizza after the game. Mary and David came with us since they watched my finale as a coach. If I only had my dad here to celebrate with me, life would be perfect.

---

**To:** Mercermur1@yaboo.com
**From:** ahmed86@yaboo.com
**Subject: Islamic New Year**
**February 22**

*Mercer,*

*It is a new year and it is time for a new beginning. May we have better and prosperous days in this new year and improve our ibadah in order to reach Allah's mercy. Today marks the beginning of the new Islamic year. Among Muslims, time is marked from when the Prophet Muhammad and his companions emigrated from Mecca to Madinah. It is marked as such because the emigration was a turning-point in Islamic history that allowed the community to prosper, grow, and develop. Emigration is called Hijrah in Arabic; thus the calendar is called the "Hijrah calendar." Muslims have our own calendar, which is based on the cycles of the moon. The calendar consists of twelve months but only has 354 days. For this reason, the Islamic New Year moves eleven days backwards through the seasons each year.*

*I have read and watched movies about your New Year's celebrations. We do not celebrate with such a festive atmosphere, but we say prayers and take the time to reflect on our life and death and Allah's blessings. I do like the tradition of New Year's Resolutions though. My resolution is to pray fervently five times a day and to support my family by playing with my cousins more. Kul 'am wa antum bikhair ("Happy New Year" in Arabic).*

*Ahmed*

**February 23** - Track is going well. I'm picking up speed and so is Gina. She could be a contender for one of the top long-distance runners on the team. I might just have to show her up, though.

I'm still working a desk job at the Boys and Girls Club. I only work twice a week (on Mondays and Wednesdays) after track, so I get to see the kids once in a while. Anna is there every day it seems. Colin hasn't been by yet – I miss him.

---

**To:** ahmed86@yaboo.com
**From:** Mercermur1@yaboo.com
**Subject: Ash Wednesday**
**February 24**

*Ahmed,*

*Tomorrow is Ash Wednesday, where we repent, fast, and remember that we "are dust and to dust we shall return." I actually like Ash Wednesday. I like walking around the whole day seeing ashes on people's foreheads (ashes were used in ancient times, according to the Bible, to express penitence.). I go out to the grocery store or the gas station and I see people with the ashes on their forehead and have a sort of connection. Anywho, we also fast on this day, certainly not as much as you do during Ramadan - I can't believe you don't eat all day until sundown for a month! We are supposed to only eat one full meal and two smaller meals and we are supposed to abstain from meat. Now for someone like Mary, who can't eat meat anyway (Did I tell you she has PKU and can't eat anything high in protein?), this isn't a big deal (although she goes beyond the minimum obligation and doesn't eat ANYTHING the whole day – I only know this because her brother told me that she doesn't want anyone to know because Jesus warned against fasting to gain favor from other people and that he also warned his followers that they should fast in private, not letting others know they were fasting. I'm telling you, Mary will be canonized a saint one day). Anywho, back to not eating meat. It's hard, but not that hard. We just go get fish sandwiches from McDonald's. Okay, so now as I'm thinking about how my best friend, who has a restricted diet anyway, fasts completely and how my good friend, Ahmed, practically doesn't eat for a month during Ramadan, but who also doesn't eat a lot of meat (because he doesn't have access to it – I'm never complaining again), I think I'm going to have to try something a little harder tomorrow. I have all this good food at my disposal – I'm going for the complete fast. Pray for me.*

*Mercer*

---

To: ahmed86@yaboo.com
From: Mercermur1@yaboo.com
**Subject: Ash Wednesday Fast**
**February 25**

*Ahmed,*

*I'm writing this to you at 8:00 and then I'm going to bed. I fasted today, which probably wouldn't have been so bad except that I ran six miles for track practice. I almost passed out, but I prayed a rosary in my head the last two miles and pushed through. Water never tasted so good. I can't wait until tomorrow morning when I can eat ten waffles with a stick of butter and a quart of syrup. By the way, I didn't tell anyone except you – does that mean it doesn't count since I told someone?*

*Mercer*

---

To: Mercermur1@yaboo.com
From: ahmed86@yaboo.com
**Subject: Re: Ash Wednesday Fast**
**February 25**

*Mercer,*

*I am proud of you, my friend, especially since you had to run. Allah will honor your sacrifice. I am glad you told me about your fasting – it inspires me to remember to fast, even in times of want. No matter the conditions here, I am blessed.*

*Mercer, you are a good soul.*

*Ahmed*

**February 27** - It was grilled cheese for lunch and McDonald's fish sandwiches for dinner. I think I could actually be a vegetarian. Wait, was I supposed to fast today? Oops.

Gina and I are running at 6:00 tomorrow morning. Now why would two intelligent teenagers run at 6:00 A.M., you might wonder? Because we ROCK.

**February 28** - Last night was a blast. We went to the basketball game and had a "chanting" fight with the West fans. We started out innocent enough with "We've got spirit, yes we do, we've got spirit, how 'bout you?" But then it got interesting. They started chanting "Jeans on Fridays" (which I'm actually proud of because when we pay $1 to wear jeans on

Fridays, we raise a ton of money for charities – plus, I don't mind having a dress code – it simplifies life) and we'd chant "Public Schooling," and so on. Then it started getting nasty. They chanted, "Fish on Fridays," which is pretty tame, but then Bear started the chant, "Welfare babies," which I personally did not participate in. Little things like that just 'T' me off. I know that crowds will do things individuals would never do, but come on. When does anyone have personal accountability anymore? Mr. Ause put that fire out in a hurry though – he grabbed Bear and took him in the hallway for a good tongue-lashing I'm sure. Bear came back a few minutes later grinning from ear to ear, but he didn't start any chants anymore. Both the boys and the girls lost.

I went to confession today at St. Pius. It felt good. For some reason I always feel good about confessing my sins.

**To:** artmurr@yaboo.com
**From:** Mercermur1@yaboo.com
**Subject: Iraqi Constitution**
**March 1**

*Dad,*

*I read in the paper that the U.S. approved the Iraqi interim constitution today. So when does that mean they will take over? They've got a constitution now and they've got a government. Let's pack it up and ship 'em home.*

*Mercer*

---

**To:** Mercermur1@yaboo.com
**From:** artmurr@yaboo.com
**Subject: Re: Iraqi Constitution**
**March 1**

*Mercer,*

*We can't pull out now – we've put a lot of sweat and blood into this country. We're not quitters. Politics back home isn't relevant to the soldier here. What's relevant is patrolling Baghdad and gaining control and bringing an end to the violence on the streets at two in the morning. The Iraqi constitution is a step in a long journey toward freedom. Today was a good day, Mercer. Our battalion found ten initiation devices (the detonators for the IED's). Every time we find one of those, I know we have saved lives. The key to success in Iraq is training the Iraqi Security Forces. We train their soldiers, integrate them with our forces, and then have them operate independently. Our goal is to hand over the power with maybe 2,000 Iraqis and 10 U.S. soldiers advising them. Then, eventually, we will leave completely. It won't happen overnight, though. The Iraqi Security Forces are not battle-trained yet. The key is "yet." Four of our men have already lost their lives – we have a dangerous job since we actually go looking for bombs, but have faith, Mercer. We're doing our work.*

*Dad*

**To:** artmurr@yaboo.com
**From:** Mercermur1@yaboo.com
**Subject: Story Contest**
**March 1**

*Dad,*

*I'm looking for hope anywhere I can find it, Dad. I believe in you, but I'd rather believe in you in Iowa.*

*On the lighter side of things, Ms. Boge asked us to write a short story for a contest, so I sent mine in. The story had to be 500 words or less and it had to start with the line, "It was Christmas Eve; Nancy dozed before the fireplace, wondering if he would come, as promised." So I entered the following story:*

### A Change in the Season

It was Christmas Eve; Nancy dozed before the fireplace, wondering if he would come, as promised. The clang of the doorbell jolted Nancy's arthritic legs to a quickness not seen since her 30's Olympic gymnastic days. She opened the door to a stout man wearing a tweed coat and hat. Her joker smile dropped to a frown as she saw Harold Jacoby, her friendly neighborhood vacuum salesman.

Harold saw the disappointment in Nancy's eyes, but quickly addressed her.

"Good Afternoon, Ms. Boyd. I won't keep you long. I just thought you might want to join me over at St. Luke's tonight for our Christmas Eve celebration," Harold said.

"Harold, you are so sweet, but my son is coming over tonight. I haven't seen him in a year, so I better just wait for him here," Nancy replied.

"No problem. Merry Christmas, ma'am."

And just as quick as he came, he trotted off. He was still agile for a man of 87, and as he glanced back, she felt a flutter. He'd been coming here for the last five years now, trying to sell her some vacuum part and to invite her to a movie or a Knights of Columbus fish fry. And as always, she politely turned him down every time.

The piercing ring of the phone interrupted her thoughts. She knew who it was and felt the tears well as she picked up the receiver.

"Mom. How are ya? Say, I'm not going to be able to make it today. A huge deal just opened up for me. You wouldn't want your son to miss this opportunity, would you? Thanks for understanding, Mom. I'll call you tomorrow."

After a restless night, Nancy forced herself out of bed to sip a cup of cold coffee. The sound of the doorbell once again sprang her to life. She walked over to the door and flung it open.

"Merry Christmas, Ms. Boyd. I was wondering if you'd like to go to Christmas Day Mass with me today. They're serving a fried-chicken dinner afterward," Harold said.

Nancy looked at his eyes and paused. "Why, yes, Mr. Jacoby, I would love to go to church with you. Will you wait a moment while I get ready?"

Nancy hurried to her bedroom and pulled out the sequined purple dress she last wore at George's college graduation. After a quick line of the eyes and lips, she was ready.

Harold's eyes widened at the sight of her entrance. "Ms. Boyd, you, you look stunning," he said with a cheshire grin.

Harold held out his hand and led her to the front door. Just as she fumbled with her key in the lock, the phone rang. She paused – she knew it was George. She looked at Harold and then looked at the phone.

"I'm sorry, Mr. Jacoby, but I need…" she paused again. She looked back at him and smiled. "I need for you to call me Nancy."

*What do you think, Dad? Do you like it? Do you think I've got a shot? Maybe I will be a writer someday – that or a barista. I'm still addicted.*

Mercer

---

**To:** Mercermur1@yaboo.com
**From:** artmurr@yaboo.com
**Subject: Re: Story Contest**
**March 1**

Mercer,

*I'm so proud of you. You've already won.*

Dad

---

**To:** Mercermur1@yaboo.com
**From:** ahmed86@yaboo.com
**Subject: Ashura**
**March 1**

Mercer,

*Tomorrow will be a great day of celebration for my people. Tomorrow we celebrate Ashura, an Islamic holiday observed on the 10th of Muharram, the first month of the Islamic year. Ashura commemorates the death of Husayn, son of Imam 'Ali and grandson of Muhammad. Husayn's martyrdom is seen by many Shi'ia as a symbol of the struggle against injustice, tyranny, and oppression. This event actually led to the split between the Sunni and Shi'ia sects of Islam, and it is very important in Shi'ia Islam. But it is also celebrated among Sunni Muslims, although for very different reasons.*

*For us the rituals for Ashura focus on public expressions of mourning and grief. Some Shi'ia express mourning by flagellating themselves on the back with chains, beating their head, or ritually cutting themselves. This is intended to connect them with Husayn's suffering and death as an aid to salvation on the Day of Judgment. Many Shi'ia parade in the streets with red paint splattered on their bodies to symbolize Husayn's blood. I will participate this year by walking with my fellow Shi'ites through the streets, although I will not put paint on my body or whip my back. I will celebrate tomorrow because I am able to celebrate.*

*Saddam Hussein saw the Shi'ia celebration as potential threat and banned Ashura commemorations for many years. This will be the second year we will celebrate Ashura since Saddam has been removed from power. I am happy today.*

*Ahmed*

---

**To:** Mercermur1@yaboo.com
**From:** ahmed86@yaboo.com
**Subject: Suicide Bombings**
**March 2**

*Mercer,*

*I am sad to be writing to you, Mercer. I am sad because our most holy feast day was marred by a dozen suicide bombers who killed more than 85 and wounded 233 others. Why must they hate so much? My father never subscribed to "suicide bombing" being something noble. Muslims are commanded to defend their right to freedom of worship, but not to "terrorize." I miss my Baba so much, especially in times like these. Who will help me make sense of this mess?*

*Ahmed*

---

**To:** ahmed86@yaboo.com
**From:** Mercermur1@yaboo.com
**Subject: Re: Suicide Bombings**
**March 2**

*Ahmed,*

*I am so sorry. I can't imagine somebody bombing our church during Easter Vigil. I am glad you were not one of those hurt though. Go find my dad and ask him for words of comfort. For some reason, he always knows what to say.*

*Mercer*

**To:** artmurr@yaboo.com
**From:** Mercermur1@yaboo.com
**Subject: Come home**
**March 3**

*Dear Dad,*

*A dozen suicide bombers just killed 250 people on the Shi'ites most holy day. What is going on? Who are we fighting? Saddam is gone and we have one sect blowing up another. What is this war all about, really? Get out of there, Dad! I just heard some guy on TV paraphrase Dwight Eisenhower on the war in Korea. He said, "Anyone who tells you we can set a timetable for withdrawal doesn't understand war." So what are we doing? Are we there forever? I knew we'd probably always have a base there, but that doesn't mean YOU have to be there. Why are we being a police force? Why are we referees in a civil war? Why do we have to save them?*

*Will you please write back right away just to confirm that you weren't one of the 250 people who were killed? I can't believe I even have to think about such things.*
      *Mercer*

---

**To:** Mercermur1@yaboo.com
**From:** artmurr@yaboo.com
**Subject: Re: Come Home**
**March 3**

*Dear Mercer,*

*I am fine, Son. Please pray for those who died and their families. Sometimes I think the suicide bombers want to start a civil war knowing that it is unwinnable. They do it for God, and the only way I know how to stop them is to bring people democracy here. I know it is hard, Mercer. Democracy in Iraq is a stepping-stone to secure peace in the Middle East, which will benefit all. America is strong because of what it values: liberty and democracy. Spreading liberty and democracy is in our economic and security interests.*

*Woodrow Wilson declared that the U.S. should enter World War I to make the world safe for democracy. President Bush, Sr., emphasized the moral justifications for defending Kuwait against Iraq's aggression. America is a big brother, whether the world wants it or not. Is that right? I don't know, but I do know that liberty is an ideal worth fighting for. I am here because I believe all people deserve to claim liberty as their right. People can argue that we shouldn't be here because no WMD's were found and that we are just letting innocent American soldiers die for nothing, but history will prove differently. I know you support me, Mercer, but you must also support your country.*

*I am proud of you. I am proud that you are using your intelligence to develop your own opinion about the war. Just make sure that the media is not your only source of information.*

*By the way, I have to eat raw tobacco periodically to kill the stomach worms that come from local foods. Remember that when you are tempted to smoke.*

    *Dad*

---

**To:** Mercermur1@yaboo.com
**From:** ahmed86@yaboo.com
**Subject: Senseless**
**March 4**

*Mercer,*

*It is senseless. This violence is senseless. Yesterday the head of Iraq's Governing Council said that the death toll from the Ashura attacks in Baghdad and Karbala had risen to 271. Our religious leaders are blaming the Americans for multiple security failures. What is happening? At least some Sunni and Shi'ite leaders stood side by side in Baghdad yesterday to urge Iraqis to avoid a civil war. Islam does not teach this hate. I do not understand. It is frustrating and infuriating and confusing all at the same time. I cannot think anymore. I feel at times that I cannot breathe anymore. Is there any hope left?*

    *Ahmed*

## MERCER 24
## WAR 28

---

**To:** ahmed86@yaboo.com
**From:** Mercermur1@yaboo.com
**Subject: Re: Senseless**
**March 5**

*Ahmed,*

*I apologize for not writing you back yesterday. I was studying for a HUGE Anatomy test last night and didn't check my e-mail. Even if I don't think the U.S. should be there, they will make it better, and they won't leave until the Iraqi government is ready to go. That may not bring peace right away either, but it sounds like it's going to be a very long process. That's why you need to come here for college. You need to be able to study in peace without worrying about whether noises are bombs or whether someone will kidnap you because you are helping the U.S. We will get you here.*

> *Mercer*

---

**March 6 -** Bear has grown a soul patch. What a nerd. They will make him shave it off at school tomorrow anyway. How can he grow a soul patch in a weekend? I have to shave like once a week, if even. Maybe Bear is growing a soul patch to hide his puffy face. I don't know what happened, but he looks bloated. Am I weird because I notice this stuff?

Last night we hung out at Bear's and played Poker again. I'm losing my touch (which resulted in a loss of money – no mochas this week).

**To:** Mercermur1@yaboo.com
**From:** ahmed86@yaboo.com
**Subject: My friend**
**March 7**

*Mercer,*

*My friend Amer just came back from Syria. He was looking for a safer home since he had been receiving death threats for helping the Americans create an Internet hookup. He is broke, but he is glad to be back with his family. Hundreds of thousands of Iraqis have fled our country. I wonder if they will come back. Amer is an IT engineer, but he couldn't find work outside Iraq (Syria stamped all the Iraqis' passports with "NO WORK"). I will try to find out if any of the Americans could use him again. It is still dangerous, but it is work.*

*Amer drove his uncle's car over to my house so we could go visit another friend, and I had to warn him to take down the pictures and stickers of Imam Ali in his car, especially in his rear window. I also took down his Alek (a religious amulet made of a strip of green cloth). He is not aware that if a Sunni sees the picture of Ali (which Sunnis consider idolatry), they will pull him over and may harm him. He has only been gone nine months, but so much has changed. He wants to go to America to find work, but it is very difficult to get a visa.*

*It is good to have Amer back. Many of my friends have left Iraq or have moved or dropped out of school to work. Amer is my serious friend. He has an intensity that I envy. When he took some on-line computer training three years ago, we didn't see him for six months. Since then he has been reading everything and anything about computers that he could get his hands on. He basically has taught himself. His is an inspiration to me as are you. Praise Allah for good friends.*

*Ahmed*

---

**To:** ahmed86@yaboo.com
**From:** Mercermur1@yaboo.com
**Subject: Re: My friend**
**March 7**

*Ahmed,*

*I'm glad that Amer got back safely. It sounds like it is dangerous just to be alive. You need to come here, Ahmed. Did the admission's counselor get back to you? I will put you down for my housing when I have to fill out the forms. It's going to happen.*

*Mercer*

**To:** Mercermur1@yaboo.com
**From:** ahmed86@yaboo.com
**Subject: Fun**
**March 8**

*Mercer,*

*Today was actually relaxing. My friends and family played beatha, a name game played with fast-moving hands and strips of paper. Someday when I come to America, I will teach you and your friends. I am the ultimate champion in beatha. Even Amer cannot beat me. Just as I'm sure I can never beat you at football, although I am eager to learn.*

*Ahmed*

---

**To:** ahmed86@yaboo.com
**From:** Mercermur1@yaboo.com
**Subject: Re: Fun**
**March 8**

*Ahmed,*

*I would like to learn beatha, although with my cat-like reflexes, I know I will be challenging you as the grandmaster soon enough. School is pretty boring these days. I'm still working at the Boys and Girls Club, but I might have to quit once we start track meets. Last week I went to a* Students Beyond War *meeting. I'm becoming a peace activist slowly but surely. We might go sit outside Senator Grassley's office sometime to protest the war. I just want my dad home.*

*Mercer*

---

**To:** artmurr@yaboo.com
**From:** Mercermur1@yaboo.com
**Subject: What are we doing in Iraq?!!!!**
**March 8**

*Dear Dad,*

*The war, which supposedly was started to protect us, has become the single greatest threat to our national security. The single greatest threat! We are losing lives and money and there is no end in sight. The war has trashed our reputation with the rest of the world (has it ever been this bad?). In the meantime, real threats suffer terrible neglect, including more terrorist attacks, jeopardized oil supplies, rising tension with China, the spread of nuclear and other weapons of mass destruction. All these things are being ignored while the Bush Administration pours the country's blood, money and energy into a futile war. I'm sorry, Dad. I just went to a* Students Beyond War *meeting, and I'm fired up. I knew we shouldn't be there. I knew your place wasn't in the desert but instead home taking care of our family. We need you.*

*Mercer*

---

**To:** Mercermur1@yaboo.com
**From:** artmurr@yaboo.com
**Subject: Re: What are we doing in Iraq?!!!!**
**March 8**

*Mercer,*

*Son, I know you are still struggling, but I am where I'm supposed to be. This war is about protecting America in the long run – our national security is why we are here. The rest of the world will understand soon enough.*

*It isn't always easy to believe in the cause. I have nightmares of having to count dead bodies and body parts from car bombings. I startle easily at the smallest noise. I am tired and frustrated, but my resolve is strong. We will succeed in Iraq. It may take ten years or twenty years, but peace in Iraq is the start of peace for the entire Middle East. Trust me. Americans are "McDonaldized." They want to drive up, order, pay, go to the next window and get a democracy. It's just not that easy. Dignity, honor, and freedom are more important than oil.*

*Dad*

---

**To:** artmurr@yaboo.com
**From:** Mercermur1@yaboo.com
**Subject: Re: What are we doing in Iraq?!!!!**
**March 8**

*Dad,*

*I know that we have different views, but why do different views have to have such dire consequences? Why can't we just differ on which college I should go to or which candidate to vote for? Mary is on your side – she always gives me the same arguments that you have (I can't argue with her – I'm a horrible debater). Anywho, she's good for me – if I didn't have her arguments making me feel at least a LITTLE better about this war, I think I'd be in jail by now.*

*I have to go get ready for the basketball game (the girls are playing in the first round of the state tournament down at Vets). Bear and I are dressing in kilts and painting our faces blue like the* Braveheart *dudes.*

*Mercer*

**To:** Mercermur1@yaboo.com
**From:** artmurr@yaboo.com
**Subject: Re: What are we doing in Iraq?!!!!**
**March 8**

*Mercer,*

*I hope you are thankful for Mary. She is a loyal and compassionate friend. Keep listening to her.*

*I welcome your arguments, Mercer. It reminds me to keep my spirits up for my soldiers. As leader of this battalion, I make my men visit a Missionaries of Charity orphanage once a week here in Baghdad. It is important to serve the Iraqis as people as well as a country. The children laugh and play with the men who teach them simple games and give them small treats. Their smiles make me miss my own family, but I am fighting for you just as much as I am for them. I am fighting for freedom – we are lucky someone already fought for ours.*

*Dad*

---

**To:** Mercermur1@yaboo.com
**From:** ahmed86@yaboo.com
**Subject: Sand Storm**
**March 8**

*Mercer,*

*Have patience, my friend. I know the desire to have your dad home is great, but he is needed here.*

*I was just looking at my journal of this war. Last year during this month we had a freak sandstorm. The air was so thick from red dust that I could only see about two meters in front of me. The government had been burning huge amounts of oil to cloud the air so the American's missiles would miss their targets. It didn't work. I couldn't see very well, but at times the night sky was a work of art. Black, purple and red shades swept through the sky and painted dark, yet vibrant pictures. Unfortunately, this burning oil cut off much of the fresh air supply. It was difficult to breathe! We also noticed that there were no sounds from the birds. I had always taken a bird's song for granted. Now I smile whenever I hear a bird sing for it means the air is clean.*

*Ahmed*

**To:** ahmed86@yaboo.com
**From:** Mercermur1@yaboo.com
**Subject: Re: Sandstorm**
**March 8**

*Ahmed,*

*I just came back from a Students Beyond War meeting, and I am livid. We are killing people for no good reason! No wonder the Catholic Church is against this war. If I had the ability, I'd go kidnap my dad, but maybe that's why you are in my life - to add balance. I get so riled up and then I read your e-mails, and I see the other side of things. Every time I hear a bird from now on, I'll try to remember to be thankful for the freedom I've never had to struggle for. Still, it's hard. I've got to go burn off some steam – five miles will work.*

*Mercer*

---

**To:** Mercermur1@yaboo.com
**From:** ahmed86@yaboo.com
**Subject: Re: Sand Storm**
**March 8**

*Mercer,*

*I will smile whenever I hear a bird because the air is clean and because I have a good friend in America.*

*Ahmed*

**March 9 -** We were on the front page this morning! Bear and I in our cool Scottish garb were pictured on the front page of the *Des Moines Register* for the tournament. Man, track has been good to my washboard stomach.

**March 10 -** I'm reading this on-line newspaper from Bangladesh called *The Daily Star*. It's supposed to be fair and impartial and have current news. I'll still read the *Register* and the *NY Times*, but this seems to cover what I want to know in a hurry, and it doesn't seem biased.

Track practice was KILLER today. We did hills forever – my legs feel like Jell-O. Gina and I picked up Larry and treated our hard-working selves to a LARGE Blizzard. I feel sick to my stomach – time to sleep.

**March 11** - Today we had an interesting Christian Lifestyles class. We're in this "marriage" unit where we get paired up with someone and create a budget. Patt (spelled with two "t's – I learned that mighty quick), my pretend wife, and I "earned" $50,000 combined (we're both teachers). We had to create a budget for rent, food, student loans, utilities, gas, phone, entertainment, etc. So this should have only taken ten minutes or so, right? We were arguing by minute three. I wanted cable, she didn't. She wanted bikes for weekend rides, I didn't. I wanted Hawkeye season tickets, she didn't. She wanted to take art classes on the weekend – I did too (but that doubled the education budget). We went on and on (in good fun) and on until we were both living in a one-bedroom apartment in the hood, but at least we had season tickets and art classes! Who knew money didn't go very far? Each time we meet for class, Mr. Schmidt will hand us a "problem" that could be a pregnancy or a letter that we're being sued. I'm so glad this is not my reality right now.

Next week we actually have a baby to take care of; well, it's a doll, but it cries loud enough. Now this is not just any doll, it's called "Baby Think It Over." It weighs about 6-1/2 pounds and is 21 inches long, so it's like a real newborn. She (Patt and I named her "Sienna" after the movie star – who?) wears a diaper and a cute T-shirt, and she cries at random, just like an infant. Sienna is designed to make young people experience what being a parent is like. I get Sienna for twenty-four hours (even in school) next Monday. No problem.

**March 12 -** They bombed the trains in Madrid – what is next? When will it come here (I can't believe nothing has happened since 9/11)? I read in *The Daily Star* that three different train stations were hit and 173 people were killed. No doubt it's a terrorist attack (someone named Eta?). I'm on my knees for my dad.

T.G.I.F. (really, I am praising God that it is Friday; I'm not taking His name in vain) Today after school I'm going to a sit-in. Peace, love, harmony.

**To:** artmurr@yaboo.com
**From:** Mercermur1@yaboo.com
**Subject: Sorry**
**March 12**

*Dad,*

*There's no easy way to say this, but I got arrested today. I went to a couple of* Students Beyond War *meetings, a group that meets weekly at the American Friends Service Committee's Des Moines office. We had to attend a mandatory non-violence training workshop last night including an overview of the theory, history, and practice of nonviolence and civil resistance (so the experience was actually educational, right?). A group of us went to Senator Grassley's office for about three hours after school on Friday to protest the war (I talked to Coach about this ahead of time and I did my track workout in the morning), and we refused to leave so we were arrested. We visited Senator Grassley's office in the hope of talking with the ranking member of the Senate Finance Committee to urge him to end his support for the war in Iraq. Soon after we arrived, a staffer said the Senator was traveling and could not be reached by phone, so we sat in a circle on the office floor and read from a list of the names of the dead from the Iraq war (I had to go to the bathroom for a while during this part). Later we passed around and read from Thomas Merton's* The Nonviolent Solution. *A spokesperson told us that: "Senator Grassley is looking for the best way possible to draw down the U.S. commitment as quickly as possible while also looking out for U.S. interests and security in the long term." I just want the war to stop. Actually, I really just want you to come home.*

*Don't worry though. We were charged with misdemeanor criminal trespass and will be processed through the juvenile court system. I was home in time to relieve the nanny at 7:00. Mom will get me off - she hugged me and said she was proud of me when I told her what happened. I'm going to go read Thoreau's "Civil Disobedience" now – I have a right and an obligation to follow my conscience. Actually, I'm going to go to sleep – protesting can take a lot out of you.*

> *Mercer*

---

**To:** Mercermur1@yaboo.com
**From:** artmurr@yaboo.com
**Subject: Re: Sorry**
**March 12**

*Mercer,*

*I am proud of you for sticking to your convictions, Mercer, but be careful not to mix your personal feelings with your convictions. Would you have protested had I not been here? Thank you for taking care of your responsibilities at home and at school. Next time, try not to get arrested, though.*

> *Dad*

**March 14** - I hope you don't read this, Ms. Boge, because Bear would be highly embarrassed, but I want to read this in twenty years and laugh my head off again. We were playing video games over at Bear's house today and Bear was slumming in sweat pants and no shirt. So we're goofing off when Bear looks down and finds a left-over Doritos chip in his belly button. So he picks it up, looks at it, and EATS it! Then he says, "I'm hungry. Let's go get some chow." EEEWWWW. I thought I was going to faint from laughter and hurl at the same time. Only Bear, only Bear.

**March 16** - 8:00 AM – Creative Writing Class - Oh, my, oh, my. I am so exhausted my eyelashes are sleeping. Every time I sit, I feel sleepiness crawl through my body. Last night was my first night with "Baby Think It Over." Sienna, my precious, cute, adorable little monster, was up EVERY HOUR last night. And I couldn't get her to stop crying! I fed her (I stuck the key in the monitor, which is supposed to simulate the average length of time it takes to feed, change, etc., and the baby won't stop crying until the time has elapsed), I changed her (stuck it in again), I rocked her, I even did squats with her while singing "On Eagle's Wings." I am never having sex. I can't handle a baby.

9:00 P.M. – After a seven-mile run WITH hills every mile, cooking Mac and Cheese for Gina and Larry, and after completing two hours of homework, I am in a coma. I am only writing this journal to remind myself how hard it is to have a baby, even for a DAY! I am going to marry someone who is patient and kind and loving and who won't mind getting up without help from me. I know, I know, that is SO sexist, but right now my toes are even tired. Not only did I not sleep last night, but the baby cried ALL day too. I had to shove that stinkin' key in the monitor and hold it there so many times I have carpal tunnel now. I seriously think Mr. Schmidt set the crying level at "colicky" just for me. I couldn't even take the battery pack out because the doll would shut down and the monitor would register abuse and I would FLUNK having a baby! How can you FLUNK having a baby? I better get a good read out (Sienna has a computer chip that documents how well you took care of her), and I better get an 'A.' In any case, I've learned that I'm not ready to be a dad, not that I'm in any danger of that happening anyway, but having a baby for a night gives me a whole new appreciation for two-parent families who are prepared to have kids.

I had to keep a journal of the experience hour by hour, and twenty-two out of the twenty-four hours I report crying at one point (ten of those hours are me crying). Sienna needs to go see mommy now.

**March 17** - I'm still recovering from my no-contact boxing match with Sienna, so I couldn't enjoy the St. Patrick's Day party that Bear put on (yes, even on a school night). He had green beer, green Jell-O shots and his mom made green pumpkin bread (which was actually really good).

Beth was there in a green mini-skirt. I guess she's not going out with Bear – she was just making out with him the other night. Is my interest waning? I don't know. I just feel this compulsion to ask her to prom. Is that wrong?

I had a weird dream last night. I dreamt I was on a beach with two boys I knew were mine, but then they kept changing into Patt's and then back to mine. Anywho, I was playing Frisbee with these boys on the beach when my wife came over. Her face was murky, but I knew she was my wife. She mentioned that she just saw someone we went to high school with so that means my wife is my high school sweetheart. I still couldn't make out her face, but I remember her laugh, her kind, gentle laugh. I also remember her hair – it was swishy and full, even in a pony-tail. What does that mean? Is Beth the one? Will I really marry my high school sweetheart?

**March 18** - Tomorrow David and I will be on a plane (with half the senior class and more importantly, Beth and friends) to Cancun where the sun and the beach will make me forget about my dad and my responsibilities and my stress. I saved up for this trip all summer (although my mocha addiction cut into my spending fund a bit, but that's okay since I won't spend any money on alcohol). Cancun, take me away.

To: ahmed86@yaboo.com
From: Mercermur1@yaboo.com
**Subject: Spring Break**
**March 18**

*Ahmed,*

*Hey, buddy. I'm headed to Cancun for a week for Spring Break so I don't know if I'll be able to e-mail. Take care of my dad. Peace.*

> *Mercer*

---

To: artmurr@yaboo.com
From: Mercermur1@yaboo.com
**Subject: Cancun**
**March 18**

*Dad,*

*I might not be able to e-mail for a week or so (which will be weird since I've e-mailed you practically every day since you've been gone). I'm headed to Cancun for fun in the sun. Don't worry – I'll be good. I love you.*

> *Mercer*

---

**March 19 -** 8:00 A.M. "Leaving on a jet plane, don't know when I'll be back again."

---

To: ahmed86@yaboo.com
From: Mercermur1@yaboo.com
**Subject: Speechless**
**March 27**

*Ahmed,*

*I ran and ran and ran. I found this coffee shop somewhere in Cancun and thankfully they had internet access. I didn't know who else to write to, but I was so upset I want to hit something, actually someone. Tonight was our last night here so we decided to go clubbing (remember it's legal to drink in Cancun if you are 18). I was having a good time dancing with a couple of football buddies when I looked over and my mouth dropped. Beth was kissing David on the dance floor! I stopped and stared. David eventually pushed her away and then caught my glance, but all I could do is stand there with my mouth agape. He knew. He knew. He knew how much I liked her. He wasn't even supposed to kiss anyone until he was married, let alone on a dance floor in Mexico. I just ran. It's 12:30 A.M. and I am sitting in a coffee shop in a foreign country. My dad will probably die in Iraq when we shouldn't even be there, I won't play football for the Hawkeyes, and my best friend just made out with my future wife. What's next?*

> *Mercer*

# 4TH QUARTER

## MERCER 24
## WAR 31

---

**To:** Mercermur1@yaboo.com
**From:** ahmed86@yaboo.com
**Subject: Re: Speechless**
**March 28**

*Mercer,*

*I am sorry I could not write earlier to offer words of comfort, but I did not read your e-mail until just now. I know you must feel betrayed. I am sorry, my friend. I hope that you went back at the hotel safe with the other students. Time will make it easier to deal with this. In the meantime, pray for David and Beth and for patience and forgiveness. Please let me know how you are doing.*

*Ahmed*

---

**To:** ahmed86@yaboo.com
**From:** Mercermur1@yaboo.com
**Subject: Speechless**
**March 28**

*Ahmed,*

*I am safe. I drank a lot of coffee that night, but I caught a taxi back to the hotel after I emailed you. I saw David the next morning and could tell that he had been up all night as well, but I couldn't even look him in the eye. He said sorry over and over and over, but I blew him off. He put his hand on my shoulder, and I freaked out. I threw it off like his hand was on fire or something and then I gave him a look that made him know how much he had hurt me. I don't care if I'm supposed to be the bigger person and forgive and say, "That's okay, best friend. I know you couldn't help kissing the girl that I've been in love with all year," but I just couldn't.*

On the plane ride home, he tried to apologize over and over again and said that he "had sinned against the Lord," and all that stuff. Then he said he had four bottles of beer and that he had never drank before and that his guard was down and that he was SO sorry again. I calmly and quietly turned to him and said, "If you can't be loyal to your own best friend, how can you be loyal to your country as a Marine?" At that his eyes widened, and he put his head down. I know that was cruel, but I wanted to hurt him like he hurt me.

I'm a mess, Ahmed. I haven't eaten all day, and I locked myself in my room. Larry, Gina, and my mom all tried banging on the door, asking me what happened, but I can't face anyone. Mary called and called and called (she stayed in town and worked during spring break), but I didn't answer. I have to go to school tomorrow. I have to face him. I have to face life.

      *Mercer*

---

**To:** artmurr@yaboo.com
**From:** Mercermur1@yaboo.com
**Subject: Prom**
**March 29**

*Dad,*

*Well, Dad, it looks like I'm not going to prom anymore. We went on Spring Break and Beth was kissing a guy AGAIN on the dance floor, only this time the guy was David. I'm speechless.*

      *Mercer*

---

**To:** Mercermur1@yaboo.com
**From:** artmurr@yaboo.com
**Subject: Re: Prom**
**March 29**

*Mercer,*

*Forgive as you are forgiven. I'll write again later.*

      *Dad*

**To:** artmurr@yaboo.com
**From:** Mercermur1@yaboo.com
**Subject: Re: Prom**
**March 29**

*Dad,*

*Our first track meet is tomorrow after school in Indianola. How can I run? How can I concentrate on anything?*

*Mercer*

---

**To:** artmurr@yaboo.com
**From:** Mercermur1@yaboo.com
**Subject: Gina**
**March 30**

*Dad,*

*I have to hand it to my little sister – she got me through the track meet. She gave me a pep talk about focusing my anger and it worked: I won both my races. It was my first track meet ever and I won, but I don't care. I'm worthless. Maybe that's why Beth likes everyone except me.*

*Mercer*

---

**March 31** - It is Day Five since my heart was sautéed and I'm going through the motions. The Simpson Invite yesterday actually went well. I won the 800M with a time of 2:15, and the mile with a time of 4:58 (coach says my times will go down when we run outside) - Gina gave me a good ribbing before the races and I actually listened to her. She didn't do so badly either - she placed second in the 800 and third in the high jump. Who knew? I'm happy for her.

---

**To:** ahmed86@yaboo.com
**From:** Mercermur1@yaboo.com
**Subject: Civilian heads**
**March 31**

*I'm still in Depressionville, Ahmed. I don't know if I can come out of this one. To make a horrible day even worse, I just looked at some nasty pictures on the internet of the Iraqi mob that killed and mutilated four America civilian contract workers today and then dragged them through the streets of Falluja. That could have been my dad's head. I never thought I'd ever have to write a sentence like that.*

*Mercer*

**To:** Mercermur1@yaboo.com
**From:** ahmed86@yaboo.com
**Subject: Re: Civilian heads**
**March 31**

*Mercer,*

*I know you are sad, but your dad is still alive. When you forgive your friend, your anger will subside. Pray for David.*

> *Ahmed*

---

**To:** ahmed86@yaboo.com
**From:** Mercermur1@yaboo.com
**Subject: Re: Civilian heads**
**March 31**

*Ahmed,*

*Maybe I'm just a sissy. Maybe I shouldn't care so much that my best friend just betrayed me and that my dad might die at any moment. I just need to buck-up. I've got to be strong and open and have a sense of my own path without letting other people bring me down, right?*

> *Mercer*

---

**To:** Mercermur1@yaboo.com
**From:** ahmed86@yaboo.com
**Subject: Baba**
**April 1**

*Mercer,*

*I am sad today, my friend. It is the one-year anniversary of my father's death. My mother spent the day praying, meditating, and mourning. I spent the morning with her, but I left after our meal in the afternoon to be alone. I went to an alley and cried and cried. I miss him so much. I thought that time would make it better, but time has worn me down.*

> *Ahmed*

*Ahmed,*

*I am sorry, Ahmed. I can't imagine. I know you are taking good care of your mom. I'm sure she is scared for you as well. Please know that I will be praying for you.*

*Mercer*

**April 1** - I was driving Larry and Gina to school today when we heard this weird alert on the radio. Apparently we are supposed to put a bag over our phone because the phone company is blowing the lines or something like that and the bag will protect the surrounding area. I began to call my mom to tell her that we needed to do this, but then I started thinking about it – how would the phone company blow lines through all that cable? Ah, April Fool's Day, I get it.

Today is the one-year anniversary of Ahmed's father's death. I can't even think about what I would do if my dad died.

*Ahmed,*

*I don't have too many words of comfort, but I do want to tell you that you are one of the strongest and most honorable people I've ever known. I'm here for you, buddy.*

*Mercer*

*Mercer,*

*Just a heads up that we're headed up to Mosul to try to detonate some IED's for the coalition base up there, so I won't be able to write for a while. I'll keep in contact with your mom, but keep praying. I love you.*

> *Dad*

---

**To:** artmurr@yaboo.com
**From:** Mercermur1@yaboo.com
**Subject: Re: Prom**
**April 1**

*Dad,*

*Good luck in Mosul. I'll survive without your e-mails – I guess I've done it so far. I'm getting stronger, Dad. I can't string your bow yet, but I'm getting stronger.*

> *Mercer*

**April 2** - It was a bright cold day in April, and the clocks were striking thirteen. I'm not even in the military and it's controlling my life. Don't die, Dad, just please don't die.

Bear keeps bugging me about why I won't talk to David. I guess David never spilled the beans and told him that I liked Beth so much. How could I tell Bear that I liked Beth when he kissed her? At least he never knew I liked her – David knew. If you are reading this, Ms. Boge, I'm sure you are confused because I never wrote what happened over Spring Break, but that's a good thing. You should just know I'm still steamed.

The D.J. from that radio station got fired today for his little April Fools' Day prank. Two hundred people phoned the phone company and asked if it were true that they needed to bag their phones. If two-hundred called in, how many do you think actually bagged the phones and waited?

I'm depressed again.

**April 3** - Yesterday I won the 800 (2:10) and the mile (4:48) at the Urbandale Relays (our first outdoor meet). I haven't been pushed yet though – I wonder what will happen when I have someone who pushes me to the finish line?

Mary came with me to Larry's Taekwondo tournament today. Larry LOVES Mary (I think he has a crush on her). He made it to the semis, so we were proud. I said I'd take him out to eat anywhere he wanted to celebrate and he paused and said, "Mercer, my favorite meal is your Chicken Parmesan. Will you make it for me?" I swear I almost started to cry (maybe I am a sissy). Mary threw me a huge smile and gave me a pat on the back and then we all trucked over to Hy-Vee for the fixin's. Gina and my mom joined us for dinner and we toasted to Larry. Today was a good day.

**April 4** - I woke up at 10:00 for 11:15 mass. It was actually 11:00 - Daylight Savings stinks (although I do love it in the fall). It's Palm Sunday today – the day when Jesus was hailed with palm branches on his way to Jerusalem. They killed Him five days later and Jesus STILL asked His Father to forgive them. I know I have to forgive David. But how?

---

**To:** Mercermur1@yaboo.com
**From:** ahmed86@yaboo.com
**Subject: Family Honor**
**April 4**

*Mercer,*

*Thank you for your e-mails, my friend. Your prayers are comforting. Although I still cry once in a while at night, I am better now. Sometimes it feels as if there is no time to cry though.*

*My cousin Samira is living with us now and she is of great comfort to me. She said she left her family because my mother and my other aunt need help, but she has told me that she was glad to leave. She said that her father has changed – he is so conservative now that he makes them wear abbayah everywhere outside the home. She couldn't even wear trousers outside the home, and she and her mother had to wear long skirts with long wide shirts covering their hips when they went anywhere. I told her that men often feel the need to protect their female relatives from being the subject of gossip and from losing the family's honor (Our society values a woman's honor as a reflection of the family's honor.). She said that she knows that, but she has already enjoyed the freedom of not wearing the abbayah and of wearing jeans and feeling free. She told me a story about a boy from school who tried to drag a girl by the hair to speak with him by claiming that he was in love with her. But the truth is that he just wanted to show his friends that he had sex with her. Samira felt bad for the girl because if her father or brother find out, she could be beaten. And if the gossipers spread a rumor, she would have a hard time getting a husband.*

*Samira is scared to even talk to boys, and not just because she might be the victim of a rumor, but because she could actually be killed in an "honor killing." Fathers and brothers of women who are known and often only suspected of having 'violated' the morally accepted codes of behavior, especially with respect to keeping their virginity before marriage, might kill their female kin in order to restore the honor of the family. Although this usually only happens in rural areas and sometimes with uneducated Iraqis, knowledge about "honor killings" works as deterrence for many.*

*Samira is actually afraid of my uncle. She is afraid for her sisters as well, although they are younger. I did not know what to say to her, except that she is welcome to live with us as long as she likes. I cannot help feeling protective of her though. I do not want her to get harassed on the streets for not wearing the abbayah.*

*Samira will do well here with our family. My mother is an excellent cook and an excellent teacher. Samira will still go to school and she plans to study in the fall at the University of Baghdad to be a doctor.*

> *Things are changing. Some are good. Some are not.*
> *Ahmed*

---

**To:** ahmed86@yaboo.com
**From:** Mercermur1@yaboo.com
**Subject: Re: Family Honor**
**April 4**

*Ahmed,*

*Whoa. Samira needs to come here, too! Getting killed for a rumor? I respect people's devotion to their religion, but the line has to be drawn somewhere. Tell Samira to come study in America where men and women are treated equally, well, at least people TRY to treat them equally (I just heard a statistic in my Christian Lifestyles class that women earn on average 70 cents to men's one dollar, even with childrearing years taken into consideration). Anywho, it's nice of you to let her live with you. How many cousins do you have anyway? I don't have any cousins – I wish I did. David and Mary both grew up with huge extended families. They always have big holiday dinners and birthday parties. Oh, well. You can be my official cousin, Ahmed.*

*I know what the whole "family honor" thing is all about, although certainly not to the extent your culture upholds it. Whenever I do anything wrong (like lie or cheat on an assignment or talk badly about someone), I am always conscious of what my dad would say - I don't want to embarrass him or make my mistakes a reflection of him. It doesn't stop me from streaking, though (warm weather is coming back – it was 60 degrees today).*

*I'll keep praying for you, Ahmed. Only five months until we're yelling in the stands at the first Hawkeye game.*

> *Mercer*

**April 5** - I talked to Beth this morning, and it was more than just our usual exchange of phrases. She asked if I was going to prom with anyone, and I said, "No." She said she wasn't going with anyone yet, either, and then stared at me (my Spidey-sense thought she was fishing for an invite, but maybe it's just wishful thinking). Then the warning bell rang so we both had to go to class. She swished her mane as she walked away – am I weird because I love hair? I looked at her again - I guess I never noticed how skinny she was. I mean REALLY skinny, like too skinny. That's okay – what she lacks in the body she makes up for in her face. Why the girl doesn't have a boyfriend is beyond me.

Bear had another party tonight for the NCAA Basketball Championship game. Connecticut easily beat Georgia Tech 82-73 (they were ahead 60-35 midway through the second half). UNI lost in the first round so the tournament didn't hold much interest for me anyway. I'm always up for a party, though.

**April 6** - Today we had the Jordan Creek Invite at Jordan Creek Stadium. This is the first co-ed track meet, so it was fun to see Beth and cheer her on. I got to see her run a lot because she is a sprinter (J.V.). Her legs are like fiddlesticks polls – they don't have any curve, not like Mary's anyway, but then again, Mary has *Rockettes* legs. She was voted "smartest," "nicest," "best smile," and "best legs" by the senior class. Which reminds me, I got voted "best dancer" and "best smile" as well, thank you very much. David got "best looking," "best eyes," and "nicest." Beth got voted "best looking." See, I have great taste in people.

**April 7** - I talked to Jerome after my shift today. I gave him my two-weeks notice because I would have to take off so much for track and end-of-the-year stuff. He asked if I liked working at the Boys and Girls Club, and I said of course. He told me that I could come back to work after I graduate in May or on college breaks or next summer or whenever I wanted to come back. He said that my work ethic and integrity made me an invaluable employee and that I could come back and work anytime. I laughed it off and said some stupid sarcastic reply, but I think he knew how much that meant to me. In fact, that may be the best compliment I've ever received. I'll definitely be back in June – who else could keep the place running?

**April 8** - David called and left a message on my cell phone. He signed up with the National Guard, but at least his dad convinced him to go to school as well at Iowa State.

I kicked some butt at the Indianola Invite today. I dropped both my 800 and mile times by two seconds each. I've got my goal on a state championship already – if I can't have my football glory, I might as well have something.

**April 9 -** It's 11:30 on a Friday night and I am writing in my journal and I don't even care how pathetic that may sound. Today was Good Friday. I feel like I want to throw up, cry, and tear my eyelashes out. Here is this man, this human who felt pain just like anyone, who endured the ultimate suffering for people who spit on Him and hit Him and whipped Him and crowned Him with thorns and crucified Him. We watched *Jesus of Nazareth* in Christian Lifestyles yesterday and today, and then a bunch of people went to *Passion of the Christ* tonight. Talk about your gut-wrencher. Jesus was perfect - He never sinned. In the Garden Gethsemane, he saw the sins of the whole world, mine included! Why would He suffer for people who tortured Him? Who am I that He would do that for me? "Judge not, and you shall not be judged."

## MERCER 27
## WAR 31

**To:** dkalsi@yaboo.com
**From:** Mercermur1@yaboo.com
**Subject: Sorry**
**April 9**

*David,*

*I know I don't usually write you e-mails, since we always see each other or pick up the phone, but I want to say everything I have to say without forgetting something. I owe you an apology. I know you would never deliberately hurt me, even though I deliberately hurt you with my words. I am sorry for that. I know you actually did push her away after a few seconds, but it was those few seconds that I couldn't see past. Sometimes it's hard being your friend. Every girl is in love with you, even my nanny. I'd hate it if you weren't such a great guy and so oblivious to it all. Anyway, when I saw Beth kissing you, all I could feel was jealousy and betrayal, no matter what you said. I've just liked her for SO long that I was crushed and jealous and mad and frustrated all at once. I forgive you, David, and I'm asking you to forgive me as well.*

  *Mercer*

**To:** Mercermur1@yaboo.com
**From:** dkalsi@yaboo.com
**Subject: Re: Sorry**
**April 9**

*No cause, no cause. I'm coming over to whip your butt in Madden NFL.*

  *David*

**April 9 -** Madden NFL was a good investment. I get by with a little help from my friends.

---

To: Mercermur1@yaboo.com
From: ahmed86@yaboo.com
**Subject: People**
**April 9**

*Mercer,*

*I do not know why, but I am sad lately. Maybe it is the anniversary of my father's death, maybe it is because I see my mother work and work and I cannot take her pain away or maybe it is because I feel like my people have changed. It is hard to describe, but they have become afraid of each other, and not just people from different sects. So many people have lost their jobs and businesses, so they just sit around and gossip and interfere in other people's lives. People are also embarrassed because they cannot afford to buy nice clothes and nice things and, therefore, it is better to wear hijab, and then they judge others who do not wear hijab. It also seems that honesty is not paying off anymore. People have become corrupt and greedy. They are looting, stealing, lying about food and possessions, and betraying even their own family members. Why? Why are we changing?*

*Ahmed*

---

To: ahmed86@yaboo.com
From: Mercermur1@yaboo.com
**Subject: Re: People**
**April 9**

*Ahmed,*

*I don't know why people change. I guess fear can make them do things they wouldn't normally do. I know I've acted like an idiot the past week because of jealousy and envy. Just make sure you don't change, Ahmed. To thine own self be true.*

*Mercer*

**April 10** - I smell. There's no denying it. I stink like musty old socks, a wrestling room after a three-hour practice, and sulfur, all rolled into one. I swear I shower at LEAST twice a day, and I still smell. I put on deodorant before I go to bed, after I shower in the morning, before track, after track, after the shower after track, and then before I go to bed again. AND I STILL SMELL. I hope no one else can smell me.

It was a pretty boring day – David, Mary, and I sat around and ate chips and watched *The Lord of the Rings* and *Pirates of the Caribbean*. Later on I watched *Finding Nemo* with Larry and Gina – I'm not ashamed to admit that *Finding Nemo* is an excellent, excellent film. I know my dad would search the ocean for me, too.

**April 11** - Today I had a major wardrobe malfunction in church. It was Easter Sunday today, and I dressed in a suit and tie, as Larry and I are always expected every Easter. Anywho, I leaned down to pick up a toy that a baby in front of us dropped, and my pants ripped. It wasn't a soft rip either. It was a loud, fabric-tearing, bright-red-cheek rip. I just sat down and took out the Missalette and pretended to read the gospel readings. At least no one laughed, not loudly anyway. I'm SO glad I wore a suit coat today.

Mary came over today and we baked cookies (low-protein cookies too) with Larry and Gina. We had fun spraying each other with whipped cream and sprinkles – Larry was in heaven. I told him he should ask Mary to the prom (woo-hoo, did he blush at that!). I and asked Mary if she was going to prom yet (I've been so wrapped up in my own life; I never even asked what was going on in her life). She turned away a little and said, "No." I teased her and asked her if she wanted anyone in particular to ask her (we've never talked about her crushes – man, am I selfish or what?). Then she seemed to get a little sad and she said that the guy she wanted to go with wasn't interested in her. I kept ragging on her all night to tell me who this guy was, but she just said I didn't know him. Must be a Jordan Creek guy – she knows a bunch of those guys from swimming. Too bad – she's a great catch.

**April 13** - I'm losing time – SAWWWEEEET! I placed first in the 800 and the mile again at the Waukee Invite today. I know that my track times will improve my chances of playing with the Hawkeyes – I just don't know how much, since I'm not a sprinter. Just keep swimming, just keep swimming.

---

**To:** ahmed86@yaboo.com
**From:** Mercermur1@yaboo.com
**Subject: Girls**
**April 14**

*Ahmed,*

*You are not going to believe this. I know you know how much I like Beth, and that I have wanted to ask her out all year, but I'm too shy, blah, blah, blah. Anywho, one of my New Years' resolutions was to ask Beth to the prom, right? Well, plans have changed. I don't think I ever mentioned Heather, the Paris Hilton wannabe. I went to Homecoming (a dance here held in the fall) with her (she somehow got me to ask her, or maybe she asked me, or maybe I said yes when I didn't mean to???). Well, she's pulled out all the stops. My little sister, Gina, is trying out for the dance team, and guess who is one of the judges? Heather. So Heather comes up to Gina after the first practice for tryouts and makes casual conversation with her (she has never acknowledged my sister's existence before, even though she knows she is my sister). Then Heather slyly says that as captain of the dance team, she has a say in who gets on the squad. Then she says, "It would be great if you could be on the squad, Gina, that is, if you are 'in.' The only way to be 'in' is to hang with the 'in' crowd...blah, blah, blah... and you would be 'in' if your brother and I were together. We can start being together by going to the prom. Are you with me, Gina?" So Gina is relaying this to me (and I believe her 100% because Gina never says anything bad about anyone, nor does she ever gossip or exaggerate – what good qualities in a female) and my mouth drops. Are we in a movie? Seriously, I thought stuff like this only happened on T.V. So I asked Gina what she wanted me to do. She said she's never wanted anything more in her life than to be on the dance team. I looked at her and I said, "But do you want to be on dance team because of Heather or because of your ability?" She said she just wanted to be on dance team. And so I gave her a hug and said that if she wanted me to, I would ask Heather to prom.*

*So it looks like I'm going to another dance with a girl I have no interest in. Oh, well. Maybe I'll ask Beth out on a date. I just had this whole vision of my senior prom being the best night of my life – a night where I finally get to spend time with the girl of my dreams. Life goes on.*

*Mercer*

---

**To:** Mercermur1@yaboo.com
**From:** ahmed86@yaboo.com
**Subject: Re: Girls**
**April 14**

*Mercer,*

*I am sure that you are frustrated, Mercer. I must tell you something as your friend. Please do not be mad at me, but I do not think Beth is the one for you. I know I have only a little information about her from your e-mails, but I do not respect her. She is pretty, that is all. The woman whom you will marry has to have integrity, and unless Beth changes, she is not the one for you. I know I am being blunt, but I do not want you to get hurt by this girl.*

  *Ahmed*

---

**To:** ahmed86@yaboo.com
**From:** Mercermur1@yaboo.com
**Subject: Re: Girls**
**April 14**

*Ahmed,*

*I'm not mad. I appreciate your concern. I know there's more to Beth than meets the eye. Maybe it just takes a little prodding to find it. I'm still holding on – I can't help it. When you are in love, you are in love.*

  *I have to go study for an Econ test.*

  *Mercer*

---

**To:** artmurr@yaboo.com
**From:** Mercermur1@yaboo.com
**Subject: June 30**
**April 15**

*Dad,*

*At least you'll be home by June 30th! I just read that the Bush administration agreed to a U.N. proposal to replace the Iraqi Governing Council with a caretaker government when the U.S. returns sovereignty to Iraqis on June 30. We're listening to the U.N. – that's a good step, right? I know you will miss my graduation, but at least you'll be home shortly afterward.*

*Things are going well here. David and I are tight again. I'm studying hard and living large.*

*I have another couple of pieces of Cliff Clavin information for you. Since most people had dirt floors way back when and only the wealthy had something other than dirt, the expression became "dirt poor." Here's another one: wealthy people had slate floors that would get slippery in the winter when wet, so they spread thresh (straw) on floor to help keep their footing. As the winter wore on, they added more thresh, until when you opened the door, it would all start slipping outside. A piece of wood was placed in the entranceway. Hence the saying, a "thresh hold." Oh, the useless pieces of information clouding the 10% of my brain that I actually use.*

      *Mercer*

---

**To:** artmurr@yaboo.com
**From:** Mercermur1@yaboo.com
**Subject: I won!**
**April 16**


*Dad – You are not going to believe this: I won that short story contest. I won $500! I can't believe it! It was sponsored by a group called **The Purple Pen** that encourages writers. WOW! I just got my check in the mail today and it's totally legit. I'm in shock. It will also be published in a compilation of the other entries. I can't wait to tell Ms. Boge.*

      *Mercer*

---

**To:** ahmed86@yaboo.com
**From:** Mercermur1@yaboo.com
**Subject: A Turn of Events**
**April 14**

*Ahmed,*

*I gotta tell you, buddy, high school life changes like a chameleon on a Kandinsky (I don't think I like that simile, but I like Kandinsky). I was supposed to ask Heather to prom tonight – at least that was the plan she "hinted" to Gina if Gina wanted to make dance team. Anywho, Bear was going to have a wild rumpus at his house again, and that was supposed to be the "event to ask her." So I'm all prepared to ask Heather, even though I DREAD going with her, and I'm waiting and waiting and waiting. She never showed! So now I'm all nervous that I won't get to ask her and that Gina won't make dance team and that my dad will be upset for my letting Gina down. But then Gina comes through the door and spits out phrases like, "Heather's suspended, can't go to prom, can't help with dance team tryouts, you're off the hook." It takes at least five seconds for me to translate, but as soon as I figured it out, I hugged my sis. I was cool, calm, collected, but inside I was flipping out. Finally, I can ask Beth – if this wasn't a sign, I don't know what is. "As the World Turns" continues.*

*It turns out that Heather got suspended from school activities for the rest of the year. She was one of the four people who planned the Senior Prank last week and she got caught. I forgot to tell you about that. Every year the seniors play a "prank" on the school or the administration. Anywho, Heather and three other guys rented some animals from a local petting zoo (they all called in sick except for Heather). Then around 1:00, Heather poured baby oil all over the hallway, and the guys brought the animals in from a truck (Heather let them in from the outside, since all the doors are locked to our school). They timed it so that the animals were let free right before the bell rang to switch classes. Imagine a goat, three chickens, a sheep, and a llama loose in the main hall of our high school, while students are screaming and laughing and everyone is slipping on baby oil. Anywho, Heather acted like she was just an innocent bystander in the hallway, and the other three seniors took off in the truck. It was almost a clear-cut get-away, but someone ratted them out. Thankfully, none of the animals were hurt in this prank. I have to admit it was pretty clever. I felt bad for the teachers who tried to get the animals – slippery, nasty, slippery, nasty, slippery, nasty. Anywho, the four seniors were suspended and fined, and I don't have to ask Heather to prom. How lucky is that?*

*Mercer*

---

**To:** Mercermur1@yaboo.com
**From:** ahmed86@yaboo.com
**Subject: Re: A Turn of Events**
**April 16**

*Mercer,*

*I do not usually advocate disrespect for authority or rules, but I have to admit, the senior prank was funny. Thanks for making me laugh today.*

*Ahmed*

---

**To:** ahmed86@yaboo.com
**From:** Mercermur1@yaboo.com
**Subject: Censorship**
**April 19**

*Ahmed,*

*Ooo,ooo,ooo. St. Thomas of Aquinas has some controversy! Yes, something to chat about in school besides prom (I'm so stinkin' nervous, I'm sweating all the time – as if I need more reasons to smell).*

*A freshman English teacher started a novel unit on <u>I Know Why the Caged Bird Sings</u>, Maya Angelou's autobiography. Then a freshman's parent* started contacting the other students' parents and within a week of starting the book, they went to the school board asking that the book be banned and that the teacher be suspended for teaching such filth to freshman in high school (apparently they object to the rape scene and some other moral issues – even though this IS a true story). So now we're in this heated debate about censorship and when to expose kids to what and how and blah, blah, blah. It's sort of cool though because the news has interviewed some students and parents and people are yelling at each other and calling each other fascists and immoral mongers and such. I read the book back when I was a freshman (they've been reading it here for years), and I liked it. I wish I had the strength to refuse to speak for several years like Maya Angelou did. So now kids are mad at each other, parents are mad at each other, and teachers are using every opportunity to bring up the discussion in class (yes!). It's going to be a good week in school.

By the way, Gina made the dance team, on merit.

Mercer

---

**To:** Mercermur1@yaboo.com
**From:** ahmed86@yaboo.com
**Subject: Re: Censorship**
**April 19**

Mercer,

It is interesting that you fight over one book. We were not allowed to fight over books – Saddam's people had to approve them all. Freedom of speech is one of the things I like best about America.

Ahmed

---

**April 20** - Can you imagine not being able to read a book? At least if I can't read *I Know Why the Caged Bird Sings* in school, I can go to the library to get it. I'm amazed that the Founding Fathers remembered to protect freedom of speech. Ahmed needs to come experience freedom – he deserves it.

Props to Mercer, pat, pat, for smokin' everyone at the Ankeny meet yesterday. My times are droppin' like kids in a pool after they whistle that the guard break is over – nah, I don't like that simile, but I'm leaving it in here to remind myself to try. I still wish I could be witty like Conan.

**April 21** - I picked up trash today, just at random. I remembered how Mrs. Meyers, my pre-school teacher, asked us (homework for four-year-olds was so meaningful – what happened?) to go for a walk with our parents and pick up litter on the ground to keep God's earth beautiful. And so I picked up litter around my block just like I did with my mom when I was four. Someone also told me that if pick up trash, you give atonement for someone else who littered. I'll have to remember that.

April 22 - Today is Earth Day. After track, Mary and I celebrated it by picking up cans for *Kids Against Hunger* and recycling them. Then we got a mocha (in our cool travel mugs – reduce, reuse, recycle…) at *Barnes and Noble* and studied for our badminton test (who knew that Lifetime Sports would have TESTS!).

I'm still keeping up on the events of the war daily. Today the U.S. announced that some Iraqi Baath Party officials who had been forced out of their jobs after the fall of Saddam Hussein would be allowed to resume their positions. Maybe we're moving away from a civil war after all.

April 23 - I just read in the New York Times that Pat Tillman was shot yesterday in Afghanistan by enemy fire. He was the only other reason I thought I could possibly support this war. After 9/11, Tillman gave up a multi-million-dollar contract to play football with the Cardinals in order join the Army and fight as a Ranger. That is patriotism. That is integrity. He gave his life for this country, for my dad, and for me.

I was on fire today at the Drake Relays. I will win state. I will play football for Iowa. I am a stallion.

---

**To:** artmurr@yaboo.com
**From:** Mercermur1@yaboo.com
**Subject: Life is GRAND!**
**April 25**

*Dad,*

*I'm on the top of Mt. Wanna-Hock-A-Loogey. If you were home right now, life would be absolutely perfect (well, actually, I haven't asked Beth to the prom yet, but I plan on doing that tonight at Bear's party). Dad, I won all three of my events at the Drake Relays, and an Iowa track coach came over to talk to me. I gave him my phone number, and he said he'd be in touch. We won the 4 X 400 (Split 48.4) total: 3:21. 95, the Sprint Medley 3:26.15 (split 400 – 47.9), and the 4 X 800 7:55.40 split (1:56.1). I had the fastest splits on each of the relays! Why I never went out for track, I have no idea, but I am pumped up. This might be my way in to Iowa football. I'm climbing the mountain, and I'm not coming down.*

*I've got to go plan my "conversation" with Beth when I ask her to prom (she hasn't been asked yet).*

*Mercer*

To: artmurr@yaboo.com
From: Mercermur1@yaboo.com
Subject: Yes
April 25

*Dad,*

*I'm going to prom with Beth. I'll send pictures.*

> *Mercer*

---

To: ahmed86@yaboo.com
From: Mercermur1@yaboo.com
Subject: Yes
April 26

*Ahmed,*

*Well, Ahmed. I'm going to prom with Beth. I know you don't necessarily like the stuff you've heard about her, but I'm sure that after I get to know her and tell you all of her good qualities, you'll change your mind.*

*I have to go over my manners. My dad was HUGE on etiquette. I had to actually go to class at Von Maur (a classy department store) to learn how to hold a knife and fork. I usually open doors for women (although I forget a lot with my mom and Gina and Mary), and I try to remember to stand when a woman leaves (ditto with M & G & M). The one thing I always forget is to walk on the outside of the street near the cars when I'm walking with a woman. It's not like I've ever had practice, not on a REAL date anyway. David and I are probably the only non-daters in our class – David by choice and me, process of elimination for Beth, I guess. Anywho, it's hard to know if I should be a gentleman – some girls get all huffy about women's rights and stuff. I certainly don't want to offend anyone. My mom and Mary and Gina love it when I open doors for them and when I help them with their coats (when I remember, that is). I don't see it as sexist; I just see it as a form of respect. Two weeks, buddy. Two weeks.*

*Mercer*

---

**To:** Mercermur1@yaboo.com
**From:** ahmed86@yaboo.com
**Subject: Re: Yes**
**April 26**

*Mercer*

*I am happy if you are happy.*

*Since your father left, I do not have a contact with the Americans here. I need to find work.*

*Ahmed*

---

**To:** ahmed86@yaboo.com
**From:** Mercermur1@yaboo.com
**Subject: Re: Yes**
**April 26**

*Ahmed,*

*My dad can't write very much, but I know he is touch with my mom. I'll tell her to tell Dad that you could help them in Mosul. I don't know if it will work, but it's worth a shot. I'll also mention it in my next e-mail to him, but I don't know if he even reads them.*

*Take care, my friend.*

*Mercer*

---

**To:** ahmed86@yaboo.com
**From:** Mercermur1@yaboo.com
**Subject: Vaseline, Eggs, and Anchovies**
**April 27**

*Ahmed,*

*"As the World Turns" continues. Remember the story about Gina and how Heather said she could make sure Gina made dance team, but then she got suspended from school and Gina made dance team on her own? Well, Heather is back at it again. The dance team outlawed hazing three years ago when Heather*

was a freshman. Apparently, Heather didn't get the memo. She and three other dance team seniors told the three freshman girls who made it that they would pick them up at 5:30 A.M. for a "congratulations" breakfast. Gina was so excited– she must have tried ten different hair styles the night before (but I was thinking – you're going to sleep on your hair anyway????). So I saw Gina at school later that morning, and she looked like a mutant from King Kong Island. Her hair was greasy and full of twigs and her clothes were all disheveled and full of grass and an odd yellow oozy substance – Ooo, she smelled. I asked Gina what happened, but she wouldn't tell me. After track I asked her again what happened, but she said she was sworn to secrecy. By then I was freaking out that something bad had happened, and I was ready to go postal on someone, when she burst out that Heather and her friends "hazed" them for dance team and that if she told anyone, she would get kicked off the team. She said they picked her up at 5:30 as planned, but they blindfolded her and put a mixture of Vaseline, anchovies, eggs, and rolled up tampons in all the girls' hair and on their clothes and then put a pillow case over their heads and rolled them down a hill! Then they made them run through the sprinklers and took them to school AS IS, where they were forced to secrecy.

Who are these people? I thought stuff like that only happened in the movies. Are people really that mean? Gina is fine, but she had to cut off ten inches of her hair and it is still all greasy. I think she's going to a stylist tomorrow to see if they can do anything.

What should I do? Should I do anything? Should I rat on Heather or forget about it? The administration made the three girls go home to shower and change, but the smell lingered that whole day and she couldn't tell anyone why. Being a big brother is hard work.

Mercer

---

To: Mercermur1@yaboo.com
From: ahmed86@yaboo.com
Subject: Re: Vaseline, Eggs, and Anchovies
April 27

Mercer,

I am sorry for your sister, but I do not think you can do anything about it. She is still on the dance team and her hair will grow. What is "As the World Turns?"

I feel like I am a big brother to Samira now. I do not want her to get hurt or to have rumors spread about her. If I do study in America, I will worry about her safety. Who will protect her? Maybe I should stay in Iraq. What will become of my mother and Samira and the rest of my family? My father is not here to take care of them. I must pray about which path to take.

Ahmed

**April 28** - Why do we call him Saddam? Why don't we call him Hussein? We call everyone else by his/her last name, well, except Oprah. I was just wondering.

I asked my mom if she found any provisions or anything to help Ahmed study at Iowa this fall. She said she's still looking. Today they awarded Pat Tillman ( my other hero) the Silver Star for his death "in the line of devastating enemy fire." God Bless America.

**April 29** - I've got to study for a test, help Mary make fifty bags of puppy chow for YELL, take Larry to Taekwondo, work with David on our Econ shirts, AND I've got the Newton Cardinals' Relays today. My dad always warned me not to over-schedule my time – what was I thinking? It's a good thing I'm taking time to write in this journal so I don't get bored today.

10:30 – I survived. I told Mary I'd help her sell the puppy chow at school instead (they want to raise money to buy books for Blank Children's Hospital), I studied for the test while waiting for Larry's Taekwondo class, and David came to the track meet to work on our shirts in between races (we made a shirt that said, "$1 jeans on Fridays, $100 a year on dress code approved attire, $5000 for an education, Being Able to Pray in Class, Priceless"). How's that for creative time management? AND I won both individual events and the mile relay with my compadres. I'm only writing in this journal now, because I just heard the news about Abu Ghraib and I'm a little nervous about how Ahmed is going to take it. Should I even tell him?

---

**To:** ahmed86@yaboo.com
**From:** Mercermur1@yaboo.com
**Subject: Abu Ghraib**
**April 29**

*Ahmed,*

*I am going to apologize right now for the American military. I just saw the news about the torture and abuse of Iraqis in Abu Ghraib prison. Have you heard? Apparently, six suspects are now facing prosecution for conspiracy, dereliction of duty, cruelty toward prisoners, maltreatment, assault, and indecent acts. A seventh suspect, Private Lynndie England, was reassigned to Fort Bragg, North Carolina, after becoming pregnant.*

*I saw the pictures. It shows a girl (Private England), who has a pixie hair cut and a cigarette dangling from her mouth, giving a thumbs-up sign and pointing at the genitals of a young Iraqi, who is naked except for a sandbag over his head. Three other hooded and naked Iraqi prisoners are shown, hands crossed over their genitals. In another, this girl stands arm in arm with a soldier; both are grinning and giving the thumbs-up behind bunch of naked Iraqis, knees bent, piled clumsily on top of each other in a pyramid. I don't know what to say.*

*The sad thing is that most of the prisoners were innocent. Most of the prisoners (several thousand, including women and teen-agers) were civilians, many of whom had been picked up in random military sweeps and at highway checkpoints.*

*One soldier made excuses that no one trained them for this sort of thing. They never taught them the rules or that they had a moral choice to say no. But don't we always have a moral obligation to the human race?*

*I'm so sorry, Ahmed. We went to stop torture and abuse and here we are doing the same thing. Please forgive them.*

*Mercer*

**To:** Mercermur1@yaboo.com
**From:** ahmed86@yaboo.com
**Subject: Re: Abu Ghraib**
**April 29**

*Mercer,*

*I cannot tell you how upset this makes me. I could have been captured in a routine sweep, especially since I help the Americans and have often been given suspicious looks by some of the soldiers.*

*During Saddam's reign Abu Ghraib was one of the world's most notorious prisons, with torture, weekly executions, and vile living conditions. As many as fifty thousand men and women were jammed into Abu Ghraib at one time, in twelve-by-twelve-foot cells that were little more than human holding pits. The Americans bragged that they had the floors tiled, cells cleaned and repaired, and toilets, showers, and a new medical center added. They were supposed to humanize Abu Ghraib. Instead, they will forever be branded with the abusive images. The abuse may not seem that bad to Americans, but in the Arab world, it is humiliating for Muslim men to be naked in front of other men, and especially in front of a woman. The American soldiers knew this. I know that my fellow Iraqis would have rather been electrocuted or burned than be humiliated. I thought the U.S. was supposed to be so supportive of human rights?*

*I know that not all Americans are so brutal, but it is scary to think that the military would allow this. How do we trust the U.S.?*

    *Ahmed*

---

**To:** ahmed86@yaboo.com
**From:** Mercermur1@yaboo.com
**Subject: Re: Abu Ghraib**
**April 29**

*Ahmed,*

*I don't have an answer for you, Ahmed. All I can say is that my dad would NEVER allow that happen. It is amazing to me that so many people were involved and that no one said anything. Maybe it goes back to the psychology of group behavior. It sounds like no one enforced any rules either – how that happened, who knows. I guess the protections granted to prisoners under the Geneva Conventions went out the window somehow. Ahmed, don't let this bug you too much. You need to concentrate on your studies and your opportunities here in the U.S. Become who you set out to be so that you can come back and make sure that nothing like Abu Ghraib happens again.*

    *Mercer*

**To:** Mercermur1@yaboo.com
**From:** ahmed86@yaboo.com
**Subject: Re: Abu Ghraib**
**April 29**

*Mercer,*

*People are upset here. I researched a little and found out that a woman named Janis Karpinski, an Army reserve brigadier general, was named commander of the 800th Military Police Brigade and put in charge of military prisons in Iraq. Maybe this is what happens when you put a woman in charge.*

*Ahmed*

---

**To:** ahmed86@yaboo.com
**From:** Mercermur1@yaboo.com
**Subject: Re: Abu Ghraib**
**April 29**

*Ahmed,*

*Whoa, whoa, whoa. Don't ever say anything like that in America, or you might get kicked where it counts. I don't know that much about Karpinski, but I can tell you that having a woman in charge has nothing to do with any abuse. She is responsible on the one hand, because she was in charge of all the prisons in Iraq, but that has nothing to do with her gender. She probably just didn't visit Abu Ghraib a whole lot, and if she did, I'm sure all the soldiers acted on their best behavior. I don't mean to excuse her – the buck stops with her (or with the general or with the secretary of defense or with the President), but don't blame it on her gender.*

*Mercer*

---

**To:** Mercermur1@yaboo.com
**From:** ahmed86@yaboo.com
**Subject: Re: Abu Ghraib**
**April 29**

*Mercer,*

*Women should not be in the military. A woman was in charge and Iraqis were tortured and abused. The young woman with the short hair cut humiliated those men and then got pregnant without a husband. American women should be at home, taking care of their families, not humiliating Iraqis thousands of miles from home.*

*Ahmed*

To: ahmed86@yaboo.com
From: Mercermur1@yaboo.com
**Subject: Re: Abu Ghraib**
**April 29**

*Ahmed,*

*I know you are upset, but you better stop while you're ahead. In America, women and men are equal. Peace.*

    *Mercer*

---

To: artmurr@yaboo.com
From: Mercermur1@yaboo.com
**Subject: Abu Ghraib**
**April 29**

*Dad,*

*I know you probably won't be able to respond to me or anything, but I have to vent to someone. Ahmed is really TO'ed about the whole Abu Ghraib scandal. He's going off about how women shouldn't be in the military and how they should be at home and stuff. I'm a little miffed myself at the situation, but I'm also a little miffed at Ahmed for his views about women. What if he came to America and started making his wife wear hijab and never letting her out of his sight? I don't know. I saw the movie* Not Without My Daughter, *where the mom and the daughter are basically prisoners of the father when they go back to Iran. When the mom wants to go back to America, the husband beats her and takes her credit cards, money and identification. So she realizes that she and her daughter have become prisoners in her sister-in-law's home. What if Ahmed came here and fell in love with Gina?*

    *Mercer*

**May 1** - I went to Larry's piano contest today (and I dragged my mom and Gina out of bed – I actually had to put shaving cream on Gina so that she would get up – it was hilarious). WOW! The kid is a young Jim Brickman. He and this other young girl made it to the "finals" and had a "piano-off" if you could call it that. I was mesmerized by his hands! My mom, Gina and I were all in awe at this little ball of musical talent. The other girl won (she won $1,000 – nice), but Larry was high on life anyway. My mom taped it so dad could see it – he'll be so proud. After the concert, I treated everyone to some mochas and hot chocolate – we laughed together today, and it was good.

May 2 - I'm actually learning something in Economics. Everyone should take Economics, or at least take a week of it so he/she can learn how to balance a checkbook. What's with our tax system? Poor people pay 30% tax while rich people pay 16% tax? Hello? We've got the Elois and the Morlocks in America. I understand the whole trickle-down theory and everything, which I agree with in part, but can't it be like 22% vs. 28%? And to top it all off, our tax money is paying for a war that might take my father. Where is Greenspan to explain things in West Des Moines, Iowa, when you need him?

I'm pigging out right now on all the May Day baskets we got from the neighbors. We have a ton of kids in our neighborhood so the candy was flowing and the popcorn was poppin'. My friend Jordan still thinks May Day baskets are a crazy idea (he moved here two years ago from Wisconsin and they never had the tradition), but I'm always up for a sugar rush.

---

**To:** Mercermur1@yaboo.com
**From:** ahmed86@yaboo.com
**Subject: Re: Abu Ghraib**
**May 2**

*Mercer,*

*I am sorry if I have offended you, my friend. I was very upset at the thought of my people being tortured, but it is more than that. I am tired. I am tired and frustrated and angry. I am seventeen, and I am forced to defend my family, my country, and hope for my own future without any idea of how to accomplish my dreams. Is there use in having dreams? Sometimes I feel there is no hope.*

*Mercer, I did not mean the things I said. I would never blame women for the problems we are having here. The Qur'an supports the notion of gender equality. Even if I do not think women should serve in the war, I do believe that women and men are equal.*

*It has been dangerous to go outside here the last couple of days. Many Iraqi people are upset because of the Abu Ghraib situation, and many are searching for revenge. We have kept the little ones inside for safety, even though they are ornery and needing exercise. Please forgive me, Mercer, and pray for us.*

*Ahmed*

**To:** ahmed86@yaboo.com
**From:** Mercermur1@yaboo.com
**Subject: Re: Abu Ghraib**
**May 2**

*Ahmed,*

*No problem, buddy. I can understand why you are so upset. I will pray for you. But just know that if you come to America and you marry my sister, she won't wear hijab. Peace.*

*Mercer*

---

**To:** Mercermur1@yaboo.com
**From:** ahmed86@yaboo.com
**Subject: Re: Abu Ghraib**
**May 2**

*Mercer,*

*Thank you for making me laugh, my friend! I promise if I marry your sister, she can decide whether she wants to wear hijab or not.*

*I must explain something about hijab. Many believe that the veil is a way to secure personal liberty in a world that objectifies women. Others argue that hijab allows them freedom of movement and control of their bodies. The hijab protects women from the male gaze and allows them to become autonomous subjects. Others have argued that the veil only provides the illusion of protection and serves to absolve men of the responsibility for controlling their behavior. It is interesting because the Christian tradition has a similar convention. In the book of Corinthians, women are asked to cover their heads as the glory of man. Nuns also used to wear a "habit," which is much like the required hijab. Islamic dress is one of many rights granted to Islamic women. Modest clothing is worn in obedience to God and has nothing to do with submissiveness to men. Muslim men and women have similar rights and obligations and both submit to God.*

*Muslims may be targeted by human rights' groups, but the males also have clothing requirements. A Muslim man must always be covered from the navel to the knees and should similarly not wear tight, sheer, revealing, or eye-catching clothing. In addition, a Muslim man is prohibited from wearing silk clothing (except for medical reasons) or gold jewelry, but a Muslim woman may wear silk or gold.*

*I apologize if I lecture a lot, but I want you to know that the Muslim religion is not about being abusive or jihad. It is a peaceful, loving religion that promotes peace and justice. I just hope that I can make Allah proud.*

*Ahmed*

**To:** ahmed86@yaboo.com
**From:** Mercermur1@yaboo.com
**Subject: Re: Abu Ghraib**
**May 2**

*Ahmed,*

*I know Allah is proud – you've already had a great influence of peace and justice in my life and I've never even met you in person. You are a good egg, Ahmed.*

*Mercer*

## MERCER 30
## WAR 38

To: Mercermur1@yaboo.com
From: ahmed86@yaboo.com
**Subject: Muhammad's Birthday**
**May 2**

*Mercer,*

*Today is Mawlid al-Nabi, a celebration of the birthday of the prophet Muhammad, founder of Islam. It is usually a big holiday in the Muslim world. Muhammad never encouraged people to make his birthday a special day, but since he established Islam as a religion and brought equality to Muslims, we honor him this day. I guess Mawlid al-Nabi is like your Christmas. Muhammad also received a vision of the angel Gabriel like your Christian Mary. Gabriel told Muhammad to serve as a prophet and "magnify thy Lord." Like Jesus, many people listened but others ridiculed him.*

*Before the war, we celebrated Mawlid al-Nabi in a carnival manner with large street processions, and some homes and mosques were decorated. We used to give out charity and food to the needy, and children would act out stories about the life of Muhammad to entertain. Today we celebrated Mawlid al-Nabi inside with the children reciting poetry about Muhammad's life.*

*Muhammad's earliest teachings emphasized his belief in one transcendent but personal God, the Last Judgment, and social and economic justice. Muhammad knew that justice would be difficult, but honoring God would be fruitful. I have to believe that the Americans will bring justice to my people. Someday we will celebrate openly as a people without fear.*

*Ahmed*

**To:** ahmed86@yaboo.com
**From:** Mercermur1@yaboo.com
**Subject: Re: Muhammad's Birthday**
**May 3**

*Ahmed,*

   *Merry Mawlid al-Nabi!!! That probably isn't right, but it fits with the Christmas tradition. Muhammad's belief in social justice sounds just like the Catholic Church. Their social justice teachings include the sanctity of human life, the dignity of the person, the call to family, community and participation, rights and responsibilities, preferential option for the poor and vulnerable, dignity of work and the rights of workers, solidarity, and care for God's creation. In other words, the Catholic Church is a tree-hugging, union-loving, family planning, bleeding heart pro-life group. Try to find that in politics today. I consider myself big on social justice, but I'm also for people having accountability. That's why the welfare system is screwed up – people need to work in order to have self-worth, but since they lose money for their kids when they make too much, it's easier to just go back on welfare. Give a man a fish, he'll eat for a day; teach a man to fish; he'll eat for a lifetime. That's all philosophy I can take for one day.*

   *I'm going to go get some Long John Silvers (great fish sandwiches). Peace out.*

   *Mercer*

---

**To:** Mercermur1@yaboo.com
**From:** ahmed86@yaboo.com
**Subject: I Am a Hawkeye**
**May 4**

*Mercer,*

   *I am excited to inform you that I have been accepted to the University of Iowa, upon the condition that a student visa can be arranged for me. I know that it will be difficult, but I also have hope. Being accepted to the University makes me happier than I have been in months. Thank you, my friend, for believing in me.*

   *Ahmed*

**To:** ahmed86@yaboo.com
**From:** Mercermur1@yaboo.com
**Subject: Re: I Am a Hawkeye**
May 4

*Ahmed,*

*That is awesome news. I'll bug my mom again about helping you get a student visa. She has your e-mail and address and everything. If anyone can do it, she can.*

*It's Tuesday. Only nine days until freedom. Freedom. It's still so easy to toss around that word. I've never known anything but freedom. I am proud to be my dad's son. Someday your country will be free, Ahmed. I believe that.*

*Bear got in a fight today – he might not graduate. If he doesn't graduate, it will be the first time he's ever had a consequence in his life (not that that makes him a bad guy or anything – in fact, he's a blast). My friend Jordan told me (I was downstairs getting my ankle wrapped for track) that this junior kid named Chris made a remark in passing about Bear "being a chunky monkey now that football is over" (he actually is a little puffy and he's got a beer gut). Apparently Bear must be a little sensitive, because he started wailing on the poor guy (who is probably 120 pounds lighter and six inches shorter). Chris could only cover his face to protect himself. A circle formed around them and the crowd started chanting, "Fight, fight, fight." Then Chris yelled, "Wait, I lost my contact," and both of them stopped, immediately went down to the floor, and started looking for the contact. The assistant principal FINALLY got there and asked who was fighting, since all he saw were two guys crawling on the floor looking for a contact (Bear found it and gave it to Chris with a pat on the back). Anywho, the assistant principal figured out who was fighting when the bloody Chris and sweaty Bear got up, and both were immediately taken to the office. Until further notice, Bear is suspended under the "Zero Tolerance" rule and might not be able to walk up with all of us at graduation. I feel bad for Bear – he seems different lately. He's not the same carefree guy anymore. I'm going to bring his homework to him after track for a couple of days. He's a good guy – he just doesn't think sometimes.*

*I'm still trying to stay focused, but it's hard. I haven't heard from my dad (well, I haven't heard his "voice" in e-mails anyway) in a month. I'm still holding out for that June 30th date – nothing official – just my own hopes. Track, Prom, School, Father Detonating Bombs in Iraq. Slam Dunk.*

*Mercer*

**May 5** - President Bush appeared on two Arab television stations to condemn the Abu Ghraib prisoner abuse today. I feel for the guy. If you are a leader, you have to trust that the people serving under your leadership will do their job, but it doesn't always happen that way. Case in point. Bush and Rumsfeld were clueless about Abu Ghraib, but it is still their responsibility. War is messy all around.

We had Conference yesterday. I won both the 800 and the 1600 and anchored the winning mile relay again. But my sister was the star today. She won the mile and the two-mile and set a meet record in both. I was so proud of her; I actually hugged her in public after her win in the mile.

St. Thomas Aquinas is Conference champs for both boys' and girls' track for the first time in TWENTY years. Who keeps track of these things anyway?

---

**To:** artmurr@yaboo.com
**From:** Mercermur1@yaboo.com
**Subject: Nervous**
**May 6**

*Dad –*
*Prom is in two days – I'm SO nervous.*

*Mercer*

---

**May 7** - Today was the Senior Awards' Ceremony. Mary received every award possible for service, academics, and at least six scholarships – she got a workout from simply getting up and walking to the podium so many times. David received a "leadership" award given by the teachers (Mary received it for the women, of course) for service by a senior. I was proud to be their friend.

**May 8** - It's supposed to be the biggest night of my life and all I can think about is my dad's head – what does his face look like? I know I can look at pictures, but I'm trying to remember the wrinkles and the moles and the scars. All I want to do is remember what my dad looked like in case he gets beheaded. I just saw on T.V. that Nicholas Berg, an American contractor, was beheaded by an Iraqi militant, who claimed the grisly murder was in retaliation for the treatment of Iraqi prisoners. What is with the beheadings? I just want to see my dad.

Tonight is prom – I have to focus. Buck up, Mercer. Mom just got a call from Artie today – he's fine, he's fine.

**To:** Mercermur1@yaboo.com
**From:** ahmed86@yaboo.com
**Subject: Mosul**
**May 8**

*Mercer,*

    *I do not know if I will be able to e-mail for a while. I am excited to tell you that I am headed to Mosul to help your father. He must have received your message because he sent word to a commander here in Baghdad that I should be transported to Mosul for help as an interpreter. The commander gave me some money as an advance for my work. That money will feed my family for a month. I am thankful for your father and thankful to you as well for watching out for me.*

    *The admissions' people at the University of Iowa are trying to help me with my student visa, but they are having trouble because Iraq is part of the "axis of evil." If I cannot come to America to study, I will study here and still be a part of rebuilding my country. I have to have hope. I will try to communicate soon. Thank you again for your help. Pray for us.*

    *Ahmed*

---

**To:** ahmed86@yaboo.com
**From:** Mercermur1@yaboo.com
**Subject: Re: Mosul**
**May 8**

    *Ahmed,*
    *Take care, buddy. Be safe. And look out for my dad, will you?*

    *Mercer*

---

**To:** artmurr@yaboo.com
**From:** Mercermur1@yaboo.com
**Subject: Prom**
**May 9**

    *Dad,*
    *Oh my, oh my, oh my. Prom was a HUGE "Oh My." First of all, Beth never shuts up. I swear there was foam in the corners of her mouth from talking so much. And she talks about NOTHING. I was so stinkin' bored; I prayed a whole rosary before she actually included me in her soliloquy. I was obviously not paying attention because I had to ask her to repeat the question, which was something along the lines of, "So what do you, 'like,' think about the war?" I told her that my dad thinks we should be there, but before I even got to my opinion, she jumped in again and went off about how she supports Barbara Streisand's anti-war position because she knows what she's talking*

about, or something like that. I was astounded. Did she not remember that MY FATHER WAS FIGHTING IN IRAQ? Everything that I thought was good and pure and holy about this goddess was crushed and I was stunned, frustrated, ticked off, and bored all at the same time.

But then, to make the start of a horrible night get even worse, Mary walked in the dance and my jaw dropped. I'd like to say that she was so beautiful that I didn't recognize her, but she was so beautiful that I DID recognize her. I literally could not move or speak or breathe. Okay, it wasn't that dramatic, but she honestly made me shudder. Her straightened hair flowed down her back like a runway model, and her wolf eyes pierced through the whole room. Then she looked at me and we locked eyes for what seemed like twenty minutes, but was really only about three seconds. I ACTUALLY BLUSHED. Then Beth said something, and then repeated her something, but I just said I had to go to the bathroom. I went over to Mary and this is a pretty good rendition of how the conversation went:

Mercer: Da, da, uh, you, uh, you look a good a, Ma-ah-reey.

Mary: (Laughs like I'm a cute kid). Thanks, Merck (Ouch, the nickname never bothered me before, but now it felt like we were just friends – which, I guess we were, but that was before I SAW her). You know my date, Andy, right?

Mercer: Uh, ya, hey, waz up.

Andy: Yo, Merck, where's your hot date?

Mercer: Uh, ya, uh, she's over there. I guess I should go back to her.

Mary: (with the cute giggle again) Bye, Merck.

Mercer: Uh, yeah, uh bye.

And I watched her walk away. How could I not notice how seriously BEAUTIFUL my best friend was? I mean, she has a kickin' booty, probably the best in the whole senior class, but I guess I shouldn't be surprised since she swims and runs, and lifts. Oh my, she was smokin'. I looked down at my feet and almost kicked myself right there. Mary was so good to me this year. She basically helped me pass my math classes, she brought me treats whenever I was down, and she's the sweetest person EVER, plus, she's movie-star gorgeous. I think I just fell in love with my best friend.

After that I went back to Beth and we danced, but I couldn't help keeping an eye on Mary. Beth didn't notice though – she just kept jabbering on without me having to say boo. I saw Andy move his hands down Mary's back, and my right hand clenched behind Beth's back, but Mary just discreetly pulled his hands north, and I simmered. What a creep. After the dance a bunch of us went to a party over at Bear's. I stayed for a while, but Mary wasn't there and I wasn't about to waste more time on Beth (as if my whole senior year pining after her wasn't enough), so I offered to take her home. She wanted to stay, so Bear said he'd take care of her. I guess Prom was an eye opener. You gotta learn somehow.

Mary asked me last week to help her at her little brother's birthday party the day after prom, but how was I supposed to know that I'd be all nervous around her now? I kept stuttering when she was in the room and she kept punching me on the arm, asking me what my problem was. Thankfully, I could go hang out with Sammy (her brother who turned seven) and his friends. Nothing like a bunch of seven-year-olds to provide cover for a love-sick *puppy. Mary looked like Mary again – ponytail, no makeup, Gap- style clothing, but she looked different too. How could I have been so blind? We both reached to get a napkin for Sammy and I brushed her hand – oh, the shivas'. What do I do? She obviously has no clue that I feel this way, and she obviously doesn't feel that way about me, but if I can suddenly change, why couldn't she? But what if she secretly likes someone else, like David?!!! He is a saint, and he's ten times better looking. How can I compete with my best-friend for my best-friend? I can't even get mad if they hook up because I love them both too much. Why is this happening to me now? Why did I have to fall for my best-friend who doesn't even know I exist "that way?" Why am I even worried about this when I haven't heard from you in a month? I'm feeling that feeling again.*

*Mercer*

**May 10** - Okay, okay, calm down. It's nothing. They would call you right away if something happened. This isn't World War II where they send a telegram. Breathe, breathe, breathe. I'm writing in this journal because I don't know what else to do. I just read on-line that in Mosul, a U.S. soldier was killed and another wounded in a mortar attack on the coalition base. The army said the wounded soldier had been evacuated to the military hospital in Mosul. It's not my dad, it's not my dad, it's not my dad.

**MERCER    30**
**WAR        45**


**May 11** - I haven't heard from my dad. Mom hasn't heard from my dad. I haven't heard from Ahmed. All this adds up to ignorance, impatience, and frustration.


**May 12** - We went out for a Mothers' Day Celebration, even though Mother's Day was last Sunday. We went to *Mojos* and ate in silence. I love my mom and we all told her that, but somehow, it seemed bittersweet today.

After the pity party at supper, Mary and David dragged me out to Barnes and Noble for a mocha and a speed-study-session for finals tomorrow. I just sat at the table and stared. I couldn't even feel tension because of Mary. I have an Anatomy test and an Econ test tomorrow. How am I supposed to memorize the arteries in a cat's arm and how the government fights recessions and unemployment using monetary and fiscal policy, when my dad could be lying in desert morgue 7,000 miles away?


**May 13** - It's 5:00 A.M. I can't sleep. The only thing I can do is write in this journal because it can't give me any bad news.

I haven't heard from Ahmed in five days, although he warned me that he probably couldn't write for a while. I asked Mom again today if she knew any lawyers who could help get Ahmed to the U.S. to study. She said it would be difficult to get Ahmed in the U.S. because of the legal red tape involved in a non-Muslim family trying to sponsor an Iraqi boy. But she said there might be a chance through a legal provision called "humanitarian parole" - she told me she's been working on it with one of her partners.

I passed my Anatomy and Econ finals, although I'll get "B-'s" in both classes. Oh, well. My straight "A's" goal seems insignificant now.

Some seniors thought that the petting zoo animals' prank wasn't enough, so three of them decided to do another senior prank. They bought 100 mice from some pet stores (you know, the kind they use to feed snakes) and hid them in their backpacks until the bell rang after the first class. Then they let them all loose in the halls (on opposite sides of the school). I could hear the screams and the running, and then I saw three little mice run by my feet. I actually laughed. Laughter means there is still hope – we don't know anything yet. Just because there was an attack in Mosul and we haven't heard anything from my dad in three days doesn't mean anything. I know this, intellectually anyway.

**May 14** - Bear came up to me today and asked, "Where's your Pollyanna girlfriend, Mary?" and I FLIPPED out on him. I actually pushed him up against a locker and said, "Not today, Bear." I guess I should probably tell people that my dad might be dead so they know I'm a little touchy, huh.

Did you know, Ms. Boge, that some soldiers tie their dog-tags onto their shoes because the feet are the body parts that are most easily identified? Why do I even know that?

**May 15** - I turned in my journals for Creative Writing II, but I started my own journal because it's my only outlet. I passed my Spanish IV final yesterday and got a "B" for a final grade. Four "A's", one "B," and two "B-'s" would make my dad proud, considering the circumstances. No more studying – now all I can do is sit around and worry.

What should I do? What is the point? Why are we really here on earth? What is my purpose in life? WWJD? I know one thing: Jesus wouldn't sit around and brood. Tomorrow I am going to get up, get dressed, go to track practice, and figure out what I'm going to do with the rest of my life, with or without my dad.

**May 16** - They called. They called Mom and told her my dad was behind a Humvee that ran over an IED. He's in surgery, and they will call with frequent updates. Okay, he's in surgery; he's alive, for now. Why doesn't the military have a hotline or something?* What are we supposed to do now?

I'm going crazy. Really. I'm seeing things or I think I'm seeing things or I'm seeing myself seeing things. I can't handle this – I need to sleep but I can't. I need to eat but I can't. I just want to know, I just want to know. Please, God, please. Your will be done, but I would really appreciate it if Your will kept my dad alive.

### * New Hotline for Injured Soldiers and Their Families

*The Army has established a hotline for injured Soldiers and their family members facing problems associated with medical care. The Wounded Soldier and Family Hotline number is 1-800-984-8523, and operates between 7:00am and 7:00pm (ET), Monday to Friday. The Army implemented the WSFH March 19, 2007 to give wounded, injured or ill Soldiers and their Families a way to share concerns about the quality of their care.*

**To:** ahmed86@yaboo.com
**From:** Mercermur1@yaboo.com
**Subject: ???**
**May 17**

*Ahmed,*

*Bear is dead. He's dead. He choked on his own vomit after he passed out from drinking. His mom found him in his bed. The designated driver brought him home and thought he would just sleep it off. He didn't. I don't even know if you will get this e-mail. My friend is dead, and my dad is probably dead. I am eighteen-years-old.*

*Mercer*

---

**To:** artmurr@yaboo.com
**From:** Mercermur1@yaboo.com
**Subject: Bear**
**May 17**

*Dad,*
*Bear is dead. He choked on his own vomit after passing out from alcohol poisoning. I guess alcohol poisoning can cause problems with breathing and the gag reflex (which prevents choking). He was so drunk that he threw up and basically suffocated. Jesse thought he would be OK – Bear didn't even seem drunk, but I just researched that a person's blood alcohol concentration (BAC) can continue to rise even while he is passed out. Jesse said he had a bunch of shots before he left the party. I don't understand.*

*If you are reading this e-mail in heaven, then you already know anyway. So why am I even telling you again? Maybe I need to tell you. Maybe I need to be able to tell someone.*

*I am scared, Dad.*

## MERCER 38
## WAR 48

**Message on Murray answering machine (May 18):**
*Mom, Mercer, Gina, Larry, this is Dad. I am okay. I am recovering in Germany. Please call me back at this number – 01-770-4533-4455. I love you all.*

---

**To:** Mercermur1@yaboo.com
**From:** artmurr@yaboo.com

**Subject: I am okay**

**May 18**

*Dear Mercer,*
*I am recovering from a head injury and the amputation of my left leg below the knee. Please pray for the fourteen men and women who lost their lives in the attack in which I was injured. The Humvee ahead of us exploded from an IED and we were ambushed by a group of insurgents. My platoon immediately went on the defensive attack. Amidst the shooting, Ahmed (who was with us as a translator on the mission) ran out of the Humvee and grabbed a fallen soldier's gun. He started shooting the insurgents. I yelled for him to get back in the Humvee, but he couldn't hear me. I started running toward him, and that was the last thing I remember. They told me a rocket-propelled grenade knocked me out and basically liquefied my leg. A medic stopped the bleeding with an elastic cord, and a surgical team stabilized me. Hours later, a Blackhawk helicopter flew me to an Air Force base near Baghdad, and that night I was evacuated to the Army's elite Landstuhl Regional Medical Center in Germany. I do not know what happened to Ahmed. I am sorry, Mercer.*
*I am in pain, but the doctors and nurses are taking good care of me. The surgeons removed my left leg at the knee. My mangled leg had been without blood for too long, and the tissue was dying.*
*Eventually they will admit me to Walter Reed Army Medical Center in Washington, where I will begin my recovery.*

---

*Thank you for your prayers, Mercer. You will get through this, we all will. Our family loved Brian, and I know you did too. I will call you later tonight. I love you.*

*Dad*

---

**To:** artmurr@yaboo.com
**From:** Mercermur1@yaboo.com
**Subject: Re: Mosul**
**May 18**

*Dad,*
*I don't know what to think anymore, Dad, but I'm glad you are alive.*

*Mercer*

---

**May 18** - Today is my worst day and my best day.

---

**To:** ahmed86@yaboo.com
**From:** Mercermur1@yaboo.com
**Subject: My dad is okay**
**May 17**

*Ahmed,*
*I am hoping that you are in some remote area and can't e-mail me, but I have to write to you anyway. My dad is safe. He lost his leg below the knee and suffered a concussion, but he's alive and well in a U.S. hospital in Germany. I cannot tell you how relieved I am. The best part is that he'll be home for good now.*
*No one is saying anything about Brian. Everybody avoids talking about it, but I get plenty of pity eyes thrown my way.*
*You were right about Beth, Ahmed. We just don't have much in common. Now I'm in love with Mary, my best friend in the world. How's that for a soap opera?*
*Graduation and the state track meet are next week. I don't know if I'll make it through either. Write soon if you get a chance. I know you are playing beatha somewhere chowing on some kebabs. I know it.*
*My dad went to war, but my friend died.*

*Mercer*

**May 18** - I was so depressed about Bear, but at the same time, so excited about my dad that I rounded up the crew to go streaking again in the rain. Jesse and a couple of others and I went out to West Glen to release some stress. It was fun for about ten seconds, but then I saw a little boy with his dad going into *I Scream for Ice Cream*. I stopped (which was dumb when you are naked) and realized that this isn't what I wanted to do anymore. I told Jesse I was going home; he nodded and said he was too. I put on my clothes, bought some ice cream at *I Scream for Ice Cream*, stopped by the movie store, and rounded up Larry and Gina for a slumber party in front of the Toshiba.

---

**To:** artmurr@yaboo.com
**From:** Mercermur1@yaboo.com
**Subject: Life in Iowa**
**May 18**

Dad,
Status report: depressed yet grateful, yet guilt-ridden because I feel grateful, 3.5 on report card, recorded the fastest 800M and 1600M in the state, proud coach of undefeated five-year-old Urban Bellie's team, in love with best-friend, Mary, and she doesn't know it, seeing a counselor about Brian (two times a week, are you serious?!!!). You are going to call in five minutes and I know the sound of your voice will be the best sound I've ever heard.
Have you heard anything about Ahmed?

Mercer

---

**May 20** - Today we had our Baccalaureate Mass, a culminating Mass for all the seniors at St. Thomas Aquinas. The Liturgy of Life Choir was awesome, even if most of us felt numb. The words to the songs had new meaning; the words to the readings had new meaning. An overwhelming feeling of gratitude came over me as I looked up to the cross. Jesus lost his buddy, Lazarus, so I know He knows how I feel. I know that many sons have lost their fathers in this war. Selfishly though, I'm glad He didn't take my dad, not yet anyway. I gave the traditional potted flower to my mother and hugged her for the longest minute of my life – she bawled, which almost made me cry, but I think I've cried enough tears for the whole senior class.

**To:** Mercermur1@yaboo.com
**From:** artmurr@yaboo.com

**Subject: Leg**

**May 21**

Dear Mercer,

I'm proud of you, Mercer. I'm talking to a counselor here, too. It's good to talk – make sure you try to talk to your other friends too. Celebrate Brian's life.

My head hurts, but I'm glad it hurts. I'm grateful to be alive, even if it means I'm in pain. The staff here in Landstuhl has been patient and comforting. One of the nurses is going to try to set up a web-cam so I can see you. I will let you know.

I'm researching everything I need to know about amputees. When I'm transferred to Amputee Alley (Ward 57 of Walter Reed Army Medical Center in Washington), I'll eventually be fitted for a prosthetic. My fake leg or myoelectric (the non-sci-fi name for bionic) leg will work off of tiny electrical signals released when muscles are contracted. Electrodes send the signals to a computer chip that instructs an electronic leg to move. I feel blessed again - injuries like mine might have been unsurvivable in previous wars.

Please pray for patience and perseverance. I have many hours of painful occupational and physical therapy to endure. Physical pain is nothing though - I miss you.

Dad

---

**To:** artmurr@yaboo.com
**From:** Mercermur1@yaboo.com

**Subject: Re: Leg**
**May 21**

Dad,

I'm sorry, Dad. I'm sorry that I'm sitting here in America while you are sitting in some hospital in Germany. I'm sorry that you lost a football player and your leg at the same time. Dad, I'm sorry. I can't wait to talk to you again.

Mercer

May 21 - Funerals should not be for kids. Bear was laid to rest today at St. Francis. I looked at him in the casket and lost it. I couldn't see through my tears, but somehow I found Mary. I remembered Okoboji, Tropical Snow, Burger King, dances, parties, movies, and running around the city. I remembered his laugh and his goofy faces and his discussions about Ancient Greece and the Iraq War. I remembered his loud snore that sounded like a broken muffler. I remembered how he always wore a green John Deere hat backward – that hat was so grimy.

Fr. Kirby gave a homily reminding us that he is home now. I smelled the incense and remembered that he is in a better place. May the Angels come to greet him.

May 22 – I can't eat, I can't sleep, I can't understand. How do I grieve while being so relieved that my dad is alive?

It's weird, but I feel funny e-mailing my dad now. I want to hear his laugh and his dry sense of humor. I think they are going to set up the web-cam tomorrow so we can see him face-to-face, or at least video-to-video. I have to admit, I'm a little scared to see my dad without a leg. He has always been this tower of strength who walked into a room like he owned it. I know he's the same person, but I'm still apprehensive.

---

To: Mercermur1@yaboo.com
From: artmurr@yaboo.com
Subject: Time
May 22

*Mercer,*

*It looks like the web-cam is a no-go for now. I'll let you know when it's available.*

*I also want to apologize because it took so long to get the news of my surgery. Part of the reason that doesn't happen is messengers are often in a race against rumors and the media. E- mail, cell phones, and near-real-time television feeds mean the family may receive half-truths before the Army can deliver a full report. The current system to notify family members of an injury simply cannot compete with the rapid flow of information heading home, and critical information is withheld within the medical community, mostly for fear of violating the 1996 Patient Privacy Act. The Army is doing a wonderful job – I'm living proof – but that doesn't mean there isn't room for improvement.*

*I'm going to go take a nap, something I don't think I've done since I was a kid. Keep me posted.*

*Dad*

**To:** artmurr@yaboo.com
**From:** Mercermur1@yaboo.com
**Subject: Re: Time**
**May 22**

Dad,
It was hard not to know what happened to you, but it doesn't matter now.
You are safe and healthy and ready to come home. That's all that matters.
Have you heard anything about Ahmed?

Mercer

---

**To:** Mercermur1@yaboo.com
**From:** artmurr@yaboo.com

**Subject: Phantom Limb Pain**
**May 23**

Mercer,
I am sorry, Son, I have not heard anything about Ahmed. I will keep asking around though.
Today my phantom limb pain seems worse. Sometimes it feels as if my toes (that aren't there) are curling tighter and tighter until they are ready to explode. I can feel myself wiggle my toes on my left leg even though they aren't there, and my whole leg and foot are burning incessantly even though they aren't there.
No one knows why amputees suffer phantom limb pain. A Civil War doc coined the term when soldiers complained after their limbs had been sawed off. Some experts believe the brain has a blueprint of body parts that persists even if they've been cut off. According to one theory, when the brain sends signals and receives no feedback, it bombards the missing limb with more signals.
Doctors said the pain might last a month, a year or a lifetime. Every amputee is different. I'm sure they'll take care of me though, somehow.

Dad

---

**To:** Mercermur1@yaboo.com
**From:** artmurr@yaboo.com

**Subject: Joe**
**May 26**

Mercer,
I was fitted for my prosthesis today. I named it "Joe." This is probably just a temporary one, but I need to learn how to operate it. The leg, made of graphite and titanium, is a battery-powered prosthetic with built-in microprocessors to improve control of the swing motion, making it more stable than previous artificial legs. I am blessed, Mercer. One in four wounded

*soldiers in Vietnam died; in Iraq, it is one in 10, but more of the survivors are left with disabling injuries like mine. Now we just need to make sure we take care of the wounded when they get home.*

*Dad*

---

To: artmurr@yaboo.com
From: Mercermur1@yaboo.com

**Subject: Re: Joe**
**May 26**

*Dad,*
*I like the name "Joe." I'm sure you'll make great partners. I'm excited to get you back to running-form so I can kick your butt in road races.*
*I talked to David's mom (remember, she's an anesthesiologist specializing in pain management) about your phantom leg pain, and she said that she might be able to help. She could implant two catheters to anesthetize the nerves or she could put in a spinal cord stimulator. Anyway, there is hope for the pain.*
*Dad, I think you should set a goal for yourself. Why don't you plan on running the Iowa PKU Foundation's 5-mile run in October? Mary is setting it up, and I know she'd love to have you there. We'll talk to your doctor and set up a training schedule. I promise I'll take you to all your PT appointments and push you just like you've pushed me.*
*Hey, here's another Cliff Clavin: Most people got married in June because they took their yearly bath in May, and still smelled pretty good by June. However, they were starting to smell, so brides carried a bouquet of flowers to hide the body odor. Hence the custom today of carrying a bouquet when getting married. I still think I smell all the time, by the way. Bear would have liked this story.*

*Mercer*

---

**May 28**th - Today is the first day of the state track meet. It's also graduation day. The ceremony is at 7:00, but I am going to Larry's piano concert at 6:00 – I hope I make it to graduation. Thankfully, Ms. Boge is my homeroom moderator, so she'll cover for me.

**May 29**th - So much happened yesterday, I don't know where to start. I'm going to list the events for dramatic effect:

1 – I won two individual state championships in the 800M and the 1600M, and we placed fifth in the mile relay. Gina and Larry and Mom were there through all my races cheering me on. I'm happy, yet sad.

2 - I went to Larry's concert at 6:00 and stayed until 6:45 (he played at 6:10, but we didn't want to be rude). Then we jetted over to the Knapp Center for graduation. I made it just as everyone was walking out to the gym.

3 –Since Mary's last name is Murtha, she sat next to me at graduation. Carpe Diem. During the principal's speech, I slowly reached my sweaty hand over and held onto her hand as we interlocked fingers. She squeezed my hand. It was probably a friendly-friend squeeze, but I can remain hopeful.

4 – During the valedictorian's speech (Mary's would have been much better), I faded. I thought about my mom, my dad, Bear, the year, the stress, the triumphs, the failures, and the future. But then I looked out in the crowd and saw little Colin, my five-year-old Urban Belly. He gave me a thumbs up and a huge smile. Life goes on.

5 – As Drake (another streaking buddy) was walking across the stage, his gown got caught on the rail and it revealed the side of his bare butt and his long black dress socks. He covered himself and waved like a champ. The crowd ate it up. Bear would have loved it.

6 – As I waited on the stage to receive my diploma, I saw Mom, Larry, and Gina waving and smiling and taking pictures – they saved an empty seat in honor of Dad. I waved and gave them a thumbs-up.

7 – After all the graduates were announced, the president of the school spoke until people started murmuring in the back of the gym. I couldn't see anything, but suddenly people started to clap. Finally, I could see what the fuss was all about. I saw a dark young man about my age pushing a full-uniformed soldier in a wheel chair. Everyone was standing and clapping, so naturally I followed. I felt a sudden sense of pride because my dad was also injured in the war and people were hailing this man as a hero. Then Mary said, "Mercer, you didn't tell me your dad was coming to graduation." I stared at her thinking to myself, "Well, of course not, genius, he's in Germany." And then it hit me.

8 – I couldn't help myself. I toppled over the people in my row

and sprinted to my father. I had the sense to slow down a little and hug him gently. I was bawling, but that's okay because 90% of the crowd was bawling too. I didn't even ask him how he got here – I just wanted to be near him. After what seemed like ten minutes, but was really only about five seconds, Mom, Gina, and Larry came down to hug him as well. Then my dad said, "Mercer, meet your new roommate for college in the fall, Ahmed Shojaat."

9 – I was speechless. My mom came through for Ahmed. The tears became animal laughs, but somehow I managed to look at Ahmed as he held out his hand to shake mine. I started to laugh again and hugged him. My dad told me to go back to my seat and make the Murray family proud as a high school graduate. I gave my mom a 'thank-you' smile and trotted back to my chair.

10 – The crowd was still clapping and cheering as I walked back. I saw David smiling with tears in his eyes, and then I swept Mary up in my arms and swung her around. While I set her back down on the ground, we stared at each other for a LONG two seconds, but then we both smiled and hugged again. The president quieted everyone, and we all sat down. I didn't even care that I was blubbering, I was that happy.

11 – As I was walking out of the gym, I saw Gina talking with Ahmed and she threw her head back in laughter. Oh, well. I couldn't ask for a better guy.

12 – After more hugs and questions and answers and more laughter and questions and answers, we went out for dinner at Café Di Scala downtown. I don't even remember what I had, but I know it was the best meal I've ever eaten. My dad asked me afterward if I wanted to go out for a mocha and a cookie at *Barnes and Noble* with him and Ahmed. I told him the cookie sounded good, but I'd have to pass on the mocha. I have to start saving my $4 addiction for college.

13 - I heard the birds singing today.

**To:** Mercermur1@yaboo.com
**From:** artmurr@yaboo.com
**Subject: Amputee Alley**
**May 30**

*Mercer,*

*I can't say it's good to be back here on Amputee Alley, but I'm ready to work hard so that I can come home sooner. I'm excited for the family to come out later this week. You can wheel me around D.C., and we'll see every monument in the city. I'll need you to push me in my physical therapy sessions if I'm going to be ready for Mary's PKU run in the fall (followed by the Army Ten-Miler at the Pentagon).*

*Keep praying for Brian and his family, and keep going to those counseling sessions. Talking is a good thing.*

*Please remember to pray for the soldiers in Iraq, but also the injured soldiers who are suffering back in America as well. People can see that I am injured because I don't have a limb, but people can't always see the psychological pain that many veterans carry daily. They can't put a prosthetic on a brain. Unfortunately psychological wounds are often considered unmanly, something not to be discussed by real soldiers. Post Traumatic Stress Disorder needs to be addressed with the same care as my amputated leg.*

*Mercer, I want to prepare you that I might go back to Iraq after I recover. They won't send me back to active duty unless I'm ready and able; in fact, I could be teaching again at St. Thomas Aquinas in the fall, but I want to go back to Iraq. I have a duty to my soldiers and to my country and to you, Mercer. We will see where God wants me, but I wanted to prepare you for whatever happens. I want God to make me choose the harder right instead of the easier wrong.*

*There's a guy here named Jim who is helping us all recover simply by talking to us. He has lived through every stage of recovery and knows what we are enduring beyond the pain: identity crises, loss of self-confidence, and fears about supporting ourselves. I am thankful for Jim. I have a long road ahead of me, but I'm glad he is here. I'm also glad that my family will be with me for the long run.*

*Dad*

---

**To:** artmurr@yaboo.com
**From:** Mercermur1@yaboo.com
**Subject: Re: Amputee Alley**
**May 30**

*Dad,*

*Ay, there's the rub. I should have known that you would want to go back. I guess that's what makes you who you are. I know you'll make the right decision. I'm still holding out that the war will be over before you fully recover, but I will support you no matter what. Thanks for being my hero.*

*By the way, I just found out that Pat Tillman was actually killed from friendly fire ( meaning, he was accidentally killed by Americans). The Army covered it up, even after they knew he wasn't killed by enemy fire. I guess people make*

> *mistakes, but here's reason number 2,041 that you need to stay in Iowa.*
>
> *Mercer*

**May 31** - Today is Memorial Day, which obviously holds a lot more importance than it used to. I don't know if we are supposed to be in Iraq or not, but I do know that I'm proud of my dad and what he's done for his country. In a way, my mom should be remembered on this day as well. She may not have served in the military, but she supported her husband and her family, and that is supporting our country in much the same way.

I will still follow the war and pray for our soldiers, but I will also remember to pray for their families. It's hard being left behind to question everything and worry all the time.

Thanks to brilliant lawyering moves by my mom, Ahmed is going to stay with us for the summer and then will be my roommate in the fall. He's going to major in chemistry, and his student visa is approved for at least four years. We've had a blast the last couple of days, hanging out and eating burgers (he eats the burger without the bun). When he first got to America, Ahmed was astounded by all the trees here. He said they made everything so beautiful and peaceful. The first thing he wants to do is plant trees when he gets back to Iraq. Who knew that something as simple as years of tree growth could mean so much?

I introduced Ahmed to David and Mary, and we all went to the movies last night after my dad's flight left. I didn't get to talk to Mary much – I guess I've got two-and-a-half months to muster up the courage to tell her how I feel. Why can't I be more like Conan?

I don't know what I will do in the fall with track and football – I guess I have all summer to think about it. I e-mailed Mr. O'Keefe my running times, but I don't know if it will make a difference. In fact, I don't know if I want to go out for football anymore. Who knows, maybe I will go out for track instead. Maybe I'll be an Olympic runner and the 2012 Olympics will be held in Iraq where Ahmed's family can come cheer me on.

I probably won't write much in this journal anymore, that is, until I have another crisis to endure. My counselor says writing is a good expression for my emotions, so maybe I'll write once in a while. Plus, I want to write down as many memories of Bear as I can think of. I miss him.

If my dad goes back to Iraq, I might have to dust this off, but it has been a great outlet for my frustration. Maybe I will be a writer someday, who knows. Maybe I will be a doctor or a lawyer or a scientist who finds a cure for PKU. In any case, I will be a man of integrity, just like the soldier who taught me.

## ACKNOWLEDGEMENTS

Praise God for this opportunity to create a work of historical fiction. Thanks to all the soldiers, past and present, who fought for freedom. Thanks to my husband, Mike, and our three amazing kids, Joshua, Jonathan, and Gianna. Thanks to my extended family for their support and love. Thanks to my mom who instilled a love of reading. Thanks to my dad who still sends me cards that make me cry. Thanks to my brother, Justin, for all the medical information and for his crazy boyhood stories. Thanks to my other brother, Thane, for being an example of Mercer's character.

Thanks to my publisher, Usher, and all at *Library Tales Publishing* who took a chance on a football book. Thanks to Tim P., Tim W., and Michelle W. who networked this book to its fruition. Thanks to all my colleagues at Dowling Catholic High School and my teachers at Aquinas High School. Thanks to the community and my "Soul Sisters" at St. Francis who have supported me through the years. Thanks to my lawyer Shelley. Thanks to Steve, the first editor and first person to read the entire book. Thanks to Jamie for encouraging me to print manuscripts. Thanks to K.D., Jamie, Julie, Tiffany, Sarah, Jason, Maggie, and Stephanie, all of whom read the book and gave good feedback. Thanks to Ms. Breuer and her Senior Honors class at Aquinas High School including Ben, Kami, Megan, Tyler, Grace, Lauren, Liz, Mike (thanks to Mike and Alex and Liz for suggestions), and especially Alex and John, whose fathers both served in the Iraq War. And finally, thanks be to God the Father, Jesus Christ His only Son, and the Holy Spirit for being sovereign.